Dave stopped midway to ~~open~~ ~~the~~ f the cargo hold and stared at me. "Were you bitten?"

I blinked. "What?"

"Were. You. Bitten?" he repeated slowly and evenly.

I shook my head. "No. The clawing zombie didn't get close enough before you hit it, you saw it. Even that last one would have had to gnaw through my boot before he got to my skin." He continued to stare at me, both eyebrows slightly lifted as if he doubted me. Bad in these end times. "What? Why are you looking at me that way?"

He popped the cargo hold and started putting weapons back in their designated areas. "I don't know. I've just never known you not to want to shop."

Praise for the Living with the Dead series

"If you like *Shaun of the Dead* or *Zombieland,* this book will probably make you happy in your zombie pants."

—smartbitchestrashybooks.com

"It's just good, old-fashioned brain eating here, and sometimes that's all a girl needs." —*Romantic Times*

"This has got to be the cutest zombie book I've ever read."

—tigersallconsumingbooks.blogspot.com

BY JESSE PETERSEN

LIVING WITH THE DEAD

Married with Zombies
Flip this Zombie
Eat Slay Love

EAT SLAY LOVE

BOOK 3 OF LIVING WITH THE DEAD

JESSE PETERSEN

orbit

www.orbitbooks.net

This book is a work of fiction. Names, characters, places, and incidents are the product of the author's imagination or are used fictitiously. Any resemblance to actual events, locales, or persons, living or dead, is coincidental.

Copyright © 2011 by Jesse Petersen
Excerpt from *Soulless* copyright © 2009 by Tofa Borregaard

Orbit
Hachette Book Group
237 Park Avenue
New York, NY 10017
www.orbitbooks.net

Orbit is an imprint of Hachette Book Group, Inc. The Orbit name and logo are trademarks of Little, Brown Book Group Limited.

The publisher is not responsible for websites (or their content) that are not owned by the publisher.

Printed in the United States of America

First edition: July 2011

10   9   8   7   6   5   4   3   2   1

For Michael, as always. And for the zombies,
without whom this would not be possible.

EAT
SLAY
LOVE

CHAPTER 1

Zombie on a diet

Have you ever felt like you were on a treadmill, but no matter how fast or far you ran, you never dropped those pesky last fifteen pounds? Yeah, welcome to my life. Only I'm not trying to lose weight (okay, I'm a girl, I'm *always* trying to lose weight); I'm trying to lose the slobbering, moaning, growling group of mindless zombies that always seems to be on my ass.

Every time I look back over my shoulder, it seems like they're right there. Their feet pound on the pavement, their clawing fingers (complete with long, dirty, dead-person fingernails—um, *manicure,* people!!) reach for me, trying to give me one scratch, one bite, one nick that spells certain death...er, living death...for me.

They never stop. And so *I* never stop. I just run and run and run...

"Sarah?"

With horror-movie slowness, I turned and there was David, my husband, my partner in crime and in fighting for our lives. He smiled at me, but it didn't comfort me because as his lips pulled back I saw that his gums were black. His teeth were beginning to rot. His eyes were red rimmed and focused on one thing. Eating me.

And *not* in the porn-movie way.

"Stop running," he said, his voice garbled with infection and transition as he reached for me.

I sucked in a breath and sat up, but as I did so, my forehead collided with something. Something metal that I smacked into hard enough to make my vision blur.

"Son of a—!" I grunted as I reached up to touch my head.

Already the knot of a bruise started to throb just under the skin. Slowly, I opened my eyes and looked around. As my sight cleared, I willed my heart to slow down because I was safe. There were no zombies near me. No reaching hands, no frigid breaths, no clawing fingers straining to tear and pull at flesh. Just a dim room filled with dusty gym equipment, including the treadmill I had apparently fallen asleep on.

"I *knew* I was on a treadmill," I muttered as I ducked my pounding head from under the bar of the machine and pushed to my feet.

"Did you say something?"

It was David's voice coming from the other room. Not garbled by infection, though. Just plain old David. I smiled as I moved through the entryway to a weight room. The lack of power made the other equipment in the gym useless except as a very uncomfortable bed, but the weight sets still did their job. No juice required.

"Nope, just dreaming," I said. After a hesitation, I added, "Nightmaring, I guess, is a better description."

I tilted my head as Dave braced himself on the weight bench and pressed a bar filled with weight plates... a *lot* of weight plates... over his head.

"Need a spotter?" I asked as I stepped closer.

"Nope," he grunted. "I got it."

Dave's face was red with strain and sweat rolled down his cheeks to drip on the dusty mat below him. He wasn't wearing a shirt and even more sweat collected on the muscles of his chest. Yeah, you read that right. My once-unemployed, gamer husband with the little beer belly now had ripples of muscle on his chest. He was even starting to get some abs.

Hot.

He held the bar above himself, suspending it even as his arms shook ever so slightly from the weight. With another grunt, he eased the bar back into place on the rack. Once it was steady, he reached up to wipe away the sweat from his brow with the back of one gloved hand. His gaze slipped over to me slowly as he did it.

"So what was this one about?" he asked as he set his hands back in place and pressed the heavy bar upward again.

This time I counted the weight plates and blinked in surprise. He had to be pushing more than 350 pounds. Pretty impressive since I don't think he ever topped out over 200 before the zombie outbreak that had changed our lives, and ruined my sleep, forever.

"Sarah?" he asked, his voice strained as he held the bar above his head.

"Huh?" I shook my head. "Oh, just the usual. You know... getting chased by a horde of drooling zombies."

He lowered the bar again and this time he ducked under and sat up on the bench. He grabbed for a dingy towel that he'd draped across another nearby machine and wiped himself off before he said, "And was *I* in this one?"

I half turned away. Dave knew about my dreams. Only because sometimes I talked in my sleep, though. Nothing like screaming out, "Dave, please don't eat me!" to let a guy know you're thinking about him.

"I'll take that as a yes," he said softly.

As he peeled off his weight gloves, he pushed to his feet. When he opened his arms, I stepped into them without hesitation, despite my troubling dream and his stinky body.

"I'm okay, you know," he whispered after he'd given me a rather sweaty hug for a few minutes.

I nodded, but out of the corner of my eye I looked at his right hand. On it was a scar, black tinged and gnarled, that covered both the top and the palm of his hand. It marked the place where a zombie had bitten him more than a month ago. If we hadn't had a miracle serum...a *cure*... my Dave would have been nothing more than a roaming, mindless eating machine.

Oh, who am I kidding? He would have been a stain on the wall courtesy of yours truly. And there are not enough self-help books in the world to get over that one. Trust me, I've had a lot of time to look.

"I know," I whispered as I pulled away with a smile I admit I had to fake. "But you might not have been."

"But I *was*," he insisted with a shake of his head as he patted the sweat off his forehead and motioned toward the dressing rooms in the back. I followed close behind.

"I know," I said with a sigh. "And I guess our personal experience is pretty good proof that the cure worked. So now we just have to get it to the Midwest Wall."

Dave was silent as he hesitated at the door marked "Men." His frown made my own fake smile fall.

Okay, so this rumor about a wall in the Midwest, one built by the government at the beginning of the outbreak to cut off the zombie infection from the rest of the country... we both knew it was a long shot. But we kept moving toward it despite our misgivings. Kept hoping it wasn't all a colossal fake out.

If it was... well, I had no idea what we'd do then. We'd have one vial of a cure and no one to give it to. Plus, since it had taken us a month to get from Phoenix, Arizona, to Oklahoma City, we had to figure it would take us another month to get to the Wall, which would put us smack dab in the middle of a Midwest winter, complete with snow, ice, and frigid temps. Fun, eh?

Yeah, sounded like a freaking laugh riot to me.

David motioned me into the dressing room without any more discussion on the touchy subject of walls, or lack thereof. Inside he had set up a portable shower we'd managed to grab from a camping supply store somewhere around Albuquerque. The shower would be cold, but it would do the job. Although since I hadn't actually worked out at the gym we'd taken shelter in, I didn't exactly need it. I was mostly there to stand guard.

Which I did (along with take a couple of peeks by lamplight at my sweetie soaping up... what? We're married and I *like* him!!) But pretty soon he was changed and we started toward the vestibule of the gym, with Dave loading up a shotgun as we went.

"Okay, so I'd like to get in at least thirty miles today," he said absently as he cocked the shotgun with one hand.

I nodded.

So I'm sure that sounds crazy to you. Thirty miles in a day? In the pre-apocalypse days we would have been talking thirty minutes, probably less if we really put pedal to the metal. But these are not pre-apocalypse driving conditions, people. There were several things that kept us from getting much farther:

1. We tried to stay off main roads. And by that, I mean, *big* roads... freeways meant abandoned cars to move, fires to put out (literally and figuratively), and the occasional highway man to avoid (when humanity goes to hell in a handbasket, it really goes to hell in a handbasket).

2. We tried to avoid cities. So I'd said we were in Oklahoma City, but that wasn't exactly true. We were actually about fifteen miles north of there in a town called Guthrie. Unlike the real city, which had over five hundred thousand residents who were probably pretty much all zombies now... Guthrie rocked a little less than ten thousand. See what I'm saying?

3. Finally, the last reason we moved so slowly became very clear as we stepped up to the floor-to-ceiling glass doors that led to the outside and the parking lot where we'd parked our big old SUV right in a pimp spot.

That reason would be the zombies.

"I guess they saw us come into town," I said mildly as I peered outside. It was early morning still and the sky was dark from dawn and from the heavy rain clouds that were gathering in the distance.

Oh yeah, also it was dark because there was a crowd of at least twenty zombies all gathered at the windows. They pressed their faces against the barrier until they smooshed rather comically, climbing up on top of one another as if they could climb right through the glass. They were growling and pawing until they streaked the windows with sludge and blood and... *goo* of an undefined nature.

Which is more disturbing, by the way. Definable goo is way better; trust me, I'm an expert by now.

"I guess they did," Dave said with a long-suffering sigh. Like it was *so* hard to beat the zombies.

Okay, it was.

He turned toward the check-in desk where we'd left a pile of our shit when we entered the gym last night. There were all kinds of guns in a big mass there, including a supercool multishot cannon that he swept up with one hand (I had to hold it in both, it was so heavy, but I guess all that weight lifting was starting to pay off for him).

"Well," he said with another heavy sigh. "Ready to do this?"

I grabbed two 9mms from the counter and slipped clips into place in a smooth motion that had taken months of practice to perfect. I was quite proud of myself for that move. It was very "movie version Sarah."

"Hell yeah," I said with a big smile. "Ready as I'll ever be."

With a half-grin in my direction, Dave flipped the flimsy lock on the glass door and let in the horde.

CHAPTER 2

Cut the zombies out of your life.
Emotional and actual.

The cannon sounded pretty much as cool as it looked when Dave slung it up on his shoulder and started pounding out wave after wave of beautiful, bloody carnage. Bullets flew outward in a rather poetic net pattern and the tall windows exploded outward in a hail of flying glass.

This, of course, effectively ended any other poor sap's chance to get in a workout at the gym, but sometimes these sacrifices need to be made. There was a Gold's Gym nearby anyway; they'd be fine.

Pretty soon the holes in the windows were filled by the flailing of zombies. They fell one on top of the other, rapidly piling up like firewood (although not as neatly) in the window holes in a mass of reaching hands and moaning calls. A few even impaled themselves on the shards of broken glass around the window panes and hung there, suspended, clawing hands still clutching toward us until Dave put a few rounds through the top of their rotten skulls and cut off whatever was left of "brain function."

I joined in the fun, firing off a rapid beat of shots from first one gun and then the other to the tempo of the song "The Final Countdown"—you know that stupid eighties song that gets stuck in your head the second you hear the first few beats (you're welcome, by the way). Blam-blam-blam-blam . . .

More zombies fell on the pile as we each took a second to reload.

"We really are *so* good at this," I said with a grin in Dave's direction.

But before he could reply, there was an echo of snarling growls and several more zombies—ones we hadn't been able to see over the mountain of dead bodies crowding the door—started over top of the pile and staggered into the gym foyer.

I fired off a shot and dropped one, but the quarters were close and the remaining two staggered within arm's length too quickly to shoot again. Dave swung an elbow around and it collided neatly with the squishy temple of the zombie closest to him. It whimpered as it dropped to its knees and then teetered over sideways. Good old zombies and their rotting skulls. It was their only real weakness.

The one closest to me opened his mouth with a harsh, empty roar and staggered against me, its biting teeth snapping as I clutched his upper arms and shoved backward.

Unfortunately, as squishy as a zombie head is, one of their benefits is increased strength. I don't know why this is; I'm guessing maybe because they're just so damned driven to get what they want and they don't care if they hurt themselves, so it allows them to hold themselves differently.

Or maybe they just get all insane in the membrane from the poison in their blood and it makes them more powerful. No idea.

Either way, this fucker was pressing against me with all his weight and, in the battle royale for my life, he was inching closer. My heart rate ratcheted up in response, even though I'd been in this position before. It's that "I could be dead in a minute thing," I guess.

But before I could meet my maker, or figure out a way to get myself free, Dave swung the butt of a shotgun down and smashed it into the head of my zombie dance partner. It collapsed at my feet and twitched once before it stopped moving.

"You okay?" Dave asked.

I bent at the waist, panting from fear and the strain. "Yeah. I'm okay."

He patted my shoulder and then moved off to collect some of our gear to move out. Of course, as soon as he was out of range, the big horror-movie moment happened (for a second time, actually).

One last zombie did a surprisingly impressive vault over the bodies of others. Seriously, he must have been a gymnast in life because it was Olympic worthy. Except for the landing, which ended up being face-first on the cheap carpet, I'd probably give it a 5.5.

Somehow he was still growling, though, even as he lay in a tangled heap at my feet.

I backed up instantly, mostly out of instinct rather than fear, but found myself pinned against the welcome desk in the foyer of the gym. It was surprising to find myself in that position, actually. After so many months of doing this, I was normally pretty good at *not* getting myself trapped against anything. Guess I was off my game after my disturbing little treadmill dream.

The zombie lifted his head, his red eyes glinting in the dim light as he reached out for my ankle. I was wearing heavy work boots but I still felt the strength of his grip as he dug his fingers into the leather.

He dragged himself closer, mouth open and ready to bite. But before he could do that, a flash of metal whizzed toward me and Dave's big bowie knife sunk into the rotting flesh and disintegrating bone of the zombie's forehead with a satisfying wet "thunk."

The poor beast crossed its eyes as it looked up, like it was trying to get a good look at the thing that had just severed its frontal lobe. With a sad little whine, it collapsed forward and drooled its last on the tip of my steel-toed boot.

I turned toward my husband as I shook away the zombie's dead hand from my ankle and kicked its broken face to the side. "You couldn't have shot it faster?"

"Didn't want to hit you." He shrugged. "This time, anyway. Plus, I ran out of ammo in the cannon and I couldn't get the shotgun out fast enough. Sorry."

I glanced down at the zombie with a shiver. We'd had way more close calls before; even combined with the biting zombie, this one didn't even qualify, but still...I was getting really tired of this. I mean, we'd been running and fighting for so long, and now that we were actually heading toward the Wall, the place where everyone said we *might* be safe, I was ready to retire from the ass-kicking business; that was for sure.

I shoved those thoughts away. Longing for "normal" was about as useful as longing for a hot fudge sundae. Mmmm, hot fudge sundae.

Oh, sorry. Got distracted there.

We both took a minute to reload before Dave nodded toward me and began to push the door. It was caught on about eight zombie bodies and it took both of us putting all our weight into it to finally get it open. By the time we managed to shove aside the heavy bodies, I was panting and sweating from the workout. Guess I should have gotten on those weights, myself.

"That *thing* drooled on my boot," I wheezed as I stepped over gray limbs and avoided a big puddle of sludge and blood that was starting to seep out from under the collection of bodies.

Dave shrugged. As opposed to my panting ass, he didn't even sound winded as he said, "You and your boots."

I shot him a look. "Boots are important."

He laughed. "Are they?" When I didn't answer but just glared, he raised his hand like a little surrender. "Okay, well, I'll get you a new pair once we get down the road further. The guidebook said there was a big mall on the way to the Route 66 interchange."

I nodded.

Here's a little tip if you're ever caught in a zombie apocalypse . . . or really *any* kind of apocalypse (there's more than one, you know): Stop at every bookstore you can find. Not only was there plenty of entertainment to be had there, but guidebooks, road maps, and survival manuals are like *gold* in these times. David and I always found the first bookstore we could any time we entered a new area and raided it for information.

Plus, sometimes they still had bags of coffee hidden in their bookstore cafes. And although I wasn't much of a coffee person, it, too, was worth its weight in trade in the survival camps along with cigarettes and, of course, chocolate of any kind. We all have our vices, right?

"Nah," I said as Dave clicked the remote entry and the doors to our SUV unlocked with a pleasing *chirp*. "I'm not really in the mood to shop."

Dave stopped midway to opening the back of the cargo hold and stared at me. "Were you bitten?"

I blinked. "What?"

"Were. You. Bitten?" he repeated slowly and evenly.

I shook my head. "No. The clawing zombie didn't get close enough before you hit it; you saw it. Even that last one would have had to gnaw through my boot before he got to my skin." He continued to stare at me, both eyebrows slightly lifted as if he doubted me. Bad in these end times. "What? Why are you looking at me that way?"

He popped the cargo hold and started putting weapons back in their designated areas. "I don't know. I've just never known you not to want to shop."

I stared at him. His lips were twitching with laughter and his eyes sparkled in the dim light.

"You asshole." I laughed as I swatted him.

"What? I'm just saying!" he said as he dodged my playful slaps and shut the cargo hold door.

We walked around the SUV together and my smile faded as I flashed back to the horrible day just a few weeks ago. When Dave had been bitten. I shivered as I put on my seat belt.

"You're funny," I said, trying to soften my tone with another smile. "But we don't joke about getting bitten. Not anymore."

Dave's own laughter faded as he got into the driver's

seat. When he looked at me, the humor was gone from his eyes, too. "I know. Sorry, Sarah, couldn't resist."

"It's just that—"

He interrupted me with a shake of his head. "I know what it is, baby. I was there, too. I felt infection changing me and it was the worst thing I've ever gone through. I knew I wasn't going to be able to stop myself from hurting anyone who was near me. From hurting you, even though I didn't want to."

He shivered before he continued. "*But* it didn't happen. I didn't turn, mostly because you're a badass and you found the cure for me in the lab. You risked everything to save me. And you did. So if we can't joke about that, I don't know what we can joke about."

I shrugged. I got what he was saying, but the whole thing was still a little too...*raw* for me. Maybe in another month or two I'd be able to crack wise about my partially zombiefied husband or start calling him Scarhand or something...but not yet. It wasn't funny quite yet.

"Besides, look what that did. Because of it we got this." He reached out and pulled on the heavy necklace I wore around my neck. From beneath my shirt flopped a vial with purple liquid inside. The cure.

"Yeah," I agreed reluctantly. "But I have to say...not worth almost losing you."

He leaned forward and kissed me. Long and hard. When he pulled away, he grinned. "It will be if we can save the world. Think about it, we'll be famous. We probably won't have to pay taxes anymore or anything."

I laughed as he started the car. "To be fair, we don't exactly pay taxes now."

"Only because all the IRS agents in this part of the country are drooling zombies intent on eating our brains."

"And that's different from before, *how*?"

As he laughed, I looked out the window. The rain was starting, light and cold against the window. It was December and even this far down south, we felt it. I didn't have a coat yet, just long-sleeved shirts and heavy sweaters we'd picked up as we got farther north, but already I was starting to want a jacket whenever we went outside. Much farther north, I was going to need one in order to stay alive.

"Maybe that mall isn't such a bad idea after all," I said.

"Why?" Dave asked as he maneuvered us back onto the main road for a short jaunt south before we headed east. Dead cars rusted on the side of the road, turned over and burned from accidents or just abandoned by zombie drivers.

"Coats," I said softly. "We're going to need them if we get much further north this time of year."

He nodded, but his mouth had thinned. See, the outbreak had started in August, when malls and other stores were still clearing out their summer gear and getting in light fall items. To be honest, we hadn't seen any heavier coats yet in all our "shopping" (translation: looting). And that meant that, like the scavengers we'd become over the past few months, we might have to start searching homes next, going through the closets of the dead and undead for their stuff.

Only every time we did house sweeps, we almost always found zombies. The ultimate "going out of business" sale of zombie apocalypse wasn't the draw you'd think it was. Turned out more people went home to hide

in the face of death than went to the mall, no matter what
Romero wrote.

Plus, I'd rather fight zombies in a Wal-Mart than a
house any day. Stores were laid out in really easy to
understand ways. They had big aisles and not a lot of hidden areas. They "flowed" so that people would buy, buy,
buy and then get the hell out.

Houses . . . well, you wander into one place where a
hoarder used to live and all of a sudden you're fighting in
a narrow hallway surrounded by some creepy collection
of garden gnomes. I don't know about you, but that's not
how *I* want to go out.

So we hadn't had much luck finding winter gear, but I
wasn't about to go on any house-to-house search until we
got a bit farther north. Might as well put off the
inevitable.

"Well, the mall is about ten miles down from Guthrie,"
Dave said as he eased along the thoroughfare. He was
slowing down because we were coming up on what
looked to be about a fifteen-car pileup. "So that's what . . .
about an hour or two on the road? We can stop off there
for a bit and then get going east!"

If he sounded excited, it was probably because we'd be
that much closer to Illinois. And Illinois was supposed to
be where we'd find this Midwest Wall. Not to mention my
mother. Before the outbreak she'd been living in a town
called Normal.

Yeah . . . *Normal.* We hadn't yet started to place bets on
whether it still was or not. I think it was one of those "off
limits to joke about" topics, despite how easy it was to
make puns with the town name.

"It's crazy that it takes so long to get from one point to

another," I murmured as I looked out the window at the burnt husks of the wrecked cars. Some of them had been nearly welded together by the heat of the fire. "We had it so good B.Z., and we didn't even know it."

B.Z. = Before Zombie, by the way. Speaking of stupid clichés...

"Yeah, well, it's getting worse, too," Dave said, his knuckles whitening as he edged our SUV between two vehicles. There was a light scrape on the back passenger side as we bumped the other cars, but then we were out and he was able to raise his speed up to a frisky thirty... at least for a minute.

"I noticed it, too. Ever since we started hard north there are more zombies and more devastation. Why do you think that is?" I asked.

He shrugged. "I guess it took longer for the outbreak to get here than it did along the coast. Think about the news coverage in Seattle in the first twenty-four hours, then multiply it by another two days."

I shivered as I thought of just that: reporters getting turned on live television, the first glimpse of the horde, limbs torn and laying in gutters. It had been mass hysteria in Seattle, and that coverage had convinced us to run like hell.

"They must have been terrified," I murmured.

He nodded, solemn. "If people had an extra day or two knowing what was coming... that meant a couple extra days to get on the road and try to run from it. A couple extra days to panic and start acting like fools and cause fifteen-car pileups. Not to mention a couple of days to gather up and become zombie chow."

I shivered as I glanced at the wreck slowly disappearing in my side mirror. "That must be it."

"The closer we get to this Wall, if it even exists, it will probably get even tighter and uglier. I mean, we've both seen *I Am Legend* and *Resident Evil* enough times to know that any promise of 'safety' translates to mass hysteria."

"Not to mention we lived in the camps for a while. They draw zombies like crazy and I imagine the Wall would be the same way. We'll have to be really careful."

I shot Dave a glance. He was staring straight ahead, his mouth a thin line. We didn't talk about this shit very often and this was why. There was no comfort in thinking you might get all the way to the Wall and then get eaten by a huge group of zombies waiting for you there. In fact, that was even more depressing, in some ways.

"Okay," I said with a shake of my head. "That's our cue to lighten up. How about we play some I Spy?"

Dave groaned, but there was laughter to his tone and that's what I'd been going for when I suggested it.

"God, Sarah, you and your travel games."

"Well, license plate bingo is probably out, so I Spy is the best alternative. At least for now." Dave was rolling his eyes and I reached out to pinch his side playfully. "Come on! You know you want to. Okay, I'll start. I spy, with my little eye ... something black."

"The only thing I can think of that is black that you might be able to see is sludge?" Dave said with a laugh.

"No. Strike one. Want another clue?"

"Sure." He sighed but I could see he was starting to relax a little.

"I spy with my little eye, something small."

His brow wrinkled and he scanned the horizon for whatever I was describing. I smothered a smile. He was never going to get it considering I was looking at a cock-roach that was crawling on the edge of our dashboard (what they say is true, by the way; cockroaches survive *everything*).

"Small...black..." he mused. "Still don't know."

"I spy with my little eye—" I began, but before I could give a third clue to the puzzle he'd never solve, I caught a flash of movement from the corner of my...er, little eye. With a yelp, I braced myself on the dash.

"Woman!" I screamed.

Dave looked at me. "Well, that doesn't make any sense with the other cl—" Then he saw the same thing I did and gripped the wheel. "Shit!"

He turned hard to avoid hitting the woman who was running up onto the road and right into the pathway of our car. And behind her? Four zombies, doing that dead jog they do in her direction. Their arms flopped at their sides uselessly and their moans were load enough to echo even in our closed-up SUV.

Despite the cooler weather, the woman was wearing a pair of jeans that had been cut off above the knee and a green tank top. Not exactly battle gear. She *was* armed, though. A gun was strapped across her chest, but it jangled against her back and she made no attempt to grab for it despite the gang behind her. Which either meant she was empty...or she'd been bitten and was no longer in her right mind enough to think about protecting herself by using her weapon.

Either way, we were about to find out because Dave screeched the vehicle to a jarring stop and we both flung open our doors to face our new friend...who we might just be killing in a matter of minutes.

CHAPTER 3

Make connections with like-minded people. Support
groups are a good way to stay fit, improve your
life…oh, and survive a zombie apocalypse.

Dave dove out of the driver's side and in one smooth
motion used the hood as a rest to fire off the first two shots
from his shotgun. The zombie closest to the woman (close
enough that when he stretched his arm out toward her, he
almost touched her) fell, his clenching fingers tightening
into a fist as he collapsed in a heap behind her.

She dove flat against the road and slid toward us, heav-
ing in a huge sobbing breath as I braced against my half-
open door and fired off the next round of shots. Between
Dave and me, the second and third zombies tumbled in a
lifeless pile.

The fourth was a little slower. Actually he was also a
lot uglier. Apparently he was an older zombie. His flesh
drooped sickeningly around his bones and he was missing
an ear, an eye, and three fingers from his left hand. He
dragged a battered and torn leg behind him and groaned
almost painfully as he reached toward us.

"Not worth wasting the ammo," Dave grunted.

He came around the truck and, stepping over the girl as he marched toward the zombie, used the butt end of the gun like a bat and took a looping swing. He connected with a sickening crunch and the zombie staggered back, tripped over the edge of the highway, and went tumbling head over feet into the berm on the shoulder. Dave followed after him, flat-footed and rather terrifying as he lifted the butt again and pummeled the pathetic creature into oblivion.

I shook my head as I reloaded, then stepped out onto the pavement. The girl was still crouched near the front passenger wheel of our SUV, holding her hands over her head. She shook like a leaf. I almost felt sorry for her. But not enough that I didn't carefully lift my gun and level it at her trembling form.

I wasn't stupid, you know. Maybe kind of bitchy sometimes, but not stupid.

"Hi," I said softly.

She tensed and then slowly rolled over to face me. She looked at me for a minute, then her gaze slipped to the gun pointed in her face. She stared at it, then her attention went back to me.

"H-Hey," she managed to stammer. "Thanks for your help. I ran out of ammo with those four left. I thought I was dead for sure."

I nodded, but didn't lower my weapon. Upon quick first inspection, she seemed okay. Her voice wasn't garbled, her eyes hadn't turned red, but she was also covered in blood and I wasn't sure how much of it had come from zombie bites and how much from...well, something else. I wasn't about to take any chances until I knew for sure.

"Mind standing up?" I asked, motioning her to her feet with the barrel of the pistol.

She nodded and grabbed for the SUV to drag herself to her feet. As she moved, she winced and I couldn't help but relax a fraction.

Zombies didn't register much pain. It was something that died along with their brains. It was part of what made them so hard to fight. You could hurt them, bad... like cut off an arm and both legs, and they just kept coming. Coming and coming until they got to you or you took their heads.

"You're awfully bloody," I said softly. "Want to show me that you weren't bitten?"

She took a glance over my shoulder toward Dave, who was starting up the embankment back toward the SUV. "Does *he* have to watch?"

I glanced at him. The butt of his gun was covered in gore.

"Why don't you clean that thing up while I take care of her?" I called to him.

"Take care of her?" he repeated with mild alarm in his tone. "You mean she's bitten."

"No!" the girl burst out with a wild look that said she knew what would happen if she *was* bitten. "Your... uh... *whatever* she is to you wants to check me and I don't really want you staring while she does it."

Dave hesitated for a minute, but then he shrugged. He knew I could handle myself. "Works for me. Tell me when it's safe to come out."

The woman's face relaxed slightly. Once Dave had gone to the other side of the SUV and turned his back, she lifted up her shirt. She had road rash something fierce from her slide on both her arms and her stomach, not to mention her knees. It looked like it hurt like a son of a bitch, too, since there were little rocks and pieces of glass clinging to her skin and filling the wounds.

But no bites.

"Turn around?" I said, continuing my inspection. She had a big cut on her back, but there was no black sludge. "How did you get that?"

She grimaced as she unbuttoned her shorts and tugged them down so I could see the rest of her. "I had a motorcycle. Veered to avoid a zombie and bashed the hell out of myself."

"You were riding a motorcycle in *that* outfit?" I wrinkled my brow as she covered back up and faced me.

She shrugged as she glanced down at herself. "I was coming up from Mexico. It was hot down there. I didn't want to weigh myself down with too much gear."

"Mexico," I said.

To be honest I hadn't put much thought into our neighbors in the South or the North since the outbreak. Free trade and immigration weren't really the issues they'd once been.

"Is it bad down there?"

"Well, there were a lot of damn zombies, if that's what you're asking." She frowned. "This thing, whatever you want to call the infection, well, it didn't seem to pay much attention to Border Patrol."

I dipped my head briefly. I guess I'd thought of this outbreak as an American problem for so long. Now I had to wonder how global it had gotten. Was it just North and South America? Or had the entire world been wiped out in the last few months all Stephen King's *The Stand* style?

"Well, you look okay, I mean besides having the shit kicked out of you," I finally said and lowered my pistol. As I holstered it, I continued, "I'm Sarah. Babe, you're okay to come out."

Dave came around from the back of the SUV with his shotgun freshly cleaned. He put it in the sling so that it lay flat against his back and approached us.

"And this is my husband, David," I continued.

"Hi," the girl said with a cautious smile. "I'm—"

But before she could finish, Dave sucked in a harsh breath. "Holy shit! I know who you are! Holy shit!"

I stared at him and then looked back at the girl. She *did* seem kind of familiar, now that I was actually looking at her face and not for evidence of zombie attack on her banged-up body. She had blonde hair, or at least it would be blonde after she brushed the dirt and blood out of it. And she had really striking blue eyes. She couldn't have crossed thirty yet, either (not that I had).

She was the kind of girl that when guys saw her on the street, they looked over their shoulder once she was past them. You know...your basic nightmare.

"Oh, you're so sweet," she said with a blush and a girl-ish...giggle (one I might have called fake, except it was adorable). "It's always nice to meet a fan, especially out here."

Dave was nodding enthusiastically and I pursed my lips.

"*Fan*? Sorry, I'm out of the loop. *Who* are you exactly and why do you have *fans*?"

Dave and the girl exchanged a "Wow, she's dumb" laugh that grated on my nerves and then she stepped closer and held out one scraped-up hand.

"Hi. My name is Nicole Nessing."

Dave grinned as I briefly shook the hand I was offered. "She's a reporter for E.N.Z."

I stared blankly.

"You know. Entertainment News Zone?" Dave added with an apologetic shake of his head for our new friend. "Sarah didn't watch your show during the day."

"I was working," I said softly. "But yeah, I think I vaguely remember it. It was like . . . tabloid TV, wasn't it? Stalkerazzi stuff where you chase some movie star all over God's half acre and then scream questions at them on camera until they explode and you get it all on tape, right?"

Nicole shrugged at my dismissive description of her chosen profession, but she didn't seem offended. "Hey, it got ratings, right? Paid for my cushy life for quite some time."

"So what in the world are you doing *here?*" Dave asked as he edged closer and motioned around. "Why weren't you in L.A. or New York?"

Her mouth thinned into a frustrated line. "I *should* have been in L.A. when the shit went down, I *should* have been covering the Jennifer Reynolds meltdown."

"Oh yeah, right before the outbreak, the Pop Princess was bashing in her ex's windows with . . . was it a lawn umbrella?" Dave asked with a chuckle.

I rolled my eyes. I can't believe that stuff had been *news* back then. What a world. You know, we kind of deserved an apocalypse.

Nicole folded her arms with a pretty little pout. "Yup, but my stupid producer gave Jenn's big, ridiculous story to my idiot of a coanchor and sent me on field assignment instead."

"Where?" I asked.

"Cancun," she said with a sigh, like she'd been delegated to Alcatraz or something. "Following Jonas Granger when he went down there to get a quickie divorce from his first wife so he could marry Poppy Stevens."

Jonas Granger, a Hollywood playboy who had been running around with a girl almost half his age, star of one of those stupid remakes of a nineties show that had been inexplicably the rage before the zombies did the ultimate Hollywood shutdown. *90210 Place* or *Melrose Beverly*... whatever. I was more of a *Fringe* kind of girl.

"Gross," I said.

"So what happened to him?" Dave asked. "Did he get the divorce?"

I blinked as I stared at my husband. Did I *know* this guy? His eyes were lit up and he actually sounded like he gave a shit. I'd had no idea my hubby had been so into Hollywood gossip.

But then again, Nicole *was* awfully pretty under all those scrapes and bruises.

For the first time since the outbreak, I felt a twinge of jealousy. I kept it to myself, though. I really didn't have a right to get pissy since I'd made the mistake of picking a madman over my husband just a few weeks before and nearly gotten us both killed. If he wanted to gawk at the pretty stalkerazzi girl, who was I to say anything? At least for now.

But if it went too far, *someone* was going to get zombiefied, and this time I would keep the cure to myself, thank you very much.

She laughed, completely oblivious to my dark little thoughts. "Oh yeah. He got the divorce all right. And then his personal assistant, who he'd treated like shit for *years,* by the way, took a chunk out of his arm. Last I saw, Jonas was munching on the entire divorce court…and my poor cameraman."

"Sorry," I mumbled.

"Well, I managed to get the video equipment from him before he totally lost his…er, head. It's back over the berm with the wrecked bike." She shrugged, but there was a brief flicker of emotion in her eyes. "Anyway, we all have our stories, don't we?"

I tilted my head. I couldn't tell if she was dismissing the death of her coworker as a defense mechanism or if she really didn't give a shit what happened to the poor guy. I had to hand it to her, Nicole was a tough read. It had probably made her very successful B.Z.

She sighed theatrically. "Poor Jonas, he was a Vegan in life, you know, so it must have been painful to him to make the transition to eating meat."

Dave laughed a bit too hard at her not particularly funny quip and I folded my arms.

"So after the shit hit the fan, you started up this way?" I asked, the chill in my tone unmistakable.

She nodded and her bright blue eyes moved back to me. "Yup, fought my way out of Cancun and started toward the good ol' U.S. of A. Unfortunately there's not much of it left."

"True," I said with a shrug. "But if you'd been in L.A., it would have been worse. They firebombed there."

She nodded. "So I heard. But *fuck*, the footage I would have gotten first. Imagine, Lady Gaga zombiefied…or Brangelina going to town at Spago!"

I blinked, disbelief rolling over me. This woman couldn't be serious, could she? "But you'd be dead."

"Maybe. Maybe not. I'm not dead yet."

"Thanks to us," I muttered.

She looked at me for a minute and then she said, "So what's your story? How did you two get to Oklahoma City-ish? Or is this where you started?"

"Nope, we started in Seattle," Dave began before I placed a hand on his forearm and stopped him.

"Hey, can I talk to you for a minute?"

He looked down at me, brow wrinkled in confusion. "Um, yeah." He shot Nicole a smile. "We'll be right back."

She shrugged. "I need to grab the camera anyway. I'm guessing with all the shooting we're going to have company within the next fifteen minutes or so and I can't lose my footage."

We moved around to the back of the SUV and Dave shook his head. "What?"

"I don't know how much we want to tell this girl," I whispered, casting a quick glance in her direction.

She was picking gravel out of one of the scrapes on her arm and wincing as she slipped up to the ditch by the road. She stepped over the zombie bodies without even looking at them and dug around in the dirt until she came up with a big black backpack that I assumed contained her camera.

"What do you mean? Why?" Dave asked with a tilt of his head.

I stared at him. "You can't be seriously asking me why. I mean, we have something pretty amazing on us and she's a reporter."

I reached up and touched the outline of the precious vial hanging around my neck under my shirt. We'd come in contact with people since getting it, of course, and we hadn't told any of them about it. I didn't really want to start getting into it now.

Dave arched a brow. "She *used* to be a reporter. Now she's just a survivor like us."

"One who wishes she'd been in the middle of Hell-A when the shit went down. Not exactly normal, David!"

"And define 'normal' again, Sarah?" he said with a laugh.

I rolled my eyes and his laughter stopped. He actually sounded annoyed when he continued, "Look, we're not telling her anything about the vial or anything else. But she asked for our story, so we'll tell her some of it. Otherwise, don't you think she'll be suspicious?"

"Maybe she'll think we're just not friendly-like," I said with a fake Southern accent that made his smile widen. "'Sides are you sure you can keep yourself from confessing everything and anything to Miss Pretty Pants?"

Dave tilted his head. "Are you jealous, Sarah?" When I turned my head, he laughed again. "Wow. *There's* a reversal. Look, I promise not to give any details about anything important without running it by you first. Okay?"

I pursed my lips and he leaned closer. "Okay? C'mon..." He winked. "Go Team Sarah and David..."

"Okay," I mumbled reluctantly as I watched him go back around the SUV to meet up with Nicole.

They talked for a minute out of my earshot and she nodded and smiled, then frowned. Obviously she was getting the short version of how we'd come from Seattle, running like hell from the source of the outbreak that had wiped out our world as we knew it. I didn't really need to hear the crib notes. I'd lived it, after all. Whether I wanted to or not.

Finally they motioned to me and I made my way back to them.

"Wow, you guys have been through some stuff," Nicole said with an impressed shake of her head. "It's amazing you're still together."

I nodded as I slipped my arm around Dave's waist (okay, I admit it was a little proprietorial, so sue me). "We're very lucky. Anyway, it's probably time for us to get back on the road..."

Dave's hand tightened on my arm and he looked down at me with a "Don't be rude" expression.

"Yeah, about that," Nicole said with a glance over her shoulder toward where she'd run from. "Look, my bike is totally toast after the wreck. I don't think I could fix it. Plus, I have to admit, my body feels like I was beaten with a bat. Do you think I could ride along with you guys for a while? Maybe even borrow some supplies to clean up these cuts before the road rash starts getting ookie?"

I bit my lip. Okay, so there aren't that many of us survivors left, right? And over the months I'd learned, sometimes the hard way, that we had to stick together... help each other... be *human*. So even though I had major misgivings about bringing anyone else along on our trek to save the world, I found myself nodding.

"Sure," I said with a short sigh. "Of course we'll help you out. Get your gear."

She held up the backpack. "This is it," she laughed. "I travel light."

"I guess so," Dave said as he motioned to the SUV. "Now we'd better get rolling. You're right that all that shooting attracted a new pod; I swear I heard some grumbling in the distance."

Just as he said the words, the roar of the zombies doubled. We all turned in unison and there, coming across a wide field that led up to the road was a pod of creatures at least fifteen thick. They were still shambling, but the shamble had purpose and we all knew from close, personal experience that it would soon turn into a jog and then a tooth-gnashing, fight-for-your-life battle. Something none of us seemed up for as we all dove for the SUV. I grabbed for the front passenger side door, but Dave shook his head at me.

"Why don't you ride in the back with Nicole and help her with her cuts?"

I might have argued, but . . . you know . . . *zombies*. So that was how I ended up in the backseat of my own SUV, picking glass out of a stalkerazzi's road rash while she and my husband chatted about movie stars, television divas (reality and scripted), and rock'n'rollers. It's a glamorous life, kids. A *really* glamorous life.

Nicole winced as I picked another pebble out of her flesh and tossed it on the growing pile on the floor. Despite my hesitation about trusting her, I felt for the girl. Having glass embedded in your flesh hurt like a son of a bitch. I'd had some experience with this kind of injury over the past few months (everyone gets road rash in a post-zombie apocalypse. It's a rite of passage).

"Sorry," I said as I patted her arm in a clumsy attempt at comfort of some kind. "But that looks like the worst of it."

"Feels like it, too," she said with a sigh as she turned her arm sideways and looked at herself with a grimace. "And I always got such compliments on my skin."

I shrugged one shoulder. What was I supposed to say, that we'd stop and get some pore minimizer?

"I'm not sure we have enough antibiotic wipes and cream to take care of all this," I said instead, mostly to avoid tension and a fight, either with Nicole or David.

She stopped looking at her battered body as our eyes met in the backseat. I felt her tense slightly. Infection equaled death in the badlands, just as much as a zombie bite did.

"I hear there's a camp about five miles east of Oklahoma City," she said softly. "Right after the interchange."

Dave's eyes came up in the rearview mirror. "Yeah? Well, they'd probably have supplies there we could trade for. What do you think, Sarah?"

I clenched my fists in and out as I thought about the question. We were supposed to make thirty miles today, but that was already way out of the question. Stopping to help Goldilocks had slowed us down considerably and if we went to this camp, that meant we would probably be done for the night by the time the trading and story exchanging was over.

But the only other option was to say fuck Nicole and keep going despite her injuries. Only we'd eventually get slowed down when she started to get an infection from her wounds. So one way or another, I guess we were screwed. That's what you get for being a Good Samaritan.

"Why not?" I sighed. "Maybe they'll even have some coats."

"Coats?" Nicole repeated with a questioning tilt of her head.

I bet she'd used that same look in a billion celebrity interviews right before she ambushed her subject with a video of them doing something incriminating.

I flinched. Shit, and I'd been the one trying to keep our

plans secret. "Um, well, we're planning to head further east and north, so we're going to need them eventually."

Nicole was quiet for a long moment and then she slowly nodded. "I guess I'm safe to assume you're heading for the Wall?"

We were all quiet for a tense amount of time, with Dave looking at me in the rearview mirror. I could have sworn I was sending him the "We still can't trust her" look, but I guess he read it as the "Spill your guts" look.

"Yeah," he said. "We're trying to make it to the Wall."

I shook my head. Well, it was out now, couldn't take it back. The best we could do was try to use the information to our advantage.

"So, you're a reporter, what do you know about it?" I asked.

Nicole shrugged and rested her head back against the seat. "Probably as much as you do, honestly. I haven't met anyone yet who has actually *seen* the Midwest Wall. I *can* tell you that the Border Wall down south is a reality. But then again, it was already pretty much there before the outbreak; *they* just had to reinforce it since it wasn't immigrants or drug coyotes they were trying to keep out anymore."

Dave nodded, but I wasn't appeased by her answer. In fact, it only sparked a whole new set of questions. "So wait, if you were in Mexico, how did you get *over* the Border Wall and back to U.S. soil?"

"Well, I used my feminine wiles, Sarah." She smiled, but it was a tight expression that didn't say, *I'm proud and happy of what I did.* In fact, just the opposite.

I stared, my eyes going wide enough in my head that if I'd been a zombie, they would have fallen into my lap.

"Yuck!" I finally burst out.

I'd never been much of the "trade sex for what you want" kind of girl. Even in our worst moments, I hadn't even withheld from Dave to get my way. So the idea of trading body for safety was pretty awful.

Even though, on a level I refused to admit out loud, I got how it might become a necessity.

"Oh, come on," Dave snorted. "She's fucking with you. She doesn't really mean—"

"Oh yeah," Nicole interrupted. "I really mean it."

Both of us stared at her silently and finally she shrugged, though she seemed less than comfortable with the subject now that she was facing judgment for it. "Oh come on! You guys are grown-ups. You know how the world works. A girl's gotta do what a girl's gotta do. I learned that ages ago in Hollywood."

I guess eventually one of us would have said something. Dave certainly looked like he had something on his disillusioned tongue, but before he could choke it out, five beaten up, sludge-covered vehicles careened onto the road ahead of us, while another three peeled up behind us, effectively blocking us in.

"What the fuck?" Dave sputtered as he slammed on the brakes and came to a jarring stop that flopped all of us forward against the seat belts.

I looked out the window. People were getting out of the cars and trucks, weapons drawn and ready. They were dressed in raggedy clothing, their hair unkempt and hanging around their faces as they motioned us to get out of the vehicle.

"What do we do?" I whispered.

My question was directed toward Dave, but it was

Nicole who answered as she reached into her bag and grabbed for her camera. "Well, I guess we get out."

"I wasn't asking you," I muttered just under my breath, but Dave was already slowly unbuckling and reaching for his door handle.

"Actually, I think she might be right, babe," he said, his voice low and steady. "It doesn't seem like we have much choice."

CHAPTER 4

There's power to positive thinking.
Also to planning an escape route.

There was one clear leader of the group who held us at
gunpoint: a tall, gangly guy who looked like he was
around fifty years old. Of course, in these dark days that
didn't mean anything. He could have been twenty and just
not taking to the zombie death march all that well. Some
people thrived in the outbreak; others...not so much.

He had a big scar that cut across his face, and it was
still red, which meant it was fresh enough to be a souvenir
of the apocalypse.

"Now everyone just stay calm," he said as the three of
us exited the vehicle with our hands in clear view. For
some reason collectively we didn't think coming out guns
ablazing would work this time. Huh.

"Hard to do when you're pointing a—what is that, an
AK-47?—at us," Dave said, his voice level and cool even
though I could see a vein popping in his neck. He wanted
to go ape shit so bad....

"It *is* an AK-47," the other man drawled with an

impressed smile. He had a Southern twang to his tone that made me wonder if he was a local who hadn't left even after the shit hit the fan. *"Nice,* city boy. Now *you..."*

He turned his attention on Nicole, who was standing behind Dave and me.

"I'd appreciate if you put that camera away."

I spun on Nicole. Fuck if she wasn't shooting all of this with a very expensive looking handheld camera and a tight little smile on her face.

"What are you doing?" I whispered.

"You can't stifle the press," she said, loud enough that everyone could hear. "This is America."

AK-47 Leader Dude smiled, but his expression was as cold as hers. "Not anymore." He pointed the gun straight at her. "Put. The. Camera. Down."

She complied with a scowl and I sighed in a mixture of relief and irritation. So much for making a good impression on our new "friends." Now we'd have to do some serious damage control.

"Look, I think we've gotten off on the wrong foot," I started as I moved forward a couple of steps.

The guys in front of us all lifted their weapons slightly and I stopped my forward momentum immediately. Apparently that wasn't such a good idea.

I lifted my hands higher. "We're not zombies; we're survivors just like you."

"You're not just like us," one of the women behind us called out. "And you're on our land."

Dave's brow wrinkled as he kept his gaze on the first guy who's spoken to us. Leader Dude. "Funny, I was under the impression we were on a public road."

"Hey, asshole, did you notice there ain't a government

anymore? That means no fucking public anything!" one of the men standing behind Leader Dude snapped. His gun lifted in a menacing fashion and I tensed as I readied for crazy-person gunfire.

"Hey, Carl, I've got this handled," Leader Dude said as he gave the one I now was calling Crazy Carl a meaningful look. Crazy Carl's gun trembled slightly and then he nodded.

"Sorry, sir," he mumbled.

Leader Dude turned back to us with a slight smile. "Public roads, not public roads, it doesn't really matter. The road you were traveling on goes through *our* territory. And we like to make sure everyone going through our territory are the kind of folks we welcome here."

I blinked at the weirdness of that statement. "Look, mister, we aren't going to stay in *anyone's* territory. We're just passing through."

"Yeah," Nicole added from the other side of the SUV. "All we want to do is stop at the camp that's supposed to be in these parts, pick up some supplies, and then keep moving. We're not trying to hurt anyone."

The men in front of us (including Crazy Carl, who got that crazy look in his eyes again) shifted and looked at one another in a way that made my heart leap. Apparently we'd said something they didn't like because they started whispering and grumbling unintelligibly in the distance.

The leader, though, he seemed less bothered. In fact, his smile grew. "Well, you're in luck then, little lady. See, the camp is exactly where you're going."

I bit my lip. Great. Once again, in a world full of pods of survivors, we'd managed to find the crazies in the mix. It was like a special gift. Like X-Men gone all fucked up.

Why couldn't I have been able to control the weather instead?

"Rod, Michelle, you two drive their SUV," the leader continued as he motioned his head toward some of the people behind us. The ones I was trying not to look at since I didn't really want to freak myself out more than I was already. He looked at Dave. "Mister, you come with me. You ladies can ride with…"

I shut my eyes. Not Crazy Carl, not Crazy Carl, not Crazy Carl…

"…Alan," Leader Dude finished.

Although I was relieved not to have Carl as my escort, I immediately started to shake my head. I wasn't about to be separated from my husband, but Dave turned toward me and gave me a quick look. He held my stare for a long moment and then smiled.

"It's okay," he said softly. "Just go with Nicole. We'll see each other at the camp."

I swallowed as he reached out and squeezed my hand, then walked toward Leader Dude and the big-ass truck he was motioning to. You know the kind, the ones you used to see on the road with the huge tires. They were ridiculous back in the "old days," but now they actually had their purposes. Like riding off road, pushing other vehicles, smashing zombie heads, kidnapping harmless survivors. The usual.

I continued to stare after them as Dave got in, but I didn't get to watch them take off because another guy, Alan I guess Leader Dude had called him, came up and shook my forearm.

"C'mon, you heard Lex, come with me."

I snatched away my arm as I looked at the guy who

was taking us...*hostage*—one way to look at it, I guess. Although that requires some kind of demand in exchange for release and there wasn't exactly anything to be traded for us...except for maybe the cure I still felt jingling beneath my T-shirt. Best to keep *that* detail to myself.

Alan was younger than Leader Dude, who now had a name. I would guess early thirties. He was blond and wearing jeans and a leather jacket. He also had a very nice set of 9mms on a double holster at his waist and some kind of machine gun gripped tightly in his hand. I couldn't tell what it was, but it was awesome.

"So, Lex," I said as I walked toward Alan's vehicle, "is he your leader?"

Alan grunted, which I guess was supposed to pass for an answer. Men. Typical.

"And what's *that* short for?" Nicole asked as we climbed into the car's backseat.

Alan got into the driver's side and slammed the door. "What?"

"Lex," Nicole repeated with a roll of her eyes. "Duh."

"It's just Lex," Alan snapped with tension in his voice.

"Like Luthor?" I asked.

Next to me, Nicole let out an appreciative snort of laughter that made me like her a lot more, but Alan just glared at us in the rearview mirror as he put the car in gear.

"I don't know what you're talking about," he glowered.

"You know, Superman?" I said but was met with stony silence. "Man of Steel's arch enemy, Lex Luthor? Don't you read comic books, dude?"

Still nothing and I rolled my eyes.

"Great, we've been kidnapped by a man with no sense of history," I muttered.

"Or at least literature," Nicole added helpfully.

Alan glared at us again. "Look, just shut up, okay. We'll be at the camp within the hour and you can talk to Lex about history or literature or whatever."

I shook my head, but I figured that was probably enough poking of the bear, at least for a little while. At least I knew Leader Dude's name, Lex, and that was something. Although I still couldn't help but think of Dave, stuck in a car with that weirdo. If we knew what these people wanted, that would be one thing, but without that info...well, we were pretty vulnerable and Dave didn't have any backup.

"So what's the deal with the highwayman act?" Nicole pressed.

I guess *she* thought the bear could take a few more pokes. And maybe she was right...she *was* the reporter, after all. Of course, several of her interviews had ended in what the British used to call "fisticuffs."

Okay, so I *had* watched her show a few times. I wasn't going to tell her, or her biggest fan, David, that.

"It's a new world, lady," Alan said with a shrug as he powered his car down a dirt road behind a line of our other "escorts." "There's no way we can take chances. We've gotten burned before."

I raised my eyebrows. Nicole might come in handy, after all, if she was able to extract tidbits of information like that from people. If this group had been burned, whatever that meant, we'd have to be extra careful until we earned their trust.

Or escaped their clutches, whichever came first.

We rattled along in near silence for another twenty minutes. I tried to keep track of all the twists and turns of the road, making note of landmarks just in case we had to peel our way out of here in a pinch. From the corner of my eye, I could see Nicole doing the same thing.

I had to give her points; she wasn't useless.

"So my friend here is injured," I said, motioning to Nicole. "Are you guys so *burned* by your sad little past with trusting people that you won't let us trade for some antibiotics?"

His gaze came up in the rearview mirror a second time. "That will be up to Lex and the council."

"The council," I repeated blankly.

"That doesn't sound good," Nicole whispered, nudging me with her bloody elbow and leaving a splotch on my shirt.

"Oh dear God," I muttered under my breath. "Not another fucking cult. I hate fucking cults."

Nicole's eyes widened. "*Another* cult?"

I shrugged. "It's a long story; I'll tell you some other time."

"We're not a cult," Alan said as we slowed down.

I craned my neck to see that we were approaching a tall gate. There were at least ten people standing guard with weapons ranging from more AKs to machetes that were already stained with what I *hoped* was zombie blood. As each car approached, they showed some kind of . . . ID, I guess.

Shit, I didn't even have a driver's license anymore (it's not like I carried a purse in the apocalypse; although I could have, Coach and Gucci had lost considerable value and were a literal *steal* now).

We passed through the gate (with the guards glaring at us like we were in some post-apocalyptic B-movie or something) and into a section where cars were parked here and there. Not too many, though, probably fewer than twenty in total, and that gave me some hope. Maybe if there were only a handful of people here, we'd be able to escape with our skin intact.

As we pulled to a stop in the line of cars, Alan said, "Okay, ladies, out." His voice was low and grim as he opened his own door.

Nicole and I exchanged a quick glance, but since this was an order, not a request, and since there were a ton of guns involved (none of them ours)... well, we didn't have much choice. I climbed out first, with Nicole right behind me.

I craned my neck, trying to find the big truck where Dave had gone with Lex. And there it was, probably a hundred yards away. Both of them were already out and walking toward us. Since Dave didn't look any worse for wear, I let out a sigh of relief.

"Pretty small camp," Nicole said as she gave our guard a little smile that had probably opened quite a few doors for her in the past.

He laughed and then another gate opened and revealed the camp within.

We were actually up on a slight incline, so as the gate swung open, we got a good view of the camp below. It was huge. At least as big as the New Phoenix camp, and that one held about five hundred people at last census. I sucked in a breath as I stared out over the sea of tents, broken up by narrow corridors. It appeared there were actually street signs at the intersections, like these people had gone so far as to name the lanes as if this was a real town.

"Holy shit," Nicole breathed.

I nodded silently, then glanced at Dave as he made his way to my side and joined us as we looked down over the expanse together.

"This is *not* good," Dave muttered.

I had to agree, but did so silently as the group who had taken us under their control got behind us and herded us like lambs into the great unknown of their camp.

Unfortunately, I felt like we were lambs going to a slaughter, not about to frolic in a field or something.

CHAPTER 5

Don't sweat the small stuff.
Half-crazed survivors, zombies after your ass...
these things are not small stuff.

Here."

I looked up as a woman entered the big army-style tent where we had been taken. You know the kind, like the ones you see in movies where the general can stand straight up and plan his attacks and pace around and shit. Not your typical "family outing" tent.

I stared at the woman. Her once-blonde hair was unkempt, hanging around her face in stringy and dirty braids. Her clothing was torn, thin like it had been washed too many times, but at least she was wearing clothing. Shoes, not so much.

Clearly, this "camp" didn't involve the trade of clothing. It was all a little *Clan of the Cave Bear* for me.

She blushed like she knew her fashion sense (or lack thereof) was being judged and scowled first at me, then at Nicole before she held out a big tube of antibiotic ointment and a box of gauze and tape.

"Um, thanks," I said, confused as I took the items.

She spun on her heel and pushed from the tent, flopping the flap behind her and leaving us alone without further comment. With a shrug, I turned toward Nicole and Dave. Outside there were three heavily armed guards (we had checked) but inside...just us.

"Well, why would they give us this if they were planning to kill us right away?" Nicole asked as she reached for the materials.

"Good point," Dave said.

He turned away slightly as Nicole lifted her shirt and started to squirt the antibiotic ointment onto her scrapes. She let out a sigh of contentment as the topical painkiller in the goo hit her mangled skin.

"Yes, we all know Nicole is brilliant." I shrugged. "But what do we *do* now? We've been here for three hours and the only person who's come in to see us is that cave-woman girl without shoes."

Nicole lowered her shirt and set what was left of the first-aid supplies to the side. If we got out of here, I was taking that shit with us. Some antibiotic ointment was the *least* of what these freakazoids owed us.

"Maybe the rest of them are in that council that the guy who drove us over here was talking about. What was his name? Adam? Arkin?" Nicole muttered.

"Alan?" I said with a thin smile.

She blinked. "Alan Arkin? The actor?"

I bit my lip almost hard enough to draw blood. "No. Just Alan."

She shrugged. "I guess so, whatever."

Dave nodded slowly and I could see the wheels turning in his head as he tried to think of a way out of this. "Lex mentioned the council to me, too. It sounds like it's their form of government."

"Or their form of crazy-person cultism." I shivered. "Are we going to have to jump off more roofs to escape? Because I'm not sure I'm up for that."

Dave chuckled as he gave me a grin, and all my jealousy toward Nicole faded. She might be cute and semifamous, but she certainly didn't have a history of running for her life or ass-kicking with my man. No one could change our messed-up past together. Who knew that the living dead would be the ties that bind?

"You guys are weird," Nicole sniffed. "What do we *do* about this?"

"Nothing," Lex said as he flipped the tent flap back again and ducked into the small room. He seemed taller than I remembered him being.

"What do you mean, *nothing*?" Dave asked.

He had tensed and now he was standing up really straight, his whole body stiff and ready to attack, even though we all knew by now that doing that wouldn't result in anything but pain and quite possibly death. We were at a distinct disadvantage with these whack-a-moles, both in numbers and weaponry.

"I mean that the council has decided what to do with you," Lex said with a look toward us that implied he thought we were pretty stupid not to understand his cryptic ass.

"Hey, jerk off," I snapped as I started toward him. "We. Don't. Know. What. The. Fuck. You. Are. Talking. About. Got me? I don't know what the hell your *council* is or why you think it has the right to decide what to do with me or my friends."

Lex had been looking at David, but now he turned, almost in slow-motion movie style, and speared me with a look that almost froze my blood. There wasn't hate in his eyes. There wasn't even insanity. There was nothingness. I was meaningless to this man. A fly or a bug that could be set free or squashed, but he would instantly forget about the decision the moment it had been made.

"There was a little town here before," he said softly. "And then outsiders came in and brought this plague that killed everyone but those of us left in this valley. Ten percent of us lived through the outbreak. Ten percent. We had to burn our own town, kill our own families and friends—"

"But we did, too," I interrupted as a brief thought of Dave's sister passed through my mind. I'd shot her months ago, and memories of that horrible moment still woke me up some nights. I knew they woke my husband up, too. "We've *all* suffered. But none of *us* caused this."

Lex shook his head. "But you *did* cause this, Sarah. People like you brought this into our town. People like *you* came to us for help and we were foolish enough to offer it. People like you, holding out your hand like we owed you somehow."

I shook my head, but it was Nicole who spoke, "But we'll trade—"

"Why trade for what you can just take?" Lex interrupted, so calm and collected you'd think he was talking about an upcoming retirement party, not the destruction of three people.

"So you're pissed at us for what happened to your people, and you have to punish us to, I don't know...appease your gods or something?" Dave said with a roll of his eyes that even impressed me, queen of eye rolls. "Does that mean your council has decided to set us free outside the camp without weapons so the zombies can sort it all out? Or are you going shoot us in the town square? What?"

Lex smiled. "Actually, it's a bit of both. But now it's getting late. Tomorrow at dawn, you'll see. You'll understand. There are cots here—"

"Wait!" I burst out. "You think we're going to go to *sleep* and just wait for our fate tomorrow?"

He arched a brow in my direction. "If you try to run, you all die. The men stationed outside of your tent are very clear on that order. But if you don't make the stupid attempt to flee, then you face the punishment and maybe some of you get to live. It's really your choice. Good night."

Then he left, the tent flap swinging shut behind him as he strode out into the fading light and the freedom he'd said we'd never have again.

The three of us stared at each other, but for a long time no one spoke. There was nothing to say, really. Outside the door were the guards Lex was so proud of, and even if we made it past them, there were another what? Probably five hundred people driven to keep us exactly where we were. There was no way we could fight them all.

Finally, it was Dave who spoke. "Okay, you know what, let's just get some sleep. At least we're safe here."

"Safe?" Nicole repeated, turning her sarcasm on him for the first time since he'd gone all fan boy on her earlier in the day. "Are you drunk? How is 'We're going to punish you in some mysterious way for not being part of our clan' anything remotely close to *safe*?"

"Look—" Dave started, but she was on a roll now. A big, fat, borderline hysterical roll.

"They're going to come in here and they're going to take us somewhere awful and we're all going to end up in some death pit like in a *Resident Evil* movie and I don't want to die wearing these ugly clothes," she said, but then the wind seemed to go out of her sails and with a broken-up sigh she sank down onto one of the cots. "This isn't safe and it isn't okay. And . . . and I don't want to just go to sleep and figure it will work itself out."

"No, David is right," I said softly as I came up to take his hand. I didn't look at him, but gently squeezed. "There are no zombies here, and if they manage to get into the camp, then there are hundreds of people outside who are going to fight them for us whether they want to or not. The freaks might be the great unknown, but at least until tomorrow morning, they *are* safe."

Nicole stared at us for a minute and then shook her head. But she didn't argue anymore. She just flopped backward onto her cot and rolled over so that her back faced us. I guess the argument was over and the pouting (or maybe it was just soft crying) had begun.

Dave and I exchanged a quick look, then glanced at the two remaining cots in the big army-style tent. There was this weird unspoken communication thing that we had now, stronger than ever since the outbreak. Without any discussion we dragged the two empty beds to the other side of the tent and pushed them together.

Hey, if this was going to be our last night on this burned-out, zombie-infested earth, at least we were going to spoon. Or fork. Maybe.

After a minute to toe off boots and shrug out of sweaters, we lay down, facing each other in the gathering darkness of the tent.

"So you think she's right. Is this it?" I asked softly. "Has the strange luck of Dave and Sarah finally run out?"

He stared at me for a moment and then smiled. "No way. We always manage to get our asses out of these situations, don't we? I'm sure something awesomely sitcom-rific will happen in the morning and save us once again."

I grinned but it fell pretty quickly. "But if it doesn't... um, thanks for putting up with me during all this. Thanks for not running off with some Swedish secretary who would have been less trouble."

He leaned forward and kissed me. "Silly girl," he whispered. "I never knew any Swedish secretaries."

I laughed even as I swatted him and we held each other as a fitful, less-than-restful sleep finally overtook our fears and sucked us ever closer to the great unknown of the next morning.

CHAPTER 6

Savor your own good life. Or just life in general.
Especially when the zombies are coming.

I woke up first. Well, technically that isn't true, but I'll get to that in a minute. Anyway, when I *did* wake up, Dave was still asleep. Light was starting to filter in through a gap in the tent flap and it hit his face. I reached out in the cool, morning air and gently touched my husband's cheek. He was calm in sleep. Relaxed in a way I never saw anymore while we were running from zombies and cult leaders and hillbillies and a ton of other dangers.

And then I noticed his breathing. One breath in, two short breaths out. One in, two pants out. Over and over. My heart dropped into my rapidly flipping, sick stomach.

Why?

Well, I'd learned some things about zombies. Just a few weeks ago when we'd met the doctor who had nearly gotten us both killed and introduced us to the cure we now carried, we'd seen the drugs he'd developed. He could put a zombie to the closest thing to "sleep" you could hope for, which allowed you to get close and actually observe them (rather than run screaming into the night as you shot at them).

And zombies didn't breathe in . . . just out.

Dave wasn't quite there, but what he was doing as he lay there, totally unaware that I was staring at him, blinking at the tears that stung my eyes, was *not* normal. For the first time since we left Phoenix, I thought about all the weird things that had happened to my Dave since he was bitten:

The superstrength when he lifted weights. I mean, he'd gone from couch potato to superhulk . . . and it didn't seem like he could have done that so quickly, at least not in a natural way. And I wasn't suggesting he was doing steroids, either. I'd actually prefer that at this point. Juiced not living dead, thanks.

Then there was the lack of sleeping. Dave just didn't seem to need as much sleep to function now, though when he crashed . . . well, he crashed hard. Like sleep of the, for lack of a better word, dead. Undead?

And now there was this weird breathing thing to add to the mix. I hadn't noticed it when he was awake, but shit, how often do you sit there and listen to your loved ones breathe?

He had been hungrier lately, too, which meant we had to stop more for supplies, part of why we'd been moving so slowly through the Southwest. We'd gone through so many Power Bars and bags of beef jerky that I'd lost count. Those things weren't brains, but still . . . it wasn't like him.

But what *was* it like?

A zombie? No. I mean, he wasn't trying to eat my

brains. Or chase me across a field moaning or something. It was like something in the ... *middle,* I guess. Not quite Couch Potato Dave, not quite Zombie Dave.

"No, no, no," I whispered, and hearing my own voice snapped me from my fog.

I sat up. I was just being ridiculous, freaking out over something that meant nothing. Dave was Dave, Dave was fine, and getting all worked up over his *breathing* was just silly.

I slung my feet off the bed and grabbed my boots. As I started to put them on, I looked across the tent to see if Nicole was starting to stir yet.

And that was when I realized that our tabloid reporter friend was nowhere to be found.

"Shit," I muttered and I reached back to shake Dave's arm. "Babe?"

His answer was a very zombielike moan, and out of instinct I was on my feet in an instant and turned toward him, hands raised defensively.

"D-Dave," I repeated while in my head I kept thinking, *Please don't be a zombie, please don't be a zombie, please don't be a—*

"What?" he grumbled without opening his eyes.

I lowered my hands with a sigh of relief and shook my head. I *had* to stop freaking out. At least about him. There were plenty of other subjects I was perfectly free to freak out about. For example ...

"Nicole is gone."

He sat up, wide awake in an instant. "What?" he snapped as he flung himself off the cot and grabbed his own boots in one smooth motion.

I waved my hand toward her empty cot and then around

the small tent. "Tada! The fabulous vanishing Nicole has performed her act once again."

He glared at my lame attempt at humor as he tied his boots. "What the fuck? Do you think she made a run for it, or that they took her?"

I shrugged as I tugged my sweater over my head, then pulled my hair back into a loose, messy ponytail. "I have no idea. You'd think if they took her that we would have heard the noise of it, right? I can't imagine Nicole being abducted *quietly.*"

"True," Dave said with a frown. "But I can't imagine her sneaking out without at least *trying* to get us free with her."

I faced him with folded arms. "Oh really? You mean you believe the smutty tabloid television reporter wouldn't double-cross someone to save her own ass? Well, of course she wouldn't. I mean, she's cute, she *must* be good, too."

He glared at me. "Snotty jealousy later, Sarah. Plan now."

I had a really good retort on my lips (okay, I was going to flip him off, which isn't really a great retort), but before I could say anything (er, motion anything) and totally crush him with my rapier wit, the tent flap pulled back. Both of us tensed, ready for a fight, but instead of a guard or Lex or something awful, Nicole strolled in with a sunny smile. Like the fact that she'd apparently been hanging outside with our (evil? crazy? both? something?) captors was totally normal.

"Hey, I thought I heard you two talking in here!" she said. "Good morning."

"Good morning?" I repeated blankly as I stared at her.

She was wearing new clothes. Ratty jeans and a long-sleeved top that covered her scratches and cuts from her meeting with the road yesterday. "What the hell do you mean, *good morning*?"

She tilted her head at me. "Um, I mean I hope your morning is good?"

"Where were you?" Dave asked and for once he didn't sound like he was ready to worship at our new friend's altar. "And where did you get the new rags?"

She looked down with a laugh. "They are a little raggedy, aren't they? Not exactly Prada. But beggars can't be choosers, as my mom used to say." Her brow furrowed for a minute. "I wonder if she's okay..."

"Where did you get them?" Dave repeated. "And *where* have you been?"

She straightened up and all her sunny, happy morning routine disappeared.

"Shit man, just calm down. Look, I had to pee. I tried to wait, but nature is nature, so I stepped outside and the guard took me to do my business. I figured I might be able to get some info from him."

"Yeah, right," I snorted. "I'm sure he was totally forthcoming."

She arched a brow. "One of the advantages of *not* being a married lady in the apocalypse, Sarah, is that I have a whole plethora of resources at my disposal that *you* probably wouldn't even think to use. I used them."

Dave and I exchanged a blank look and then I flinched as her meaning became clear. "Ew!"

"What?" Dave asked, suddenly all innocence. I almost felt sorry for him. If my hunch was right, and I totally knew it was, hello disillusionment!

I dropped my voice to a whisper, as if somehow that made what I was going to say better. "You mean you slept with him?"

Nicole wrinkled her nose in disgust. "No!"

"Oh, good," I sighed.

"I did...*something* else," she said with a shrug.

"Ew!!" Dave and I both squealed at the same time and I swear Dave actually turned a little green at the thought.

"Don't *ew* me," Nicole said with a wave of her hand that dismissed the entire reaction like *we* were the crazy ones. "It not only got me new threads, which I desperately needed, but it got me"—she reached behind her and pulled out the familiar bag she'd had before—"my camera back!! And all the footage is still intact."

I staggered back a step. "Oh God. Please don't tell me you filmed what you and the guard...did."

"Ew!!!" Dave said, his face twisting with disgust.

"No!" Nicole shook her head like we were stupid. "I didn't get the camera back until afterward. But I did find some shit out. Do you want to hear it, or are you nellies too offended by the way I got the info?"

I looked at Dave and he shrugged before he did a shudder from head to toe, like he had bugs on him or something. I couldn't blame him. I mean...come on! *Standards,* Nicole!

"Yeah, we want to know," I said, reluctant to take such ill-gotten gains. But we needed them, so there you go.

"Okay, so like Lex told us last night, the people here all lived in the same town. The zombie outbreak got here about five days after it started in Seattle. They battled it for a while, but we all know how that goes."

"Never well," Dave sighed.

Nicole nodded. "Eventually they burned the town to the ground themselves and headed out here to the plains. And ever since, it's been fucking Tombstone. Like mob justice and shit. So they started the council about a month into their exile so that they'd be more 'organized,' but it's still a vigilante throw down; they just call it the law."

"Yeah, I think we figured all that out already," Dave said with another shudder. I think he had been permanently maimed. "*So* not worth what you did for the info."

"Okay, Judge-y McJudgerson, well then how about *this*," Nicole said and she was starting to look annoyed that we weren't more behind her tactics or her information. "Yesterday afternoon Lex and the council voted for one of us to be made an example. I guess it's some kind of new tradition. *But* they also voted that the other two would be set free so that we'd spread the word that this 'camp' isn't one to stop near or trade in. They do *not* want outsiders coming here; that's for sure. They're totally xenophobic."

I blinked. I was trying to process all this, I really was, but there was a lot to think about. "An example?"

"Yeah, they're going to do something called The Pit to one of us." Nicole shrugged.

"The . . . *Pit*?" Dave repeated as his eyebrows elevated slightly. "And what is that?"

"I don't know for sure," Nicole said with a dark glare at us. "I was *going* to find out and then you two started making a bunch of noise and Ryan got all freaked out and made me go back inside."

"Ryan?" I repeated.

"Well, yeah. The guard. He has a name," Nicole said with a shrug. "He's not so bad."

"Keep telling yourself that," Dave snorted. "So which one of us gets The Pit?"

"Dunno," Nicole sighed. I stared at her and she glared back. "What? I can't get *all* the info. You go out there and do something and see if you can do better."

I swallowed at the idea. "Well, I guess it's something anyway. Um, thanks?"

Nicole sat there for a minute and I saw just a hint of regret on her face. "No problem. You know, it's just a part of Hollywood, so it's not like I haven't done...*that* before. How do you think I moved up from beat reporter to anchor on E.N.Z. in just a few months?"

"Shit, man," I said and I felt a weird urge to pat her or hug her or something.

But I didn't.

What? I had no idea where she'd been. Actually, I *did* have an idea of where she'd been and I didn't want any part of it. I have standards, and they were slightly different from hers, I guess.

"Don't give me the pity look," she snapped as she got up and slung her camera bag onto her back. It flopped against her spine, she did it so hard, and I wouldn't be surprised if she'd have a bruise later. "I do what I do and I did what I did and I don't feel bad about any of it. Got me?"

"Yeah," I said, lifting my hands in the universal gesture of "Chill out, bitch," "I got you."

"Okay, okay, ladies," Dave said as he slipped between the two of us like a referee of a fight about to start. He may have been right on that one. "So we know these freakazoids have a plan for us and that one of us is going to get chosen for this...*punishment* or whatever it is. Can we focus on that instead of who annoys who the most?"

"We can *try,*" Nicole muttered with as dark a look as I'm sure was on my own face.

But before we could really formulate some kind of serious plan to battle the great unknown that was The Pit, the tent flap pulled back again and three guards entered the area, guns lifted in a serious display of "Don't fuck with us."

"Hey, Ryan," Nicole said in a little sing-songy voice that was meant to taunt. I guess she didn't understand the message the guns were sending. Or she didn't care.

I stared as the youngest of the three guards, a kid probably barely into his twenties, shrank back slightly with a deep, dark blush. One of the older guys snapped him a dark glare and then returned his attention to us.

"Okay, time to move out. Let's go."

Instead, Dave sank down on the cot and leaned back on his arms, relaxed as can be. It seemed like *he* wasn't really clear on the "Don't fuck with us" message, either. Seriously, were the two of them *trying* to get us all killed? Because we hadn't taken a vote on that or anything and I wanted a say before some looney toon blew my brains across the side of the tent, thank you very much.

I was about to open my mouth and tell Dave to knock it the hell off, but before I could, I actually looked closer. I really saw the way he was laying and the look in his eyes. And in that moment, I realized what he was doing was all an act. The vein in his forehead was throbbing, after all, and that *never* meant good things as many a zombie, some crazy cult leaders, and an equally insane doctor had found out over the past few months.

"Where to, guys?" he asked. "Letting us head out with supplies in hand? Kind of you to be so neighborly."

He said the last with a perfect mimicry of their Southern accents that had me smothering a smile into my hand. We might all get shot because of him, but at least he was entertaining, which went a long way in the Badlands.

"Just get up," barked the guard who had spoken before. Neither of the other two had made even a peep, so clearly he was the mouthpiece of this brain trust.

But Dave stayed just where he was, pushing the boundaries and causing major headaches. He was really good at that. I should know; I'd been on the receiving end of a few of them in the past.

"Sure. Tell me where I'm going and I'm happy to come along."

Without even a word of warning, the younger guard, Nicole's friend Ryan, strode out in front of the others, swung the butt of his rifle, and smacked Dave right across the stomach with it. I gasped as I stepped forward, only to have one of the other men grab me by my arm and pull me back with enough force that I felt the strain in my shoulder.

Dave grunted and his arms came across his stomach. But damn, that blow seemed like it was pretty hard and he basically just looked annoyed. The kid who had struck him looked just as irritated that he hadn't hurt Dave as much as he wanted to.

"Get up," Nicole's boyfriend said, his voice cracking like he was twelve rather than around twenty.

Slowly, Dave pushed himself from the cot and got to his feet. It was a menacing sort of unfolding of limbs. Also kind of hot, as was his low tone when he said, "I'm going to tag you back for that, kid. Count on it."

At least Ryan had the sense to back the hell away from

Dave's purple-faced rage, but our other two escorts exchanged a look and then laughed like they knew something we didn't. And I guess they did. After all, we had no idea what The Pit was or which one of us would be today's happy participant.

Was it wishful thinking to hope it was a big shopping spree? Yeah, I thought so.

"Come on, then," said the guard who had been doing all the talking when he'd stopped giggling like a moron. "You want to know where you're going? Then let's get to it. You'll see soon enough."

Clearly there was no point in arguing anymore; even Dave saw that. With a collective sigh, we all fell into line and followed directions.

Nicole went first, trailing along behind the talker and her boyfriend. Dave slipped up beside me and we followed, with the third guy right behind us. Occasionally the barrel of his gun poked my back, like he was trying to remind us who was boss. Um, I got it. I was *not* boss.

I gave Dave a side-glance. "You okay?"

He nodded, his mouth a grim line.

I looked at him again. "Are you sure? That hit looked pretty hard."

He shrugged. "It was, but it didn't hurt that much."

"But—"

His warning glare cut me off. "Sarah, I'm fine. Don't worry about me, just keep an eye out. We're going to need to know the lay of the land when we get out of this mess."

I bit back whatever other comments I had about his health and nodded. He was right. There would be plenty of time later to ask him why a shotgun butt to the stomach hadn't elicited any more from him than an aggravated expression.

At least, I *hoped* there would be time.

We weaved our way through the camp, down side "streets" and past worn-out tents and burned-out campfires. There was a pervasive smell of sweat and, um, *other* bodily odors; when they mixed together in the air, it was pretty sour. Hygiene didn't seem to be a top priority here in Freak Town (it's like Funky Town, but not as catchy).

People lined the little lanes, all dressed the same way as the girl who had given us our antibiotic ointment the night before. Sort of a cross between a hobo and a caveman seemed to be the style of the day. Weird since there were malls and houses so close by.

Even if these people were totally terrified of the zombies (which seemed pretty unlikely considering how well armed they were), it would have been easy to send a big party out to scavenge whatever they needed. There was no reason to be so raggedy. And that made their choice to dress like this, look like this, even creepier.

And their blank, empty looks as we passed by? Yeah, also pretty fucked up. Evidently they'd seen this march before because it didn't seem to faze any of them one iota.

Ahead of us, Nicole yelled at them in a cracking voice that revealed her fear despite her surprisingly admirable bravado. "We didn't do anything wrong! You have to see that punishment with no crime is tyranny! You could be next!"

Her words meant nothing to them. One by one, they either fell into step behind us to see the show or went back into their messy tents. My heart began to throb, double time, triple time, hard enough that it hurt and felt like it could burst past my rib cage at any moment. With every step that brought us closer to this mysterious Pit punishment, my fear increased.

And I hated that. I'd sort of gotten good at the fear-mastering thing. This was a setback, for sure.

And then Dave slipped his hand into mine and that gentle touch calmed me. I glanced over at him and he was giving me a look, the look that said, "It's all going to be okay, babe."

And I guess after all this time I believed him. He had never let me down before.

We turned one last corner and down a long, empty stretch of land. I glanced around the still-protesting Nicole and past our entourage of guards and saw a group of people, probably at least a hundred and fifty, maybe even two hundred, gathered around... *something*. As we approached, they parted like the Red Sea and I saw what that *something* was.

The empty shell of a deep swimming pool, dirty and moldy, dark with blood and sludge smears that dragged up the high sides. There was a set of stairs that led into the pool, but a big kind of wooden gate had been set up in front of them in the pool so that they were rendered useless.

"Oh shit, this must be The Pit," I muttered.

And inside The Pit, waiting for whoever was going to be chosen from the three of us to be the example and take the punishment?

Of course it would be zombies. Somewhere around thirty drooling, sludge-vomiting zombies.

CHAPTER 7

Try something new. Hint: *Not* sacrificing
yourself to the zombies.

Dave gripped my hand even tighter, tight enough that my fingers squished together, but I hardly felt the sting. I was too busy watching our good, old buddy Lex step through the crowd. As he moved, some people reached out to touch him, while others stepped back in deference to whatever position of power the asshole had. It was like he was a cross between Jesus and the president.

Across the pool he climbed a short ladder that lead out over the diving board. The zombies below milled about hopelessly. They must have been in there for a while, because they didn't move toward the steps that were blocked by the gate. I guess they'd already figured out that they couldn't get out that way.

But the moment Lex came into view, they woke up from their zombie fog. In a frenzy, they ran to Lex's side of the Pit, jumping and clawing and moaning as they tried to reach him on his precarious perch.

But Lex didn't seem to care. He was cool as a cucumber

as he stared out over his zombie captives, past his fellow townspeople and toward us, standing like lemmings at the edge of the pool, ready to go over the cliff and into certain doom.

"A society must have rules," he said in a big, booming voice that cut any light chatter from the crowd. Even the zombies growled a little softer, it seemed. I guess they recognized the boss just as much as the townspeople did. "Otherwise it falls into chaos."

"What do you call this, asshat?" I screamed out.

The crowd gave a collective gasp and a couple hundred faces swung toward me in disbelief.

What? Had no other "prisoner" ever dared to question Superman's arch villain? I guess not, because Lex glared at me with a look that could have killed. And I gave one right back and wished like hell that my superpower was being able to burn a hole in someone with my eyes.

Unfortunately, my strength was killing houseplants, which wasn't so helpful either prezombie or post.

"Our rules are simple," he continued as if I had said nothing. "*No* outsiders. We've learned they only bring plague, heartbreak, and villainy. These outsiders have broken our rules and now they must be made an example."

"What is this, *Mad Max Beyond Thunderdome*?" I asked, once again yelling my thoughts out loud enough so that Lex could hear me.

And it seemed Nicole was inspired by my outbursts. She added, "Bust a deal, spin the wheel!"

"Nice reference," I said with a nod in her direction. Quoting the movie definitely raised her value in my mind.

Dave was curiously silent during the Sarah and Nicole

Comedy Hour. He just kept his slow and steady stare on Lex.

"I won't do the Gulog! I've heard the mask is bad for the skin," I said, to which Nicole elbowed me and snorted out an appreciative laugh.

Lex smiled, too, but it wasn't filled with humor. More like menace. "As punishment for trespass, the man, David, will go into The Pit for five minutes."

The laughter Nicole and I had been sharing came to a screeching halt as Lex's order echoed in the valley. The crowd around us let out a half-hearted cheer, but I didn't hear any of it anymore. Instead I looked at David. His jaw was set and he hadn't even flinched at the handing down of what amounted to a death sentence.

Sure, I still had a vial of serum around my neck that had saved his ass once before, but if he got into that Pit, the zombies would tear him apart. There wouldn't be enough of him to scrape together for burial, let alone "cure."

"No!" I cried out and started toward him, as if touching him or something would fix this situation.

Just as in the tent when Ryan swatted him with the gun, one of our guards grabbed me. But this time I was far more determined to reach my husband. I pulled against the other man's arms and was almost free when a second, maybe even a third,—person grabbed me.

I didn't exactly see them. I only saw David. But he wasn't looking at me. He was staring at Lex.

"I've been told that if one of us does this 'Pit' thing with the zombies that you'll set the other two free," he called out. "Is that true?"

Lex stared across the expanse at him and I swear there

was surprise on his face. "Yes. That's true. The women will go free after the punishment has been served." He glared first at Nicole, then at me. "And they'll tell anyone they come in contact with that this camp is not to be bothered and our borders are not to be crossed."

"We'll *all* tell them together if that's what you want. We'll leave right now and start spreading the word far and wide. There's no reason to hurt David!" Nicole insisted.

I didn't look at her, I couldn't bear to take my eyes off David, but in her voice I heard her fear. And also her empathy, though whether for me or for my husband, I didn't know. Probably both.

"It's the law," Lex said, as flat as if he was a cop issuing us a parking ticket that we couldn't talk our way out of.

"But you *make* the law, you could change it!" I insisted.

"Do you give me your word in front of all your people that you'll let Sarah and Nicole go unharmed once this punishment has been meted out?" David asked, ignoring our attempts to reason with Lex. I think he must have seen the writing on the wall that *reason* wasn't this guy's strong suit.

Lex tilted his head, and I saw a grudging respect on his face. It didn't make me like him anymore, of course.

"Yes," he called out after a long pause. "The women will be released unharmed. We'll even return some weapons and a vehicle to them once we deliver them to our border."

David hesitated and then, to my utter shock and horror, he *nodded.* "Then I'll take your punishment."

"David!" I screamed in utter disbelief, and next to me I heard someone else wail. I realized later it was Nicole, but in that moment I couldn't understand anything that was happening in this fucked-up situation.

What had happened to "some crazy thing will get us out of this"? What had happened to us fighting our way to Illinois and something resembling normalcy together?

He finally looked at me. *Really* looked at me. Like he was trying to memorize my face or something.

"Babe," he whispered, "this is the only way for you to get out."

"No," I said, shaking my head hard enough that my neck was starting to hurt. "Fuck no. We go together. If you die, I die."

He tilted his head. "And what about our duty? What about what we promised to do?"

"I don't care about that!" I snapped, blinking at tears. "If I get in the pool with you, we can fight—"

"I've counted twenty-eight zombies in there, Sarah, and we don't have any weapons," Dave interrupted. "I have a lot of faith in you . . . in us, but I don't think we could take more than maybe ten of them before we get ripped to shreds."

I shook my head even though I knew everything he was saying was gospel truth. "I don't want to do this without you," I whispered.

He looked at me with this weird, peaceful, accepting smile and suddenly I felt like a child. Not like he was condescending, but more like he saw the situation with a clarity I couldn't yet achieve.

"Sarah, we have things to do. Important things. Are you just going to forget about all that so you can die in a rusted-out pool with me?"

His words and his look shook me and I looked down.

The vial of cure was lightly outlined under my T-shirt. It looked like a necklace so the guards hadn't checked it out or confiscated it.

"Everything we've done in the last month will be in vain if you jump into the pool with me," he continued. "But not if you turn around and get into the car these people give you and keep on heading east. Nicole will help you, won't you, Nicole?"

I had all but forgotten our reporter friend, but now I blinked as I looked at her. She was staring at our exchange with a mixture of confusion and a touch of heartache. I found myself wondering who she had lost that made her eyes look like she understood what I was going through.

"Y-Yes," she finally whispered with half a nod. "I'll help Sarah any way I can...if she'll let me."

"Good." Dave smiled.

"Enough," Lex said.

Honestly, I was surprised he'd let us go on so long, but there had been something almost mesmerizing about what Dave said and how he said it. Everyone around us was staring; people were blinking like they understood what was happening in their world for the first time.

And when I looked at Lex, I realized he saw that, too. And he had to nip it in the bud. He didn't want these people to wake up from their fog of shock and fear. He needed them to stay like...well, mindless zombies (without the brain eating) if he wanted to keep his power and isolate them from everything else. And maybe he meant well. Maybe he really thought he could protect them this way.

It didn't really matter. I hated the guy and I wanted him dead for his order that would take Dave from me. His order that would change my life even more permanently than even zombies and apocalypse had done.

"Put him in The Pit," Lex snapped.

The guards who had been holding me shoved me aside and took a step toward Dave, but before they could reach him, he lifted a hand.

"I'll get in on my own, thanks," he said as he edged toward the pool.

"I love you," I shouted.

He looked at me evenly and then he smiled. "I know."

I blinked and for a moment the tension faded. "Are you quoting *Empire Strikes Back*? At a time like this you're geeking out on me! Seriously?"

He smiled and then in one swift movement he spun around, sat down on the edge of the pool, and jumped in.

CHAPTER 8

Set boundaries. It's the only way
the zombies and the crazy people will learn.

I couldn't hold back a scream as Dave's head disappeared from view below the edge of the pool, and this time when I ran forward no one tried to stop me. Or maybe they did, but I didn't feel it. The fact was, at that moment I didn't feel *anything* but pure, unadulterated terror.

I stared down into The Pit and there Dave stood, looking out across the dirty pool at the zombies who were still gathered underneath Lex's diving board.

Dave was panting, his skin pale and his eyes focused yet still filled with the fear he'd been trying not to show me earlier. I wanted to grab him and pull him out, but I couldn't reach him and I knew damn well even if I could, he wouldn't let me. He'd decided to make some kind of fucking noble sacrifice like we were in a romance novel or something. Only there wasn't going to be a happily-ever-after ending because the zombies were coming.

Well, they *should* have been coming. Only, as my initial fear and focus on Dave faded, I realized something remarkable and totally inexplicable.

They weren't.

For some reason, the zombies remained on the other side of the pool. They continued to mill about below Lex's diving board, moaning and reaching for him. They hadn't even noticed Dave, or at least it didn't seem like they had.

"Shit, do I have to do everything?" Dave muttered as he edged further into the middle of the pool toward them. His face was lined with intense concentration and anticipation of what was about to happen.

And yet, still, *nothing* did. Even as he moved closer and closer, a tantalizing morsel of a man being dangled right in their reach, the zombies stayed focused on the leader of this fucked-up band of Not-So-Merry-Men (and women, since he was an equal opportunity douche bag).

It seemed the refugees were starting to see the same thing I was, too. Around me people started muttering, the sound of which grew louder as Dave moved closer. Yet the zombies completely ignored him.

"What the hell is going on?" Nicole whispered, right next to my ear.

I jumped. I hadn't even noticed her move toward me, I was so focused on my husband.

"I don't know," I said back, leaning forward as though somehow I could get closer to him, somehow I would understand what was happening, er, *not* happening below us.

The whispers and mutters around us were getting louder and louder and occasionally I heard them clearly. "Does he have a power?" asked a male voice.

"Why don't they see him?" This time it was a little girl

who spoke, and the fact that she was here to witness an execution troubled me as much as her question did.

"Maybe they don't want to eat us anymore?" a woman said, her voice laced with hope and hysteria.

"Don't be stupid," a man answered. "They're still trying to reach Lex."

Yes, that was true. The zombies still clawed and moaned as they made every effort to get a hold of the man high above them, balanced on a precarious piece of bouncy wood. They were ravenous and drooled sludge in a pool beneath him. Nothing was different about their behavior.

They just didn't seem to want David.

Now you'd think any normal person would just wipe their brow and say, "Phew!" and take the gift they were being offered. But I could still see Dave's expression pretty clearly and rather than being happy or relieved that he was not, thus far, zombie shish kebab, he looked . . . *annoyed.* Worried. Confused.

And then he did something really stupid.

"Hey!" he shouted, waving his arms at the big group of zombies.

"David!" I yelled. "Stop that! Don't encourage them."

He ignored me and kept waving his arms around. "Hey, drooly!"

I froze as his yelling and gesturing finally seemed to connect with the zombies just feet away from him. A few turned away from the main crowd and looked at him. Well, toward him. Zombies don't really look *at* anything. They aren't so much *focused.*

"Yeah you, Ugly!" Dave continued before he tapped his chest all macho-man style. "Here I am."

The entire crowd, including Nicole and me, seemed to hold their breath as the zombies who had turned toward Dave's voice staggered closer to him. Close enough to touch him. I saw every muscle in his body tense, and mine were doing the same.

The group stared at him, looks of confusion and blank despair on their rotting faces. This was followed by the usual zombie head tilting and sniffing of their air that I'd always found so doglike and utterly disturbing.

"Oh God," Nicole whispered as she reached up to grip my upper arm in both hands. "Oh God."

I couldn't answer. I couldn't even breathe as the zombies stared at Dave and he stared back. I kept waiting for the throng to finally wake the fuck up, dive forward, and tear him to shreds.

Instead, the three zombies who had noticed him finally gave him one last look and then slowly, unexpectedly, turned back toward Lex on the diving board and continued their half-ass attempts to get to him.

I staggered backward as David turned toward me. Our eyes met and I saw the same questions that burned inside of me boiling in him. Mostly they consisted of, *What the fuck???*

"What is this?" Lex roared. His voice now sounded frightened and confused even though his angry expression was still pretty intimidating. "Why don't they attack you?"

Dave stared up at Lex and shook his head. "I don't know."

"Bullshit!" Lex was purple now, shaking his fists. He was so precarious on that diving board, I kept waiting for him to tumble into The Pit and get himself killed.

But we weren't going to be so lucky, damn it. I'd never won when I bought scratch tickets, either.

"It's true, I don't *know* why they're doing this!" Dave insisted as he stepped away from both the zombies and the very angry leader of the town.

"Fuck that." Lex backed down the diving board, almost like he didn't want to put his back to the zombies... or maybe it was David who he was afraid of. "Shoot him. Shoot all three of them."

"No!" Dave shouted as he spun toward me. The fear that had been lining his face at the thought of zombie death now doubled. "You promised me."

Lex stepped down from the board and shook his head. "But you didn't tell me you had some way to keep the monsters from attacking you. You're not safe."

He nodded toward his guards and they lifted their weapons toward Nicole and me while a few others pointed their guns at Dave in the pool.

What happened next felt like a slow-motion action sequence from a movie. Think *Matrix,* but only the first one before they all went to hell in a handbasket.

At the same moment that the guards along the edge began to fire their guns at Dave, he started to run toward the gate that blocked the steps leading from the pool. I was so busy staring that I was totally off guard when Nicole dove toward me and we both toppled to the hard, concrete pool edge as bullets whizzed by our ears.

But the guards stopped shooting at us the moment that Dave hit the gate with all his body weight. The wooden structure couldn't take the strain and it fell, breaking into shards that flew up and around the pool edge like rain.

The nearly thirty zombies who had been gathered on

the opposite side of The Pit in a disorganized and disinterested mass finally woke up. They may be dumb, but they're really good at what they do. You know, killing people.

They rushed toward the now-unblocked stairway with a collective roar and started climbing over one another to reach the dismayed people above them.

Everyone but David, of course. They continued to utterly ignore him as they staggered up the stairway around him. They even jostled him as they rushed the survivors above and didn't seem to register that he was food. Instead, they started grabbing victims from the confused, horrified crowd.

Screams echoed in the air around us as people were either grabbed or ran for their lives and scattered gunfire joined in on the cacophony of noise and horror.

Zombie carnage pretty much plays out the same way when an attack starts in a group of any legitimate size. There are some people who fight, there are some who flee ... there are some who shove eighty-year-olds with walkers to give themselves extra time to get away (which was well played, but highly distasteful).

Normally I was right in the fray of all this glorious panic, but at that moment I couldn't seem to move. I just continued to stare upward from the place where I'd landed on the ground, watching everything around me. David should have been dead. Nicole and I should have been negotiating an escape with these whack-a-doodles.

But instead, here we were. In five minutes everything had changed ... *again*.

Then Nicole was shaking me, hard enough that my shoulders hit the ground underneath me.

"Sarah!" she screamed and her voice sounded strained, like she'd been repeating my name more than once before I woke up from my fog.

"What?" I asked.

"Come on," she insisted as she grabbed my hand and half pulled, half dragged me to my feet. "Run! We have to run!!"

Her words finally registered; this time when I looked around I actually *saw* what was happening around me. The zombies who had escaped from the pool were tearing people limb from limb, sinking their teeth into flesh and working for brains.

Worse, some of the first victims of the attack were already staggering back to their feet, flesh graying and eyes sparkling red. Pretty soon there weren't going to be thirty zombies, there were going to be three hundred. And at that point, we were pretty well fucked.

I managed to get my feet under me and do what Nicole ordered. I ran like hell. But not *away* from the chaos as I think she'd been suggesting. No, I turned and headed straight for Dave.

"What are you doing?" she screamed, but she was right on my heels despite her apparent disapproval of my choice. "Are you crazy?"

I ignored her (very valid) question and just kept my focus on my husband.

He was still standing at the top of the pool steps, looking around at the bloodbath with a dazed expression. There were two zombies standing right next to him, tearing and pulling at what had once been a person, though I could no longer tell if it had been male or female. They still didn't seem to care that Dave was there.

Me, on the other hand, they cared about. As I got close enough, one of them dropped the severed arm he was gnawing on and faced me with a primal growl that had been saying, "You are my food source" for thousands of years in the animal kingdom. I guess it was my turn to be at the bottom of the food chain.

"Fuck," I muttered.

Here I was, totally unarmed, and clearly whatever was keeping Dave from being dinner was *not* a sexually transmitted disease because the zombies most definitely wanted *me* as a tasty treat.

"Dave," I said as I did a little dodgy dance with my zombie friend.

You know what I'm talking about, that shuffle you do when you're approaching someone head on and you can't figure out which way to go to avoid hitting each other. Except my new zombie friend totally wanted to hit me. And I wasn't the only one attempting not to get eaten in our group. Behind me I heard Nicole grunting as she swung a pretty nice high-leg kick at a zombie who had turned his attention on her.

My voice snapped Dave from his fog and he looked at me.

"Shit!" he barked as he finally recognized my problem and then he was in the fray. My hero, as always.

He slammed forward and sent the zombie who was interested in me sprawling away. The thing growled, but then he saw another potential victim and was distracted as he trotted off after the screaming man who had caught his eye.

"Are you okay?" Dave asked, his stare still even on me. I nodded and then cocked my head. "What about *you*?"

"We don't have fucking time for this *Dawson's Creek* feelings bullshit! We have to get out of here," Nicole bellowed as she gestured at the pandemonium around us before she slammed an elbow into a freshly minted zombie from among the camp members who hadn't gotten away from the initial attack. "Now, now, *now!*"

Dave shook his head and all the weirdness faded from his expression. He was back to normal, all-business, get-us-the-fuck-away-from-zombies-Dave now. I had a feeling that would disappear before too long, though. Some shit had gone down and we would have to discuss it at some point.

But Nicole was right. Here, in the middle of zombie hell, *not* exactly the time nor the place.

"Come on," Dave snapped and he motioned toward the place we'd come from that morning. I didn't argue, anything away from the massacre happening around us was a good thing.

We scurried up the slope that went back into the main part of the camp. Slopes are good, actually. Zombies have trouble with hills, which can be pretty damn funny to watch if you get the chance. Ultimate physical comedy, especially if they lose body parts when they fall. It's like *Jack and Jill,* but with missing arms and a lot more moaning.

Of course, you get enough of them and some of them are bound to figure it out, but still. It slows them down and sometimes that's enough to get away, or at least catch your breath in the middle of a fight.

Unfortunately, hills didn't really slow down humans. Unless they're *really* fat (and most of the fatties hadn't been able to get away from zombie attacks and were the living dead already—yeah, Zombie Weight Watchers was going to catch on big time someday). However, now that the bulk of the zombies were still behind us, partying down with the campers who had come to witness our "punishment," humans had become our biggest problem.

As we scampered up the hill, a small group of about twenty people who were left up in the "village" part of the camp, the ones who apparently hadn't figured out all living dead hell was breaking loose, stopped their various chores and stared at us. There was a brief moment of stunned quiet and then there were twenty guns pointed at us.

"You're supposed to be in The Pit," one of the women snapped as the group as a whole rushed us.

"Look, look—" Dave started, his hands raised.

My heart lodged in my throat. It seemed like every time we almost escaped these people, things got worse and worse. Annoying, to say the least.

But then a few of the people looked past us and down the hill. The wind was blowing toward us, blowing away the sounds of the chaos, but there was no avoiding seeing it when you actually looked.

"Zombies!" the same woman screamed and her dirty face twisted with horror and fear.

The three of us were instantly forgotten as the bulk of the remaining villagers started down toward their friends and neighbors. Some of the sharper ones ran *away,* too. "No man left behind" didn't really apply in postzombie existence. Well, at least not normally. Dave and I still seemed to practice it, sometimes to our detriment.

"Come on before they remember us," Dave said.

"The zombies or the people?" I asked.

"Does it matter?" He grabbed my hand and started pulling me through the twists and turns of the camp.

Okay, so he had told me to pay attention earlier that morning. I'm sorry to say, I hadn't. Too worried about The Pit, you see. Thank goodness he was on top of it, because he seemed to know exactly where he was going and how to get there in the quickest and least-attention-grabbing manner.

Pretty soon we were back to the entrance of the camp. There were two gates. We were at the first. Beyond it was the small collection of vehicles we'd seen when we came in earlier. Beyond *that* was a second gate.

Unfortunately, the entire area was crawling with guards, at least one for each of us, and unlike zombies, guards could think. Also, they could shoot and we'd already been shot at more than once today. It was starting to get *really* old.

Dave pursed his lips as we all flattened against one of the tents so that we remained out of sight of the guards at the inside gate.

"We need a car if we're going to have any chance to make it the hell out of here," he whispered.

I peered around him. Shit, they were really heavily armed. "Well," I began, "we could try—"

But before I could finish, there was a voice screaming through the quiet at this end of the now-almost-deserted camp. Nicole's voice, to be more specific.

"Zombies!" she screamed, and I swear if I hadn't been looking right at her, face as calm as could be, I would have thought she was truly terrified. "Oh God, help, they're everywhere!"

"What the hell are you—"

But before Dave could finish the question, Nicole reached up, covered his mouth, and motioned to the guards. They were abandoning their posts, running into the camp like crazy people. All we had to do was keep to the shadow of the tent where we'd been hiding and poof, we were free!

"Nice," Dave whispered as Nicole lowered her hand and motioned for the gate and the cars beyond it.

I nodded. "Yeah, good thought."

"Sometimes it's the simplest things," Nicole said, but I almost thought she was blushing at our compliments. "But we don't have time for this. Let's get a car and get the fuck out of Dodge before the zombie thing gets contained and these freaks start looking for us."

Without another word, we all rushed forward. The gate was unlocked and we were able to get into the place where all the group cars were parked. Unfortunately, our SUV was not among them.

"Fuck," Dave muttered as we searched. "I really liked that car."

I nodded. "And it had all our awesome weapons and GPS and stuff, too."

Of course, this wasn't the first time we'd lost a vehicle, our weapons, nearly our lives, but it was more and more annoying every time. You just don't know, until you've lived through your own apocalypse, how much you come to depend upon that kind of stuff. The car becomes your home, your sense of normalcy.

And once again, that was gone for us.

"Just pick something," Nicole hissed with a quick look over her shoulder. "Zombies! Freaks with guns! *Focus!*"

"All right, all right," Dave muttered. He scanned the

area until he found the big-wheeled truck that Lex had
been driving when the group picked us up the day before.
He grinned. "You know, if that little bitch is going to steal
my baby, I think I have to return the favor."

He motioned toward the truck and we were each about
to open one of the doors when the sound of a handgun
cocking echoed through the air. All of us froze and slowly
we turned to face the person who had gotten to us just
moments before we made our escape.

And who was it but Nicole's boyfriend, Ryan? He was
holding a bloody Colt .45 that was leveled right at us.
Well, at *Dave* to be more specific.

"Y-You stop," he stammered. His hands were shaking.
"You stop right there."

"Oh for God's sake," Nicole sighed. "Don't you have
better things to do than stalk me?"

The boy blushed almost purple, but he actually lifted
his gun higher. "Back away from the vehicle."

Dave did step away from Lex's truck, but he didn't
stop there. Instead he stalked right toward the kid who
was holding the dangerous weapon leveled right at my
husband's head.

The motion shocked all of us, including Ryan, who
didn't even make an attempt to stop him as he stared.

"Hey," he finally whimpered, but Dave had already
reached him.

In one swift motion he pulled the handgun from the
younger man's fist and then swung it. The handle connected with Ryan's temple and the boy crumpled unconscious at Dave's feet.

"Told you I'd get you back for smacking me," Dave
said with a smile. He sunk the gun into his waistband and

turned back to us. "Now let's go. And be sure to buckle up."

We swung into the truck, Dave driving, Nicole in the front seat beside him, and I in the back. He grinned as he gunned the truck's big engine a couple of times and then floored it.

We hit the outside gate and burst through the chain link like it was nothing. There were two guards sitting outside in the shade and both of them jumped up as we careened past them. Their faces were almost comical with shock as they watched us fly by. It took them a few seconds before they started firing at us. They were halfhearted, though, and not even close to hitting us or the truck as we screamed down the dirt road and out of range.

So once again, we had gotten away from deranged survivors and rabid zombies without a scratch on us.

Or so I thought, until Nicole's eyes went wide and she barked, "Shit, Dave! You're bleeding! You've been shot."

CHAPTER 9

Get out of your own way. Try to get out
of the way of stray bullets, too.

I jammed myself up into the narrow space between Nicole and Dave in the front seat of the truck and looked where she was pointing. Sure enough, the left shoulder of Dave's black T-shirt was soaked. I reached out to press my hand to the stain, praying it was water or sludge or pee or *anything* but blood.

But when I pulled back my palm, it was coated in dark, sticky redness that I'd come to know all too well since the outbreak. And to think…I'd been a bit squeamish about stuff like needles before the zombies attacked. Silly, silly Sarah….

Dave glanced over at my bloody hand, but his face was surprisingly calm considering I had his, you know, life source all over my fingers.

"David, stop the truck," I said, trying to remain as calm as he seemed to be. It was a struggle.

I kind of wanted to smack the doofus for getting hurt… *again* and scaring the shit out of me… *again*. I mean, it was all about me, right? No.

Well, crap.

He didn't answer and I gritted my teeth. "Dave, *please* stop."

"I can't stop," he insisted as he continued to drive at the same breakneck speed.

Superdangerous considering (a) we were on the highway and it was littered with destroyed and abandoned vehicles that he was dodging like we were in a video game and (b) he'd been FUCKING SHOT.

"Stop the goddamn truck!" I bellowed, forgetting calm and politeness.

"No. Those weirdos could be after us any second. We have to get as far away from here as possible," he said, and it sounded like he was gritting his own teeth at this point.

"Shit, man," Nicole cried. "You got shot in the shoulder! How the fuck can you be so chill?"

"Practice?" Dave asked with a half smile.

I guess I should have been happy that he was so in control of himself, but I wasn't. It was actually scary. I reined in my emotions, though. Freaking out and yelling and generally acting like a weepy girl weren't going to help in this situation.

"Please," I growled between tightly clenched teeth. "I need to look at the wound."

He glanced at me and I guess I must have looked like I wasn't fucking around. He nodded once.

"Nicole, I'm going to slow down. Take the wheel, okay?"

She opened her mouth and I saw protests forming on her lips. Reaching forward, I grabbed her upper arm and shook none too gently.

"Drive. The. Fucking. Truck," I ground out.

She hesitated for a brief second and then she nodded as she unbuckled and took the wheel. Dave grunted as he unhooked his own belt and slid himself out from the front seat to climb into the back.

The truck swerved slightly, the front wheels drifting onto the rocky shoulder before Nicole got herself situated and managed to jerk us back onto the highway. Dave staggered into the backseat as she twisted the wheel and I reached up a hand to steady him. He was cool to the touch, almost cold, and I caught my breath before I forced a smile. All my earlier anger was completely forgotten.

Of course it had been replaced by stark terror, so I'm not sure it was a good exchange. Equal, but not good.

"Sit here." I motioned to the seat beside me. "And take off your shirt."

"Are we going to make out in the backseat?" he asked.

"Please don't," Nicole pleaded from the driver's seat. "I've been traumatized enough already today."

"Let's see how badly you're hurt and then we'll talk about whether or not I want to make out with you," I said as he scrunched his T-shirt up and over his head.

There was so much to see that I could hardly take it all in. First off, there was a big, dark bruise across his stomach where Ryan had slammed the gun butt that morning. You know, when he'd barely registered even irritation even though the strike had clearly done some damage.

But the bruise wasn't our immediate problem. No, higher up was our bigger issue, the gaping hole in his shoulder.

It looked like a rifle shot and it had gone through and through from the looks of the entry and exit wounds. It wasn't the worst thing I'd seen since the start of the zombie issue, but without treatment, it could still kill David.

As could the shock he was apparently in since he didn't seem that fazed as he took a glance at the hole in his shoulder.

"Huh, look at that," he muttered.

"Look at that?" I repeated in disbelief. "You have a hole in your body that does *not* belong there and the best you can do is 'Look at that'?"

He pursed his lips but ignored me as he reached up toward the wound. I watched in disbelief as he let the tip of his index finger dip into the hole.

"Do we need to dig out a bullet here?" he asked as he poked the wound ceaselessly.

"Stop it!" I snapped as I slapped his hands away. "Don't poke it."

"He's poking it?" Nicole asked, her eyes coming up wide in the rearview mirror. "Don't poke it! Poking it can't make it better!"

"Calm down, you two," Dave said, but he did stop poking the seeping hole. "I'm fine. It doesn't hurt."

"It *should* hurt," I muttered as I grabbed for his discarded shirt and used it to cover the wound and apply pressure. "You have a hole in your shoulder. If anything should hurt, it's that."

Dave rolled his eyes and was about to argue, but Nicole interrupted.

"I think we should stop and see if we can get anything to treat that. I still have some antibiotic cream in my camera bag, although I'm not sure how helpful it will be with a gunshot wound. Will it need stitches?"

I blinked. Damn, I hadn't even thought of that. I looked

down at the hole. It wasn't yawning or anything, but it wasn't really a scratch, either.

"Yeah, probably," I sighed.

"Okay, so we definitely need to stop to get more supplies." Nicole shook her head and muttered, "Considering we have one gun and at most six or eight bullets, we *have* to stop."

I stared at the handgun that Dave had set between the two front seats when we got into the truck. I'd been so distracted by his injury that I hadn't thought much about our lack of protection.

"Okay," Dave sighed like he was *so* put upon and making *such* a sacrifice to agree with us. "I guess we do need to stop at some point in the next little while."

"Thank you so much for making that noble concession, Your Highness," I snapped.

He shot me a look. "*But* I think we need to get further down the road before we find a place to figure this out and spend the night. I don't want those camp people to find us, and the more miles we put between us, the better."

"Do you really think they're looking for us?" Nicole asked as she tossed us a fearful glance in the rearview mirror. "When we last saw them, they had bigger problems. Bigger, drooling, murderous, brain-eating problems."

Dave shrugged the same damn shoulder he'd been shot in without even batting an eye. "Well, maybe you're right, but I'm not willing to take the risk. I'm guessing if they *do* find us, this time they aren't going to wait to kill us like they're the bad guys in some kind of James Bond movie."

I smiled. Lex had all but monologued on us back in the

camp. It was a bit Bondish. "You *did* unleash zombie hell on them. I would guess you're right."

"They deserved it! They tried to kill me in an abandoned pool, for Christ's sake," he muttered.

"Okay, okay. I wasn't judging, just making a point, sheesh." I shook my head and decided to change the subject since my husband was apparently a tad touchy about this one. "What highway are we on, Nicole?"

She craned her neck and found a sign that was half-bent over alongside the road. It was covered with sludge, but the numbers were sort of visible through the goo. "Looks like 44 East."

"Perfect," Dave said with a smile.

"*Perfect?* We don't drive on the highways! Zombies, remember? Huge burning crashes? Highway men?" I said as I motioned outside with my free hand.

Along the roadway there were dozens and dozens of moaning, walking corpses, eyeing our vehicle as we zipped past. It was only our high rate of speed that kept them at bay, but if we had to slow down to clear a wreck? Or take a pee break? Or worse, had some kind of breakdown?

Well, we were boned.

Dave shut his eyes and I could almost see him counting to ten in his head before he spoke again. "Well, *today* we're driving on the highway. Rules were made to be broken. Drive for another hour, Nicole, and then we'll find a place to stop for the night, okay? Can we all agree on that?"

I stared at him, but it was obvious this was a rhetorical question. Whether or not I thought we should stop in two days or two seconds, Dave had a plan.

And I'd learned a long time ago not to argue with him when he had a plan.

"Fine." I sighed. "But at least keep pressure on the wound, okay? I'd hate to have you bleed to death before I could kill you for scaring the shit out of me."

He smiled as he reached up to press the shirt against his shoulder. Our fingers briefly intertwined and I have to admit that it was reassuring.

"I wouldn't deny you that pleasure, dear. I know it means a lot to you."

Our eyes met and despite the fact that we'd been sniping at each other a bit, the connection between us was stronger than ever. He got me, he got my autopilot reaction of going bitchcakes when I got scared because it was the only way I could function without falling apart. And I got him, too. Every brave, fantastic, awesome inch of him.

Without another word, I gave him a quick kiss on the cheek, then climbed up into the passenger front seat. After I'd buckled in, I popped open the glove compartment to see what treasures our friend Lex had left for us.

Not a lot. No ammunition, damn it, or even another weapon, which was highly disappointing. You find so many of them in glove compartments nowadays, but apparently Lex didn't like having a backup. At least not in the glove compartment. I'd have to check under and behind the seats once we stopped.

There was no GPS, either, but I guess that made sense. The Lex Camp had decided to shut itself off from humanity as a (completely misguided) way to keep the apocalypse at bay. They didn't care to find anything close by or even far away.

He did have a bag of beef jerky in the glove compartment, though, *and* something useful: a map!

I pulled it out and started unfolding it carefully. To my surprise, it was marked with a thick, red outline around a ten-mile-square area that was apparently the "territory" of Lex and his minions.

"I can't believe they were willing to kill us—"

"Me!" Dave interrupted from the backseat. He was leaning against the door, eyes half-closed. He still didn't look pained, though, or like he was getting woozy, so that was something. "They were going to kill me."

"Well, you did volunteer for Pit Duty," I said with a half-smile for him. "But I can't believe they were willing to kill *you* over a relatively small chunk of land in the middle of butt-fuck nowhere Oklahoma."

"It's not so surprising," Nicole said from the driver's seat. "I mean, people have been killing over land since the beginning of time. At some point, we probably stole that ten-square-mile piece of land in the middle of nowhere from the Indians, right? So it's not the first time there's been blood spilled over it." She hesitated. "But probably the first time with zombies."

I stared at her until she glanced at me with a blush.

"What? It's not like celebrity news is all I know. I'm not stupid."

"No, you are not," I conceded, and I admit I did so a bit reluctantly.

I hadn't really liked the girl at first, but she *was* proving to be useful in many ways. Plus, she had helped me save Dave. So that gave her massive points.

I settled back to watch the road and help her navigate with my handy-dandy map, and we were all quiet for a while.

Time moves weirdly in an apocalypse. An hour can feel like a day if you want it to pass quickly or it can feel like a moment if you need the time. Today, it was somewhere in the middle and soon enough the afternoon had gotten longer. The shadows began to stretch across the road and the sun dipped lower on the horizon.

"We're actually making decent time," I said as I checked the map and compared it to the road sign. "We've actually gotten close to forty miles in an hour. That may be a new postzombie record."

"How depressing," Nicole said. "I used to have this Camaro back before the whole zombie thing and I could make it fly on the highway. I'd get a hundred miles in an hour if I was really feeling frisky."

When I looked at Nicole, with her cute blonde hair and her bright eyes, I could totally see that. Probably she was one of those girls who batted her eyelashes at cops and got out of tickets, too.

I nodded. "Yeah, well times have changed."

Dave leaned forward. I was surprised, to be honest. He'd been so quiet, I'd thought he'd fallen asleep, but apparently not. He reached for the map and I let him take it without any argument.

After a few minutes of scanning the paper and checking what was left of the mile markers, he said, "So we're going to start bumping up against the southwestern part of Tulsa soon and I think we can all agree that roaming into the city at dusk would be a bad idea."

Both Nicole and I nodded. Shit, I did *not* want to deal with cities. Honestly, after the past twenty-four hours, I didn't really want to meet up with *any* people, zombie or otherwise.

"But," Dave continued after our silent acquiescence, "I also think we need to find a big enough place to stop that we can actually find some supplies."

He pushed the map back toward me. "How about right there?"

He was pointing to a city on the map named Plain-spark. The city was a dot with a circle around it on the map, which the key in the bottom corner said meant it had had about twenty-thousand people before the outbreak. A lot of potential zombies, but it was better than the nearly four hundred thousand in Tulsa.

"That just might work," I agreed.

I took back the map and tried to figure out the best exit. Despite our luck with GPS units, I'd also gotten much better at navigating with maps. The hidden talents you don't know you have until a zombie apocalypse. I wonder if I could dance now, too? Or play the ukulele...

"Plainspark," Nicole muttered as she glanced at the city name. "Why does that sound so familiar?"

I shrugged. "Don't know. I mean, it's not really a bus-tling metropolis. Not a lot of star sightings there." I motioned to the upcoming exit. "Take that one."

"Yeah, I guess," she mused as she steered us off the road.

I breathed a tiny sigh of relief. Whatever Dave said, I really hated traveling the highway.

She shook her head. "Still, I swear I've heard the name before."

To be honest, as we turned toward the town, I found myself surprised. Small or not, this had obviously once been pretty nice. Maybe some kind of Tulsa suburb where the slightly upper class lived. There were a plethora of nice shops and big, classy houses.

Well, the houses and shops that were still *standing* were lovely, anyway. There had been a fire at some point after the outbreak, probably *much* after since apparently no one had tried to stop it. Those damn zombie firefighters, never showing up, always on a "Braaaains" break.

Whatever had started it, though, about half the town had been devoured by flames. Husks of buildings slumped into overgrown yards and broken and blackened bricks were scattered across the road. Even the ashes along Main Street were smoldering in places.

Had anyone still been alive when this happened? Er . . . strike that . . . not undead alive. Like really alive.

"Still," I muttered as we turned into a neighborhood called Village Green that seemed to be off the main track of the fire. "It could be a lot worse."

Of course the moment I said that, three zombies lumbered from the half-dead bushes around one of the big houses and stood on the sidewalk, watching us drive by. They were recent converts, too. How do I know?

Clothing is always the giveaway. Ratty, rotting clothing = old zombie. New clothing = new zombie. These zombies had on jeans that were only slightly sludgy and bloody and all their naughty parts were covered by fabric. Which you do have to mention because sometimes . . . they were not.

Ew.

"Shit," Nicole muttered as she sped forward and careened around a corner so the zombies wouldn't be able to find us. "Looks like that neighborhood is out."

"Hey, what about that?" Dave said, motioning in front of us.

There, in the distance, was another building. But this

one wasn't a house. It was a hospital. Small but easily marked by the blue cross on the sign leading up to it.

"Plainspark Medical and Surgery Center," I read the sign. "Well, they'll probably have some good supplies. But it's a big enough building that it might be risky. What do you think?"

I turned toward Dave. He had pulled the T-shirt away from his bare chest and was back to poking at the hole in his shoulder.

"David!" I snapped.

He jerked his gaze to me and his expression was absent and distant. "What? Oh, yeah. There will be medical supplies probably, but not a lot of food and weapons."

Nicole eyed him in the mirror and her frown spoke volumes. "Right now I think medical is more important. I vote hospital."

"My vote is hospital, too," I said, waving at him to cover the wound with his T-shirt. "And we might get lucky with some of the other stuff. You never know."

Dave shrugged. "Sure. Just pull up to the emergency entrance and we'll try to pry the door open."

"*I'll* try to pry the door open," I corrected him as Nicole slid to a stop by the big blue EMERGENCY sign. "*You* will sit in the truck and think about not bleeding to death."

Before he could respond, I grabbed the handgun, got out of the truck, and slammed the door in his face. Holding the weapon at the ready, I looked around with the familiar tickle of fear and wariness pricking the back of my neck.

In the shadow of the hospital with the sun dipping out of my sight, it was dusky and cool. And quiet, so damn quiet. Even after all these months, I hadn't gotten used to how silent the apocalypse was. At first, I hadn't minded. I mean, I had always hated city noises and complained incessantly to David about wanting to live somewhere quieter. But what I wouldn't give now for honking horns and chatting people and low-flying planes.

Really anything that said, "Civilization has survived. Congratulations."

I pushed away those thoughts and carefully slipped the pistol into my waistband as I examined the automatic doors. They weren't sliding, though of course they wouldn't be. No power. I slipped my hand into the rubber stoppers between them and shoved, then I shoved harder... then I threw all my weight into the act and grunted with effort... but the door still didn't move. Not even a fraction.

"Shit," I muttered because the fact that I couldn't get the door wedged open meant that some brilliant person inside had shut it down and locked it when the shit hit the fan outside.

I was guessing that hadn't worked out for the best in the long run. In a zombie apocalypse, being locked in wasn't a good thing.

I looked around for some kind wedge device I could slide between the doors and force them open. I eventually settled on a big stick that had fallen from one of the old trees planted around the hospital perimeter. I was heading back to the door when Dave slung himself out of the truck and strode up beside me.

"You're not going to be able to get it—" I started as he slid his arm into the area between the doors. He gave a little shove, and I mean *little,* and the space between them yawned open wide enough that we could all get through.

I dropped my stick as I finished my sentence. "Um, open."

Dave glanced at me and it was furtive. Like he, too, realized that it was not okay that I couldn't get the door open without resorting to a system of pulleys but he could do it without even making so much as a grunt. But we couldn't discuss it because Nicole shut the engine down, locked the truck, and came around to the doorway.

We all looked inside at the darkness. Without lights and with evening rapidly approaching, there wasn't much to see.

"Wish we had a lantern," I muttered.

Dave pursed his lips. "We did, in the SUV. Stupid jerk-off campers."

I ignored his pouting. "Any flashlights in that truck?"

Nicole looked at us and then she walked away. I kept my gaze on the hospital foyer. It was the best thing. If there were zombies in there, they'd be coming soon to check us out.

In a minute Nicole was back and she had not one, but two flashlights. I smiled as I took one. "Where did you find those? The glove compartment was useless."

She shrugged. "I noticed a storage box in the back when I came around and one of the keys on Lex's ring opened it."

"Anything else useful in there?" Dave asked. "Like, I don't know, a submachine gun or a grenade?"

Nicole laughed. "No. Just a couple of screwdrivers and some work gloves. It was pretty well cleaned out."

"I guess Lex was more of a psychopath than a handyman," I said as I clicked on the flashlight and shone it inside. "Ready to do this thing?"

There was a brief hesitation and I couldn't blame either one of them for it. I mean, the hospital was big and dark and something straight out of a Stephen King novel. Except there were real monsters lurking inside. Nicole looked like she was ready to bolt and then she shot a side-glance at Dave. The T-shirt he was holding up to his injury was soaked with blood.

She nodded and there was resignation in her tone when she sighed, "Okay, let's do this thing."

CHAPTER 10

How to make friends and influence survivors (but not zombies).

took the gun from my waistband and made sure the safety was off. "Since I have the gun, I'll lead. Nicole, follow behind me and be ready with that light. Dave you follow us."

He rolled his eyes but nodded. He probably wanted to argue since Dave wasn't exactly a "follow the leader" kind of survivor, but my face must have convinced him otherwise. Tonight was not the night to fuck with me, that was for sure.

I slipped through the open space between the doors and managed to get into the foyer of the emergency room, where I turned on my flashlight and scanned the area for the flash of red, hungry eyes.

All I saw was death. Dead people still propped up in waiting chairs, sprawled on the floor and in pieces sprinkled all over the place. The stench was pretty nasty and I won't go into great detail here because it's damn gag-worthy. I'd just like to point out that you don't get used to the smell. Don't believe it if people tell you that you do.

"Shit, if this isn't a statement on American health care, I don't know what is," Nicole whispered as she stepped up next to me.

I smiled despite myself and despite what was all around me. You can judge if you want, but you have to find humor in these situations or you'll go freaking crazy. Er, crazier. I wasn't so certain the crazy train hadn't already come and gone for the three of us.

I turned to compliment her on the quip, but my words died on my lips. Nicole had her flashlight raised, but also her annoying camera.

"Seriously?" I said, motioning to the red blinking light that said Recording.

She shrugged one shoulder (which didn't even disturb the camera, she was just that good).

"Gotta document for posterity," she said. "And my Peabody. So, Sarah, how do you *feel* right now?"

I glared at her.

"A little like punching a blonde, actually." That elicited nothing more than a laugh from Nicole. Guess I wasn't that scary. I turned away from her. "Turn that fucking thing off."

She smiled. "No can do. Just act naturally; you'll forget it's here in a minute or two."

I wanted to argue, but decided against it. Just too much energy.

"What about the door?" I muttered as I looked at the sliding doors, which were still jammed open. The last thing we needed was for a passel of zombies to come in behind us and mess up whatever areas we'd already cleared. That was how people became zombie sandwiches.

But Dave was one step (or five) ahead of me. He tugged the doors shut with as much ease as he'd opened them (which was pretty scary since closing those things when they were locked shut was even harder than opening them).

"Problem solved," he whispered.

I shrugged and turned my back on him. This stuff that was happening with/to him was going to have to be dealt with at some point, but not yet—half because I had bigger fish to fry and half because . . . well, I just wasn't up for it. If I dug into what was happening with him, I might not like the answers.

In fact, I was pretty sure I wouldn't.

"If only," Nicole laughed, apparently oblivious. And that was good. The last thing I needed was for her to put her tabloid mind on the mysterious case of David's superpowers.

"Come on," I said, motioning to the swinging doors to the emergency room. "Let's go."

I led with the other two behind me. After a deep breath (through my mouth, not my nose), I pushed into the emergency treatment zone.

The back area was worse than the front. Blood and sludge slashed the walls; body parts and rotting flesh were everywhere, in the pools of fluids left behind.

I shuddered as I stepped over what remained of a leg and kicked aside a few scattered fingers, still clenched like they'd been ripped off while in a fist.

"Man, this must have been bad," I whispered after a long, heavy pause. I said it more to myself, but Nicole answered anyway.

"The result of mass hysteria surrounds us," she said

and I realized she was documenting for the camera. Her voice even sounded different. "Death and destruction hit this hospital on the most base level."

"One or more of them must have had the virus when they locked the doors," Dave said, his voice hushed and reverent, like we were in a church. I guess it was pretty much a graveyard, though, so close enough.

"And they might still be here," I snapped, and my harsh tone made both of them straighten up. "So let's not dillydally."

We moved forward a few steps.

"Dillydally?" Nicole said from behind me as she peered around the camera lens to spear me with a look. "Dillydally? What are you, eighty?"

I ignored her and instead focused on one of the drawn curtains in front of me. They created the semiprivacy within the rooms where doctors had once treated minor injuries and tried to save people from accidents or heart attacks.

They hadn't been expecting what had come into their hospital just a few months before. They hadn't been ready for it.

None of us had.

I stood in front of the curtain for a moment. We had to go past it, but I just didn't want to do so. I didn't want to deal with whatever was behind curtain number one. Finally, I drew some deep breaths, threw it open, and shone my flashlight inside.

I was prepared for many things. Dead body, sure: Zombie, absolutely, though I was hoping we could avoid that, at least until the "Dave's been shot" situation had been taken care of.

What I was *not* prepared for on any level were the two dead bodies positioned over the emergency-room bed. A man and a woman. The woman was still in her nurse's uniform, although it was pulled up over her waist. The dead man behind her had been wearing scrubs, which he'd pulled down around his ankles along with his tighty whities.

They had clearly been . . . um . . . well, humping.

And in the middle of that last, desperate screw? The man had shot her in the head and then himself. The gun still dangled from his cold, dead fingers.

"Sweet!" Nicole said, startling me from my half-shocked staring. "A gun."

She snapped off the camera and reached around me to grab the weapon from the dead man's hands. Of course his fingers sort of held it, the rotten flesh breaking as she tugged and finally freed the cold steel from equally cold flesh.

"Seriously?" Dave said from behind her. The horror on his face was equal to mine. "You're focusing on the *gun* in this scenario?"

Nicole glanced at the dead couple; her expression showed a brief flicker of sadness and disgust before she wiped it away and shrugged. "Well, we need the gun more than they do."

I rolled my eyes. "If they don't bother you so much, then help me roll them into the hall so we can stitch Dave up."

Nicole slipped the gun into her waistband, set aside her camera, and did as I asked without so much as a moment's hesitation. With the three of us working together, we managed to get the not-so-happy couple's supergroddy corpses out of the room. Of course we all ended up covered in gross before we were done.

Blood. It's just not a compliment to most outfits. Sludge, surprisingly, is. I guess everyone looks good in black.

"All right," Nicole said as she changed the bloody paper covering on the hospital bed with the efficiency of the most experienced nurse. "Sarah, have you stitched a wound before?"

I blinked. "Um, actually, no."

Nicole smoothed the paper across the dirty bed and then turned to stare at me with wide eyes. "Really? Even after all this time?"

I felt myself blushing, which was weird. But damn, she was looking at me like I'd sprouted a second head.

"You guys *are* lucky," Nicole muttered as she patted the semiclean bed. "Come on up, Mr. David, and I'll do it. I've done it a few times before." As she spoke, she motioned to a scar on her arm. "See, it's not even that bad looking. I don't completely suck at it."

I pursed my lips. It was totally petty but it kind of annoyed me that Nicole could help David in a way that I couldn't. And that she had a cool scar she had apparently treated herself. That was badass and suddenly I felt like Avril Lavigne in all her fakeitude standing next to a *real* punk rocker.

Dave had no hesitation, though. He was up on the table before Nicole had even finished her request. I held the flashlight in silence (trying not to seethe since she was saving my husband's life) as Nicole cleaned the wound with some disinfectant pads she'd found in a drawer and then threaded a needle and started the stitching.

I've seen people get their heads blown off. Correction: I've *blown* their heads off. I've kicked aside severed limbs like they were pebbles. I've stepped over rotting bodies.

And yet the view of the needle going into Dave's flesh was enough to make me a little queasy. I guess I hadn't gotten over my needle thing after all.

"You okay?" he asked, his voice almost cheerful.

I glared at him, but before I could respond, there was a sound in the distance, down the hall deeper into the hospital itself. All three of us froze, not even breathing as we listened for the sound again.

It came after a moment, the bang and crash of something being moved or metal cabinets being thrown open. Whatever it was, it was loud.

"Could be rats," Nicole said under her breath.

I met Dave's eyes and his lips were pursed thin and tight.

"No," I whispered. "I don't think so. You keep stitching, I'll go look."

Dave opened his mouth. "No way!" he insisted, almost too loudly before he checked his tone. "Come on, Sarah, that could be a zombie and you know it."

"I have the gun and I'll scream like a banshee if it is," I insisted. "Besides, if I stay here I'll totally puke and you don't want to clean that up, do you?"

That shut his mouth. Dave doesn't like puke. It makes him yak, too. He glared at me since he knew I was using his weakness against him. Whatever, all's fair in love and zombies.

"Keep stitching," I ordered Nicole as I moved toward the door.

She did just that, barely grunting as I made my way out

into the hallway. It was so dark, I could hardly picture what it must have been like when there was light. I had a weird moment when I wondered if it had *ever* been lit. Like the hospital hadn't existed before these dark days.

To clear that bizarre thought, I shook my head and focused as I moved toward the sound, which continued at the end of the hall. I kept my flashlight low as I slipped along the wall, taking breaks in the closed doorways like I was on some cop show or something.

The noise was getting louder as I drew closer and my heart leapt. Shit, it was still too hard to tell if I was dealing with one zombie or ten. And ten would be bad, by the way, in case you hadn't figured it out. Even with two guns, we were at a serious disadvantage. Especially since I had no idea how many rounds Nicole had in her newly acquired suicide pistol.

But then, through the eerie dark and quiet of the hallway I heard words. *Real* words in a raw, raspy British accent.

"Bugger me!"

Relief flowed through me. Zombies don't talk. They especially don't talk in accents (though an Aussie zombie might be fun). They certainly didn't say "bugger," which had always been one of my favorite swears from across the "pond."

But as relieved as I was, I couldn't let my guard down. We'd just been reminded in the harshest way possible that human survivors did not equal friendly allies. If my Brit friend was as loopy as the campers (or God forbid, *one* of the campers) we'd just escaped, it could still be very ugly.

The room he was in was a closet of some kind at the end of the hallway. I slipped closer and carefully lifted both my gun and my flashlight. As the light hit his back, I expected him to turn on me, but he didn't. He just kept slamming doors open and closed and dragging boxes off the shelves like a wild man.

"Shit, fuck, bother!" he burst out, running both hands through wild, shoulder-length brown hair.

"Hey!" I snapped.

My voice startled him and he spun on me. The light hit his face and I saw a brief glimpse of pale skin, wide eyes, and a heavy shadow of beard on his chin.

"'ello," he said, calm as if we'd just bumped into each other in a mall. "Wish you'd put that light out of my face. It's a bit bright."

"If you make a move, I *will* shoot you," I promised as I very slowly did as he asked.

"All right, all right," he said, blinking as the light moved from his eyes. "You don't have to freak out, little bird."

I scrunched my brow as I got a fuller picture of the closet. It was a medicine closet apparently and the boxes he'd been throwing around were empty but had once held painkillers, antiseptics, and blood thinners. There were pill packets all over the floor, some open, some shut, and the half-drawn drawers contained more of the same.

There was also a pistol on one of the shelves, but the Brit made no move to grab it. In fact, he didn't even look at it.

"What you doin' here?" he asked me as he reached into his pocket.

I braced myself in a wider stance and raised my gun level with his face as I prepped for a weapon to come out of that pocket.

"Hey!" I snapped.

"Don't worry, just getting a ciggy," he said, holding up a cigarette with a curious nonchalance. "Want one?"

"No." I bit out. I had quit smoking the year before, though I *seriously* wanted one now.

It had been a long fucking day. A visit to Marlboro Country sounded like heaven at present.

"Sarah?" came Nicole's voice from down the hall. "You okay?"

I kept my gun trained on the Brit. "Yeah. I found someone down here."

"Zombie?" Dave's voice replied, thick with worry as it scuttled closer. In my mind, I could almost see him racing toward me, my knight in shining armor.

"Not a bloody zombie," the Brit answered loudly enough that his voice would carry to my companions.

The scuttling stopped abruptly.

"Look, I'm going to lower my weapon," I said softly. "But if you move for that pistol on the shelf, I will kill you without hesitation."

The Brit blinked and his gaze moved over to the shelf. With a nervous, high-pitched laugh he said, "Forgot I had that. Damn."

Both my eyebrows went up as I slowly lowered my own gun. How could you *forget* your gun, especially in these times? Of course the closer I looked to this guy, the more I was starting to realize he might not even remember his own name.

His pupils were dilated and his skin was pasty and sticky. He was on . . . *something*. I probably didn't want to know what considering how many choices he must have had in the hospital. I mean, despite the fact that he hadn't been able to score in the closet we now stood in didn't mean he didn't have some luck elsewhere.

Suddenly Dave was at my side with the pistol Nicole had taken from the corpses leveled at our new friend.

"Who the hell are you?" he asked in the low, dangerous tone he had somewhere perfected over the months of badassery. Beyond hot, I admit it.

The Brit leaned back against the closest shelf and gave Dave a bored and cocky look. Apparently he was not as impressed by my husband's tone as I was.

"Who am *I*? You can't mean that. Who the hell are *you*?" he laughed. "Have you been living in a hole for the last few years?"

Dave wrinkled his brow and I lifted the flashlight to examine our new friend's face a bit closer. Apparently we were supposed to know him, though I have no idea how. There weren't many survivors left, sure, but we didn't exactly have a census or something.

Yet.

But we didn't have to wonder long. Nicole solved the puzzle pretty quickly.

"Colin McCray?" She stepped around David and stared at the Brit with wide, disbelieving eyes. "Is that *really* you?"

"Now there's a bird who knows where it's at," the Brit, apparently Colin McCray, grinned. "At your service, love." He waggled his eyebrows suggestively. "In more ways than one, if you know what I mean."

"Wait," Dave said as Nicole rolled her eyes and folded her arms across her chest. "Are you saying this is Colin McCray? The lead singer from Lead Tongue?"

Shit, Lead Tongue! That had been one of my favorite

bands in high school. Dark, heavy rock in the age of boy
band idiocy! I'd listened to their debut album, *Tongue
This* like, a thousand times.

I tilted the flashlight and looked even closer. Damn, it
was him, complete with leather pants, a black shirt that
was slightly faded and torn, but still unbuttoned to the
midchest level. He was wearing a big silver medallion
just like he had on stage for years, though at thirty-five, he
looked way closer to fifty.

But he had even before the apocalypse. The band had
slipped into obscurity after their third album flopped mis-
erably and McCray had become something of a joke.

I was sort of surprised he'd made it this far. Especially
since the dude was waaaay strung out. In the zombie-
verse you needed your wits about you.

"Always nice to meet fans," the Brit drawled. "Want an
autograph?"

"I'm not a fan," Nicole said, squeezing her arms over
her breasts even tighter. "I'm surprised you don't recognize *me,* actually. My first assignment was to cover you
guys. I did it for a few months, you know, before you
imploded and became totally *irrelevant.*"

McCray's mouth twitched slightly, but his jovial tone
didn't change as he said, "Sorry, love. I don't remember
the groupies."

Nicole was turning red, even in the dim light. "Not
a groupie, asshole. I'm a reporter. Does E.N.Z. ring a
bell?"

McCray tilted his head and looked her up and down. I
noted he hesitated quite a bit longer on her chest and her
ass than anywhere else. Classy.

Finally he shrugged. "Sorry, all you reporters look

alike. Blonde, brunette, red heads . . . just big tits and I can find better in the crowds."

Nicole arched a brow. "When you *had* crowds, you mean. You hadn't had a hit album for two years before the shit went down. And even afterward, you didn't have the wherewithal to get out of the middle of Oklahoma."

McCray sighed. "Oh Lordie, you do sound like a reporter. Does that mean you were stalkerazzi-ing me?"

"No," Nicole said through obviously clenched teeth.

Dave and I had been watching this exchange like it was a tennis match, swiveling our heads back and forth as the two adversaries snapped out rude comments. But finally Dave stepped between them.

"Okay, okay, enough," he snapped. "Seriously, I'm just not willing to babysit."

"Dude, did you know you aren't wearing a shirt?" McCray drawled.

Dave shut his eyes briefly and released a slow sigh. "Yes. I am aware. I got shot, if you didn't notice the stitches in my shoulder. We were just here to fix me up and then we're off again. What's your excuse?"

Nicole snorted out a burst of rather nasty laughter, but it was strained. I think she was a bit stung that McCray hadn't recognized her, actually. She looked the rocker up and down with a sneer.

"Oh, didn't you hear? McCray was down here for rehab. Cocaine, wasn't it? *That's* why I remembered the name of the town. We did a five-second sound bite bulletin on it on our show." She glared at him. "As filler when we didn't have a real story."

I nodded. Although apparently David was the entertainment news junkie, I did know a thing or two. "That's right. I remember hearing something about that. Didn't your whole band check in together?"

Colin's crooked grin (good Lord, that British teeth thing was true) fell and he glared at Nicole, though he answered me. "Something like that."

"So where are the rest of them?" Dave asked as he peeked over his shoulder into the hallway like any minute the whole band was going to materialize and start to rock out. Which would be pretty cool, I admit it.

McCray shook his head. "Branson ran off the minute the rehab center lost its security. He was a zombie within hours. Ellsworth OD'd a few days later. That left Keller and me. The original band members, actually." His eyes went flat and hard. "But he killed himself when we ran out of drugs. I'm all that's left."

Even Nicole, with all her snark, had the decency to stay quiet as we all stared at the former rock star. He looked a little smaller as he stared at the floor. And I could see, from bitter experience, that he was reliving every last moment of his friends' lives in that second.

But then he lifted his head and grinned at us. "But as the French say, *Que sera, sera,* eh?"

I didn't believe his nonchalance for a moment, but what could you say?

Dave shifted uncomfortably and then said, "Well, er, we should probably finish up in the room, guys. I'm still bleeding and all."

I spun on him and lifted my flashlight. Nicole had finished stitching only half his wound—leaving the needle and heavy thread hanging. But Dave wasn't right. The hole was still partially open, but there wasn't any blood.

I bit my tongue as I stared, though Nicole wasn't as quiet.

"No..." she said, lifting her gaze and her light from his injury to his face. Her eyes were narrowed and her gaze focused entirely too hard on him. "Actually, you aren't. You aren't bleeding at all."

CHAPTER 11

The only person who can reject you is you. Unless they find out you're a zombie. But then it's not so much rejection as extermination.

Turns out that finding Colin McCray had its advantages. He had been living in the hospital for over a week and once we got him to focus his squirrel-like brain for more than three seconds, he actually knew the ins and outs of the corridors.

Within ten minutes of our meeting, Nicole had finished stitching up Dave (while glaring at him the whole time) and we were standing in front of a half-empty vending machine. At some point someone had smashed the glass. Shards were scattered across the hallway floor and collected in the retrieval bin where a person would normally get their candy.

The selection was less than stellar. Some dried-up gum and a few gross candy bars were all that were left clinging to the metal pegs inside.

"Eh, Whatchamacallit," I grunted as I reached past the glass and took one of the bars. "These were awful even before the apocalypse."

"At least it's chocolate," Dave said with a smile.

No one else reacted. McCray was too busy weaving and Nicole had turned her focus back on David. Her suspicion made my pulse increase and my stomach clench. This was *not* good. I really didn't want to have to kill her, not when I was just starting to almost like her.

"Is there a place to sit?" Nicole finally asked, turning her gaze from my husband to McCray. She couldn't hide her disgust... or maybe she just wasn't trying that hard.

McCray didn't care. He blinked. "Huh? Oh yeah. There's a dining hall this way."

Dave jerked a little. "Hey, maybe a dining hall isn't such a good idea—" he started, but McCray was already halfway up the hall.

We exchanged a quick look, but then followed him. There was still safety in numbers. Of course the same was true for the zombies, and unfortunately they had us way beat in that particular department.

After a couple of quick turns, McCray stopped at a set of swinging doors. He turned back toward us and then motioned at them.

"Here we are: dining hall."

For a moment we all stood there staring at one another. Waiting for... I don't know what. And then Nicole shook her head.

"So, um, are we going in or what?"

McCray blinked again, his glassy eyes focusing for a brief moment. "Oh. Sure."

Without hesitating, without even taking a peek inside to check his perimeter, McCray shoved open the doors and disappeared into the dining hall. As the doors swung shut, we all got a glimpse of a big room with tables lined up in rows three wide. The cafeteria had obviously taken some damage, though; many of the tables were flipped and I think I saw a rotting leg (maybe the match to the one I'd seen earlier) before the door swung shut.

"Oh shit," Nicole muttered, then she caught the swaying door and slipped in behind McCray.

I glanced at Dave. "I don't like this."

He nodded. "Me neither, but here we are." He reached out and patted my arm. "So let's go. But be careful."

I lifted my gun a fraction and did as he suggested, leading our way into the dining hall. The lights were out, of course, and the room was almost pitch black thanks to the windows being so high above us and the fading light of sunset.

"The flashlights aren't going to cut it in a room this big. Any suggestion on lights?" I asked through clenched teeth.

McCray nodded. "Sure."

He stepped out of view for a second and then the soft glow of a lantern suddenly brightened the room a fraction. McCray stepped forward holding a Coleman in his left hand while his gun hung loosely in his right. Clearly he wasn't one for worrying too much about zombies. How the *hell* he had survived this long was beyond me.

"Well, aren't you full of surprises," Dave said as he looked around. "I'm surprised you didn't have that with you when you were searching the medicine closets."

McCray's eyes went wide as he stared at the lantern, like he hadn't ever thought of that. "Bugger, that's a great idea."

He moved like he was going to leave with the light and continue his search for a high right that very moment, but Nicole reached out and caught his arm.

"Hey, druggie boy, let's focus, okay? I know it's hard for you, but right now we need to eat and come up with a plan. If you want to go OD after that, well feel free. One less ass to cover."

McCray's brow wrinkled. "If you don't care if I die, then why do you care if I leave?"

I smothered a grin as Nicole's face fell. Guess she hadn't thought through that logic too carefully. Turned out McCray had a brain when it wasn't fried on drugs.

"Because you have the light," she said softly. "And a gun. So sit down and just chill out."

McCray shrugged and set the lantern on one of the few tables not overturned or covered in blood and body parts. "Whatever."

Nicole sighed and joined him at the table. Dave and I took the other side and all of us began eating slowly. It had been so long since I ate at a table, I wasn't even sure how to do it anymore. Even with a candy bar, I felt sort of awkward.

After we had all eaten in strained silence, McCray propped his elbows up on the table and leaned on his hands like a kid in school.

"So, I know this one was a stalkerazzi, but what's the deal with you two?" McCray asked.

"Yeah," Nicole said, her tone dark and dry as she tossed her candy wrapper on the blood-stained linoleum at her feet. "What *is* the deal with you two?"

Dave glanced at her and he looked confused. Clearly he hadn't noticed her suspicions. Which was not a good thing. He could easily talk himself into a problem, especially since the girl had a gun.

"What do you—" he started.

"Wow," I interrupted as I jumped to my feet and faked a big, fat yawn. "I am just beat. Why don't we discuss this in the morning after we all get a good night's sleep, huh?"

Dave shot me a weird look, but got up when I grabbed for his arm and yanked him.

McCray shook his head. "I thought we had to come up with a big, hairy plan before we did anything fun like going off to bed."

I shook my head. "Plans can wait. See you all tomorrow." I tugged at Dave again. "Come on, honey."

"Don't you want to all go together?" Nicole asked evenly, her eyes locked on mine.

"Nope," I said as I backed toward the doors. "We've got a flashlight and you have one and McCray has his lantern, so I think we're good. We'll just see you in the morning. Nighty-night."

I didn't wait for her to argue or call us out or draw her weapon; I just hauled off toward the double doors and the hallway, Dave trailing behind me with a look of confusion. But we'd been together long enough that he didn't question me. He might have thought I was crazy, but he wasn't going to ask me about it until we were alone.

Good boy.

Once we got out of the emergency area of the hospital, some of the rooms actually weren't so bad. Deeper back were even a few that barely had any evidence of zombie activity.

That was where we decided to take up residence for the night.

We picked a room and set up by the light of the flashlight.

"Here, you get in bed," I said as I dug around in our

pack for some supplies. "You need the rest after getting shot."

Dave shrugged, then got into one of the two narrow hospital beds. As he covered himself up with the thin sheets, he looked at me.

"So what was all that about, Sarah? You're acting all weird and so is Nicole."

I sighed as I turned my back on him while I rechecked my weapon. I really didn't want to deal with this, but it had to be done.

"Here's the thing, babe—" I started, but before I could finish, I heard the rasping echo of a snore.

I turned around and found that Dave's eyes were already shut in a restless sleep. I shook my head with a sigh. I guess it had been a longer day than I thought.

Putting my gun on the stand next to the bed, I slipped in next to him. I lay on my side, staring down at Dave. I watched as once again he took one breath in for every two breaths he pushed out. That ragged, unnatural exchange only served to freak me out even more than I had been all day.

Clearly there was something wrong with him.

I shifted on the uncomfortable hospital bed and tried to rest my head on the pillow beside his, but before I could get even remotely relaxed, there was a light knock on the door.

I turned as it opened and revealed Nicole, holding one of the flashlights aimed at the ground.

Shit. So much for my clever escape plan.

"Hey," she said softly. "Can I talk to you?"

I glanced at Dave again, but he was still asleep, his eyes darting beneath his eyelids as he dreamed of . . . well,

I didn't want to know what since I was sure it was zombie related, whether it was him being chased by a zombie or, you know, him eating flesh and liking it.

"Sure," I said as I carefully slung myself out of bed and motioned to the hall. "But let's go out here. Dave's asleep."

Nicole cast a quick yet pointed glance at my husband and then nodded as we stepped into the hallway. I shut the door behind me and looked at her with what I hoped was no worry or fear.

"So, where's McCray?" I asked.

Nicole rolled her eyes and my stomach settled. Apparently the British rocker was a topic that could be used as a distraction for our reporter friend—a tidbit I filed away for future use.

"He took . . . *something* and passed out on a couch in the waiting area down the hall." She shook her head. "How that idiot survived this long is nothing short of a miracle."

"Well, I'm sure we'll hear the whole story tomorrow," I said with a low laugh. "McCray doesn't seem like the secretive type."

"Unlike some others in our group," Nicole said, and her gaze settled on my face evenly.

I glared at her. "What do you mean?"

She arched a brow. "You've been dodging this long enough, Sarah. What's up with Dave?"

I slipped my hands behind my back and clenched them there, hard enough that my ragged nails bit into my palms. But my voice didn't even crack as I said, "I don't know what you're talking about. You'll have to be more specific."

"I'm not blind. It's pretty clear there's something *wrong* with him, Sarah."

I shrugged. "Well, he got shot, so I guess that's a pretty big *something*. He'll be fine, though. A good night's sleep and a dose of those antibiotic pills McCray had and he'll be right as rain in no time."

She shook her head slowly. "That's not what I mean. And you know it."

I shifted. There was clearly no putting her off this trail now that she'd gotten her damned bloodhound nose on it. But I was determined to try.

"I don't know anything," I insisted with an empty batting of my eyes I'd learned from our friend Amanda. Poor, dead Amanda.

Nicole's lips pursed. "Bullshit. I've noticed things since we met up. Little things, but freaky, nonetheless. Like when the zombies in that pool didn't bother Dave. Or when he got hit and then shot, it didn't even faze him."

"Of course it did," I insisted with a tight laugh.

"He was poking the hole in his shoulder like it was nothing!" she snapped. "And I saw that big scar on his hand. The one that looks remarkably like a healed bite wound."

I backed up as I fought not to toss a look toward the room where I'd left David. I didn't want to give her any more reasons to be suspicious, but Nicole was pretty much listing out every single thing I was currently terrified about.

But I couldn't tell her that. Even after all we'd been through since we met her, she was still essentially a stranger. And definitely a reporter. If she knew the truth, there was no doubt she'd use it all against us at some point down the road. If she suspected Dave might be infected, she might even hurt him.

And *that* wasn't going to happen.

"I don't know what you're going on about," I said softly as I moved toward the door. "But maybe after you have a good night's sleep, you'll forget all this foolishness."

She stared at me and for a brief moment I thought I saw something like pity in her gaze. But then she shook her head.

"Sarah, I'm a reporter. I'm going to figure this out eventually."

With that she turned on her heel and stalked down the hallway. I watched her go until she disappeared into another room in the distance, then I went back into our room. If only we could lock it. Lock out the zombies and Nicole and her accusations.

I stared down at my panting husband with his freshly stitched shoulder and his scarred hand.

"Yeah," I muttered as I got back into the bed and wrapped my arms around him. "I just hope I figure it out first."

CHAPTER 12

Your history strengthens your future. Remember
that time when you killed that zombie...?

One thing about a zombie apocalypse, dawn comes at
the same time as it did before. *And* our hospital room had
no shades; they'd been ripped off during the attack, as evi-
denced by the bloody fingerprints all over what was left of
the blind cord and the windows, so when the sun rose, it
flooded right into our faces and woke us up better than
any alarm clock.

Well, it woke *me* up. When I opened my eyes, I found
Dave lying on his side staring at me, and he looked like
he'd been lucid for a while.

Weird, he'd never been a morning person before. Playing video games until three A.M. did that to you, I guess.

"Hey, sunshine," he said with a grin.

He *could* grin. He had no idea of all the shit going
down with Nicole. But we weren't going to be able to
avoid that subject, not anymore.

"You talking to me or that horrible orb in the sky?" I
grunted as I rubbed mucky sleep from my bleary eyes.

Yeah, also *I'm* not much of a morning person. Especially when I've been tossing and turning all night freaking out while my husband slept peacefully beside me. Dumb jerk and his blissful ignorance and weird zombie sleep.

"You, of course," he said and bent his head to kiss me.

I'll admit, when we parted, I was waaaay less pissy. I was even able to smile at him. And then I remembered our sticky little situation and pushed into a sitting position.

"Dave, we have to talk," I started.

His smile fell and he let out a heavy sigh. "Oh, no. You're leaving me for some football star, aren't you? I knew this day would come eventually. I hope he's at least on a good team. Are there any good teams left or are they all zombies now? Zombie football, there's a new sport…"

I slugged him in the arm mostly to shut him up. "Dude, seriously, not the time for jokes."

"There's always room for jokes." He laughed. "And Jell-o. Mmmm, Jell-o."

I glared at him, partly because he wasn't being serious and partly because he knew I liked Jell-o and when he mentioned it, I missed it. Add that to the weird list of foods I missed in the apocalypse.

"*David—*" I started, determined to get this conversation started whether he wanted to goof around or not.

But I wasn't able to finish because at that same moment there was a knock on the door and Nicole's voice called out from the hall.

"Ready or not, we're coming in. Hope you're decent!"

McCray's British accent, heavy with annoyance and sleep piped in, "I don't!"

Then the door swung open and the two of them walked

inside. Nicole was pulled together. She had fixed her hair and even put on some make-up, though where she'd gotten it from I have no idea, and perhaps I didn't want to know since it probably involved searching dead bodies. Ew, dead-lady lipstick is not my thing.

McCray was the polar opposite. He looked like someone had hit him in the face with a frying pan. Repeatedly. Dark circles rimmed his dilated eyes and his skin was sallow and clammy. His shaggy hair stuck up at weird wavy angles and his scruffy beard needed trimming big time.

"Shit man, you look like hell," Dave said, cheerful as he swung out of the bed.

"It's bloody nighttime, mate," McCray moaned. "I should be fucking or asleep."

"Or fucking asleep," Dave laughed.

Nicole rolled her eyes at the fallen rocker. "It's dawn, jackass. A perfectly reasonable time to start the day in a goddamn zombie apocalypse. And if you weren't still so strung out from whatever it was you were snorting last night, you'd be fine."

McCray glared at her, his face long like a petulant child who had his toy taken away, but said nothing else. It surprised me, to be honest. The guy didn't seem like the type who was ever short on words.

Dave shook his head and looked around for his bloody shirt, which I'd draped across a chair in the room the night before. Now it was dry but stiff and smelly from the blood still slashed across it. *Not* attractive to wear, I promise you.

Before he could attempt it, Nicole held out another one. "Here, found this in a room."

I pursed my lips. Nicole saves the day again. Yip. Ee.

And yet Dave smiled his thanks before he carefully lifted his arms and tugged the shirt over his head. I brushed off my jealousy (yes, I admit, I was still jealous of the girl) and Nicole and I watched him with equal intensity. I mean, with stitches in his shoulder, that act should have made him wince.

It didn't, and from her pinched expression, it appeared that Nicole noticed his lack of pain as much as I did.

I frowned. I *had* to talk to Dave about this and soon. He seemed oblivious to her suspicions, and that could prove as dangerous to us as the drooling monsters outside the hospital. And probably *inside* the hospital, if you wanted to be honest about it.

But there was no way we could have any kind of open forum on the subject with Nicole interrupting every ten minutes and watching my hubby like a hawk. Or a zombie. Or a hawk zombie. Actually that was a good name for a band, but I digress. As usual.

"Look," I said. "I think we need to do an area search for supplies. We need guns, or at least ammo for the few weapons we already have."

Dave nodded. "Yeah, and we need more food and gas for that monster of a truck."

Nicole stared at us evenly. "Good idea. So I guess we'll be spending another night here in the Hospital of Horrors."

I shook my head. I wanted time alone with Dave, not to keep living out my nightmares by spending another evening in the gorefest of a hospital. All we had to add were scary clowns and I'd be pretty much certifiable.

"I have no intention of staying here," I said with a shudder. "And we won't have to if we split up to do our search. In teams of two we'll cover twice the ground and could be on the road by noon if we work hard."

"I shouldn't even be *up* at noon," McCray whined. "You people are bloody barbarians."

I ignored him. I needed to get this done and his irritating interruptions weren't helping.

"Why don't *you* take McCray and search here in the hospital since he has more knowledge of the building?" I suggested. "And Dave and I will do the surrounding area."

Nicole's eyes went wide and she moved toward me. Lowering her voice, she hissed, "You are *not* leaving me alone with that asshole. I'll go with Dave."

I shook my head. "No!" I snapped, far louder than I'd meant to. Then I stepped back and slipped my hand into David's. "We go together."

He smiled down at me. "Sounds like a plan to me. Are you okay with staying with Nicole, McCray?"

The rocker had apparently zoned out because he was staring at the pattern of linoleum on the floor like it could tell the future or something. But when Dave said his name, he lifted his head with a start.

"What?" he bellowed. "Yeah, one bird or another, makes no difference to me."

Nicole glared at us, then at him. She was outnumbered and she knew it.

"Charming," she growled. "Fine. We'll meet back here in two hours and compare what we've found."

With that, she grabbed McCray by the collar and hauled him out the door. There was no denying how pissed off she was. On one hand, I couldn't blame her. If our positions were reversed, I would have wanted some one-on-one question time with the half-zombie guy, too.

But our positions *weren't* reversed. Instead, I was married to Mr. Zombie Properties and I wasn't about to let anyone, especially some skinny little reporter, hurt him.

I tossed on the clothes I'd worn the day before, though I made a major mental note to grab some new ones the first chance I had. Running, fighting, and nearly dying sort of gave clothing an...odor, let's call it. Eau D'Terror by Estee Lauder would maybe be the way I'd market it, though I doubt anyone would want to wear it. I certainly didn't, though I had little choice in the matter.

"Okay," I said as I tugged my tangled hair into a scrunchie in my pocket. "Ready to do this?"

Dave waggled his eyebrows at me. "Sure you don't want to just get back into bed and tell them we couldn't find anything?"

I stared at him. "Not that I don't appreciate the horniness, but seriously? Um, death, destruction, zombies, no guns...oh and our little friend suspects that maybe you got bitten by a zombie. Just FYI."

Dave stared at me and the eyebrow waggling came to a sudden halt. "What?"

"You heard me." I folded my arms.

His eyes went wide. "Okay, *which* little friend. I'm guessing McCray wouldn't notice if a zombie was biting *him,* so I'm assuming you mean Nicole?"

"Ding, ding, ding!" I said with sarcasm dripping from every syllable. "Give the man a cigar."

He smiled, but only slightly. "Do you have any cigars? I bet they'd be worth bank in the camps right now."

I rolled my eyes. "Come on," I said with a sigh. "Let's start looking for supplies. We can talk Nicole and obtaining tobacco while we search."

He didn't argue, just followed me into the hospital corridor. I pulled the gun from my waistband as we entered the hallway, though I had only a couple of bullets left. We were pretty much screwed if anyone was around looking for trouble...or brains. Or both.

But the corridor was clear, aside from, you know, the rotting dead bodies. And within a few minutes, Dave had pried open the emergency doors and we were back outside in the cool morning air.

I shivered as I rubbed my arms absently. "Still need a jacket."

"Noted," he said as he took a side-glance at the truck we'd parked at the entrance the night before. "That thing really is a gas guzzler."

I nodded. "Yeah, we'll probably need to switch off at some point. But for now it's what we have. Oh, my life for a hybrid. Or a solar-generated car would be even better."

He laughed as we crossed the parking lot, still half filled with rusting cars and sludgy pools of goo. If push came to shove, we'd search the vehicles, but that kind of thing rarely went well. Cars = smelly bodies, rotting crap, and often zombies.

For now we just kept going toward the neighborhood we could both see in the distance.

"Maybe we can work on that technology when we get over this zombie thing," he suggested.

"Oh yeah, we'll just cure zombie-ism and then get to work on the energy crisis."

I rolled my eyes, even though I found myself reaching up for the vial around my neck. Still there.

"Look alive," Dave said as we reached the edge of the

neighborhood behind the hospital. "Or look for dead, I guess is better."

I did as he suggested. The area was clearly middle class, with neat rows of houses before us. We were entering from the back, so all I could see were dirty swimming pools and knee-high grass, but it was clear that these homes had once been the very nice residences of proud inhabitants.

Now . . . not so much.

"Which one?" I whispered.

Dave looked up and down the row. "If only we had a crystal ball to see which one of these families had weapons and dry goods."

"Maybe we can invent that after the zombie cure thing and the car thing," I snorted. "Look, that one there has a swimming pool and right next to it are some fake plastic deer. Want to try that one?"

Dave gave a shudder as he looked where I was indicating. The lawn ornaments had faded with the weather, but they were definitely plastic deer.

"Creepy, so why not?" he muttered as we moved that way.

"Be careful of the grass," I whispered. "Good zombie cover, especially for the legless ones."

Dave nodded. Since he didn't yet have a weapon, he kept close to me as we made our way to the edge of the lawn. We needed to solve that problem pretty quickly, though. One gun and two people generally equaled one zombie snack and one crying survivor.

We both scanned the area and finally he waved at the perimeter of the house.

"Shovel," he whispered. "That will suffice as a weapon

for me, at least until we find something more deadly. Not that I don't trust your ample shooting skills, my dear."

"Thanks, but I totally understood," I whispered as we entered the grass. "Besides, I don't want to have to cover your cute ass anyway."

He stifled a laugh and kept right on my heels. I kicked in front of me as I entered what had once been a lawn but was now closer to a jungle. I had to try to clear out some kind of path through the dense growth as we made our way slowly but surely to the house. Somehow we made it, though, all in one piece and with no zombies in sight.

So far.

Dave swept up the shovel as we got to the cracked patio pad. There was a rusty barbecue on one side and some rotted furniture on the other. Since half the chairs were covered with sludge, I was guessing survivors were out the question.

We both stared at the sliding glass doors. Normally glass windows in shops and glass sliding doors were the first to go, either broken by rabid zombies trying to reach their prey like they were shopping in the supermarket freezer section or by survivors trying to get away (and basically dooming themselves by leaving an opening for the zombies). By some miracle, though, these windows were still intact.

Still, the glass was covered with bloody handprints.

"Are those inside or outside?" Dave whispered.

I stared at the glass. We needed to know the answer to his question, but I really didn't want to touch it.

"Come on, Sarah," he whispered behind me.

I squirmed but I reached out to touch the glass. Of

course, goo came out over my palm when I pulled it back. Gross. I fucking hated goo. Still. Forever.

"Looks like both inside and out," I sighed as I looked closer at the smeared glass in the dim morning sunshine. "Want to try a different house?"

He shrugged. "I would guess pretty much anyplace in this neighborhood is going to have zombie friends waiting for us. Might as well be here as anywhere else."

"Good point." I wiped my hand on my already dirty shirt and once again swore to find both Handi Wipes and a new outfit ASAP. Have I mentioned the dislike of the goo? Yeah, it's a failing in a zombie apocalypse. I'm aware of that. But it's not exactly like you can find a good therapist out here. We'd killed our last one so I'm sure we were on a list somewhere anyway.

Dave lifted the shovel and reared back. I grabbed for his elbow.

"Hey, hey cowboy, whatcha doin' there?"

He stared at me, shovel still poised. "Um, breaking and then entering."

I shook my head. "After all this time, haven't we learned to *try* the door first? Might as well not bring zombies running like crazy if we don't have to."

Dave rolled his eyes, but he lowered the shovel slowly. "Fine. You never let me have any fun."

"I know," I said as I reached for the gooey door handle, "I'm mean that way."

With a deep breath, I tugged the handle; to my great surprise, the door slid open on its rusty tracks with only a slight extra tug thanks to the sludge that had molded it shut.

"Huh," I said. "Did *not* think that would work, to be honest."

"Me neither," Dave said as I stepped over the threshold and entered the dark house. "Be careful, please. Unlocked doors are never a good thing."

"Neither are locked doors," I whispered. "We're in a zombie apocalypse."

Thanks to the colder weather, inside the house was cool, but the air was still musty and close. There was a faint odor of rotting food and death all around, a wonderful combination that seemed to be the air freshener of choice now. Febreeze, people. It's never the wrong choice and there is plenty of it now that the world has ended.

"Dead dog," Dave said, his voice flat as he looked into the living room area.

"Eaten or just dead?" I muttered without looking. Did not want to see dead dog, thanks. Actually, I was pretty topped out on all dead things.

"Looks just dead," he said.

We crept into the dining area and through to the kitchen. It was quiet and still, but there was not going to be any guard-letting-down. The second you do that, the zombies come. Might as well be superstitious about it and maybe avoid them all together.

"Oh, reusable bags," Dave whistled as he shifted his shovel into one hand and grabbed a couple of them with the other. They were from a local grocery chain and had flowers on them that spelled out "Love Our Mother."

"Great, so it's a green family of zombies. At least they were worried about the earth," I said as I took the bag he held out to me. "Want to start with those cabinets and I'll work on these?"

He nodded and took one side of the kitchen, opening cabinets and clearing out any food we could use, along

with big knives and any medication and first-aid materials. I did the same, but the pickings were pretty damn
slim.

"I'm guessing someone hid out here after the outbreak," Dave said as he turned away from the last cabinet
on his side of the kitchen.

"Yeah, why?" I asked, absent as I threw open each
drawer in the hopes I'd find something more useful than
faded Christmas hand towels and aluminum foil.

"Well, all that's left in the cabinets is diet food," he
said.

I turned to find him holding up some bars with "Lose
Weight Fast" scrawled across them in bold red letters.
They had been stacked next to some empty bags of cheese
poofs and candy wrappers. I wrinkled my nose.

"Looks like they went off their diet in the end." I sighed
as I closed the last drawer and looked in my bag. I'd managed to get some batteries and aloe, but that was about it.

"Well, it's the end of the world," Dave said with a
shrug. "Why not let yourself go?"

I frowned as he tossed the diet bars into his bag.
"You're taking those?"

He nodded. "They're mostly carbs. Eat enough of them
and you'll still live."

"Is that really *living*?" I muttered as I turned to leave
the kitchen. I hadn't made it two steps, though, when a
movement from the laundry room made me stop.

"I dunno," Dave said, completely oblivious to what I'd
seen. "I guess it's better than the yummy all-protein brains
diet—"

"Shhh," I snapped, motioning toward the laundry room
with my hand.

He halted, set his bag down, and slowly lifted his shovel.

There was a moment of eerie silence and then all hell broke loose. Four zombies, what appeared to be a family of them, actually (aw, a mommy, a daddy and two adorable little monster children...the new American family, ladies and gentlemen), tore into the kitchen from the laundry room.

And they were *not* looking for diet bars.

CHAPTER 13

Happiness is not an accident.
Neither is a zombie apocalypse.

It wasn't often that I was surprised anymore. The shock value of the apocalypse had been played out at least a couple of months ago and most of the time my reaction to a zombie, even a zombie horde was… "Crap, here we go again."

But I don't know… this morning I was tired and worried about the whole Nicole thing (which I realize I hadn't addressed yet, but I was getting there! Hello? Zombies!! Stop pressuring me). I guess my reflexes were a little off from the last couple of days because I bit back a scream, a real actual *scream,* and staggered away from the family of zombies with my boot-clad feet tangling with each clumsy step.

The lead zombie, who looked like circa-1950s Housewife Zombie—since she was wearing what appeared to be what my grandma had always called a housecoat and still had a couple of curlers tangled in her otherwise ragged and thinning hair—swung at me with a dead, looping hand.

I fired off a shot but she caught the barrel of my gun with the flat of her palm and the bullet went wild. It tore through her shoulder instead of her forehead and blew a quarter-sized hole in her rotting flesh. She merely whined as she looked at the injury and kept coming in a quick set of plodding thuds.

I scampered backward. She was just too close to really get off a decent second shot and there was too much chance at getting a slice from her dirty nails or a nip from her gnashing, black teeth. She hadn't been flossing, that much was more than clear. Her dentist was going to be *pissed*.

"Back up, back up, back up!" Dave yelped.

I dove out of the way; as soon as I was clear, he swung the shovel. Unlike freaked-out me, he had good aim and connected solidly with Housewife's gray face.

Zombies are rotting. Have we mentioned this before? Yeah, I think we have and if you don't know that already, than you're not much of a zombie expert. But the point is that when you connect shovel to rotting flesh, the flesh never wins. This was no exception to that simple rule.

Dave's shovel sank about six inches into the woman's skull like it was a hot knife in soft butter (mmm, butter). The impact sent a spray of brains, goo, and blood out from the wound to coat half his shovel *and* his clean T-shirt. See, *this* is why we couldn't have nice things.

The female zombie whimpered, crossed her eyes as she looked upward at the shovel now embedded in her skull, and then went limp. Because his weapon was sunk so deep, she didn't disconnect from it, instead dangling from Dave's shovel like a sad marionette whose strings had been cut.

Dave pressed a boot into her chest and started the struggle to detach said shovel from said zombie head, but the rest of the family wasn't going to wait for us to clear one zombie (zombies have no sense of honor in a fight).

Daddy Dearest Zombie, dressed in what appeared to be the remnants if a *very* nice suit, was already heading our way, waving his floppy arms around in the air (like he just didn't care and I guess he didn't) with a series of guttural, throaty grunts and groans.

I dove over the kitchen island for some semblance of protection and a vantage point to aim better. I positioned myself carefully, then fired off a shot. I hit Dad right between the eyes; he took one final step toward Dave, still struggling to detach from Housewife Zombie, before toppling forward. Luckily as he fell, his body hit his former wife's (they were a cute couple, by the way, all matching dead skin and empty eyes) and his added weight helped Dave finally pull his shovel free.

Dave staggered back as the shovel sprayed even more gunk all over the walls and refrigerator, but regained his footing almost immediately and took another swing, this time at the teen boy zombie who had piled himself up right behind his dad (what can I say, they don't normally have much theory of positioning, which is a good thing— we'd seen some "bionic" zombies recently, and zombies with the ability to plan are not something you want to fuck with).

You know, normally I'd feel badly about killing a kid, even though we had to do it from time to time and it wasn't anything personal. But *this* kid had a Justin Bieber haircut, so I actually smiled as Dave thunked his shovel into the boy's neck.

The zombie kid made a garbled grunt, but kept coming despite the fact that his head was half severed from his body.

"Shit," Dave snapped as he shuffled out of the way of the boy zombie. "I hate when that happens."

I fired off another shot and hit Justin Bieber wannabe, dropping him in a pile where he stood. But as I turned the pistol on the final zombie, another boy, this one much younger, the gun only clicked.

Empty.

"God damn it!" I cried as I put the useless gun in my belt. "I'm out!"

Dave shrugged. "That's all right, I got it."

The little zombie boy was dressed in footy pajamas. At least they would have been footy pajamas if he still had both of his, er, footies. One of his feet was totally gone, gnawed off probably at the beginning of the outbreak and possibly by a member of his own family (I'm looking at you, Bieber Boy).

The lack of appendage didn't seem to bother the child, though (not that it ever does with zombies). He made pretty good time as he hobbled around the kitchen in a limping gate. He charged, head down like he was a bull in Spain, but Dave dodged pretty easily. The boy swung around and started forward again, so Dave lined himself up like he was batting for the Yankees. As the child got within his range, he swung the shovel.

The force of the hit sent the kid flying. Like literally *flying* backward across the kitchen. He hit the fridge and the door popped open, dumping rotting meat and warm ketchup all over his small, broken body and sending a waft of disgusting odor to fill the air around us.

"Ugh," I said, lifting my arm to cover my nose. "Freaking people who don't eat their perishables first!!"

Dave stared at the carnage, though the smell seemed to bother him less. "Well, they got turned into zombies, so I guess *that* was their punishment for lack of planning."

We were both quiet for a moment, looking at the wreck that had once been the kitchen. Dave sighed as he wiped sweat off his brow with the back of his hand.

"So, I'm hungry."

"What?" I motioned around us wildly. "After *this,* you're hungry?"

He arched a brow as he folded his arms and stared at me. "Aren't you?"

I was ready to deny it, but then my empty stomach let out a loud gurgle. Dave smiled a "Ha, told you so!" smile.

"Fine," I muttered.

"Want to eat some of these diet bars?" he asked.

I shuddered. "Is that really all there is?"

He grinned and then grabbed for the bag he'd left on the floor when he started playing gravekeeper with the zombie family. He dug around in it for a minute, then pulled out some pudding cups. You know, the kind that don't have to be refrigerated.

"Oh my God," I muttered as I staggered toward him in an almost zombie fashion. "Have I mentioned I love you?"

Dave laughed. "Not lately. Why don't we go upstairs, maybe climb out on the roof to get a better vantage point, and you can tell me all about it."

I grinned as I followed him up the stairs. "Deal."

The rest of the house was blissfully empty, including what had once been a beautiful master suite. Unfortunately, judging from the sludge stains and the blood pools on the floor, someone had been turned in that bed. Which really ruined the ambiance, I'll tell you.

The survivors had tried to help themselves by barricading the windows (though the zombies weren't going to climb up to the second-story window, so I'm not sure how that was going to help, but people do weird things when they're panicking and being turned into monsters). Plywood covered in bloody handprints was haphazardly nailed to the wall to cover the glass.

"Sheesh," Dave sighed as he grabbed a big mag light tossed on the floor at the foot of the bed and used it as a crowbar to pry the nails free. They plinked against the hardwood and the plywood section dropped free, flooding the room with light.

"Ah, much better," I sighed, but when I looked around me, it wasn't really much better. Truth be told, I think post–zombie apocalypse world is sort of better in dim light. It's not a pretty plague.

Dave didn't answer, but popped the lock on the window he'd uncovered. It slid open easily, sending wonderfully fresh air into the stuffy house. He kicked out the screen and smiled as he motioned outside. The window opened onto a lower roof, perfect for our purposes of observation and pudding eating.

As we climbed out, I tossed my husband a side-glance. He'd been afraid of heights before, but now he didn't even seem fazed. In fact, I was the one clutching for his arm as I inched down the slanted roof and sat down.

Dave was right, the vantage point was great up here. Through the overgrown trees we could see at least a mile, including across the parking lot to the hospital we'd come from and a series of parks, businesses, and schools that composed this fucked-up hamlet.

Oh yeah and zombies. We could see a lot of damn zombies, milling in the distance, roaming aimlessly through streets, groaning loud enough that we could occasionally hear them when the breeze shifted.

Dave popped the top on one of the puddings, gave it a quick smell, and then passed it over to me, along with a plastic spoon. That boy comes prepared, you have to give him that one.

"Thanks," I said as I stared down in awe at creamy vanilla awesomeness. I would have preferred butterscotch, but beggars couldn't be choosers, I guess.

"Good God, that's good," Dave grunted as he licked his spoon clean. We were both silent for a moment (aside from my little orgasm noises as I ate) but then he sighed. "Okay, so all morning I've been thinking about what you said at the hospital."

I blinked, still starstruck by vanilla-y, sugar-y, processed goodness. Later I'd pay with a sugar crash and a massive headache, but for now...*heaven*!

"Huh?"

"About Nicole having suspicions about me," he explained before he tossed his pudding cup over the edge of the roof.

My appetite fled in an instant (luckily, I had already licked my pudding cup clean) and I followed suit before looking at him.

"She's noticed your...um...*odd* habits."

He blinked and it seemed like he really didn't know what the hell I was talking about. "What do you mean, odd habits?"

I stared at him. "Come on, you know what I mean." When he didn't answer, I blinked. "You have to know what I mean, Dave."

He slowly shook his head. He was looking at me like I was crazy and if I hadn't had such a clear list of all the weird things that had been happening since he was bitten, I might have been convinced he was right, too. But unfortunately, I *did* have that list in my head.

I shifted. Shit, I hadn't thought I was going to have to actually say everything I'd noticed out loud, but he really seemed clueless. I didn't really *want* to say it, it made it more real. I wanted to pretend it away a bit longer.

"Sarah," he said softly.

I nodded before I took a really deep breath and started talking.

"Okay, so ever since you got bitten by the zombie in the lab and I gave you the cure, you've been..." I shifted again, trying to find the right word to describe my fears. "You've been *different.*"

"Well, I did survive what should have been certain death." Dave shrugged, but his eyes were hard and had no humor in them. They also didn't quite focus on me. "I guess if that doesn't change a guy, I don't know what does."

"It's more than that," I whispered, but I looked away from him over the dead town.

At the zombies roaming mindlessly in little pods, looking for any sign of human life. I shivered and it wasn't something I could have controlled for the life of me.

"Since you were bitten, you're stronger."

He blinked. "Stronger."

I nodded. "David, you were lifting *so* much weight in

that gym a few days ago. And last night, you opened the locked sliding door at the hospital like it was nothing. And we both know from personal experience that those things are a bitch to cram open when they're locked."

His brow wrinkled. "Come on, Sarah, you've got to give me some credit for being in *way* better shape now than I was when all this first happened. You're a lot stronger, too."

"Not bench-pressing-almost-twice-my-body-weight stronger," I whispered as I dared a quick side-glance at him. "Plus you've been hungrier, and then there's the sleep thing."

"The sleep thing?" he asked, but now his voice was clipped and irritated.

Shit, I remembered that tone. I'd heard it tons of times during therapy before the zombie outbreak. I really didn't want to hear it again.

"You breathe out more than you breathe in," I whispered. "It happens every night."

"So let me get this straight, you and Nicole suspect me of . . . *something*. I'm not really sure what, because I can lift more weight, I'm hungry in a world where we're nearly starving, and I might need one of those night-breathing machines now?" He shook his head. "That's sort of crazy, Sarah."

"The zombies in the pool didn't come near you, David," I choked out and finally I looked at him head-on. "We didn't talk about it afterward, we never even acknowledged it happened, but shit, you can't pretend it *didn't* happen! The zombies *ignored* you. They swarmed around you to get to other people. The only things they do that to are . . . are . . ."

I dragged my sentence to an end, but David didn't stop looking at me, straight in the eye.

"The only things they ignore are other zombies, you mean," he finally said in a flat, dead tone that hurt as much as his irritated one.

"Yes," I admitted softly.

He was silent for a long time. So long that I started to shift from discomfort and to search helplessly for a new topic of conversation just to fill the void.

"Do you think I'm a zombie?" he finally asked.

He no longer seemed mad, which I guess I should have been happy about. Though how you could be happy about anything in this scenario was beyond me.

I shook my head immediately. "No, not a zombie. But... something happened when you got bitten, honey. Something *changed,* even though you didn't turn. You have to know that's true, even if neither one of us wants to admit it."

He looked away from me finally and out into the town like I had been. He was watching the same zombies I was, and I guess he was probably having the same thoughts as I'd been. Of how close we had been dancing to the edge of death since the outbreak.

And how much closer we'd come to it when he was bitten. There were so many more ugly, nameless, terrifying "what ifs" now.

"I feel like me," he said and then let out a long, heavy sigh. "But different, too."

"Different," I repeated.

He nodded. "Yes. I didn't want to say anything to you because..."

He stopped, but I knew what he meant. My white

knight wanted to protect me and I smiled regardless of how painful this topic was.

"But I'm not a zombie," he hastened to add as he looked at me another time. "I swear to God, I don't want to eat people, I can't smell brains like some of those people who were changing said they could. If I thought for a second that I was a danger to anyone, especially you—"

"You would tell me," I interrupted, mostly because I wanted him to know I knew it without him having to say it out loud. "But I don't want you to keep things from me in order to protect me. We're in this together, right?"

I reached out to cover his hand, the one with the bite scar on it. It disappeared under my fingers and we both breathed an almost imperceptible sigh of relief.

"Right," he promised.

"Good," I sighed. "But we still have a problem."

"Nicole," he said softly.

I nodded. "Everything I've noticed, she's noticed, too. Especially the 'zombies didn't eat Dave' thing. Last night she pretty much flat out said she thinks you were bitten and that we're hiding that and a whole lot else from her."

He shut his eyes. "We haven't known her long, but I'm guessing she's not going to just let a potential 'story' go, is she?"

I shook my head. "No. So how do we put her off the scent?"

"Well, I'll try not to be a zombie weirdo as much as possible," Dave laughed. When I didn't join him, he cleared his throat and stopped. "And, well, we can always hope McCray distracts her. He's a big star, right? And that was her beat."

I nodded. "And she *does* hate the guy. We could probably feed that."

He nodded, but his mouth had gotten thin and tight the way it always did when he was worrying about something.

"What?" I asked, almost afraid to know the answer.

"Sarah, I'm not a zombie, but the cure I took . . . maybe it wears off. Or maybe the virus developed an immunity. There's got to be some explanation of why I'm . . . *different* now. We don't really know what's going to happen down the road."

"David—" I started, with a strange urge to cover my ears and scream "Lalalalala!" until he stopped talking.

But he didn't.

"Just listen," he said, his tone sharp and silencing. "If I do ever change, Sarah, I want to know that you'll . . . take care of it."

I looked at him, blinking at tears that suddenly stung my eyes. Stupid boy, making me want to cry when I hadn't done that in weeks. I thought I was over it.

"Shut up," I whispered.

"Promise me that you'll kill me if I ever become a threat to you."

I bit my lip. This was a conversation a million couples all over the Badlands had probably had by now. The ones who answered the question wrong were dead (er, undead). But it was one thing to have a vague "what if" scenario conversation and it was quite another to be asked to swear an oath to a man while holding his zombie-scarred hand in yours.

"Promise me," he repeated.

I looked into his eyes. Green, not red, still. They were

filled with desperation. Fear for me. Fear of himself. And I knew I might very well be lying to him when I nodded.

"Yes, I promise."

He looked at me funny. Like he sort of knew I was lying. Or that I'd at least hesitate before I did what I'd said I'd do. But he didn't get a chance to press me on the subject like he seemed to want to do because in that moment we both saw something that totally distracted us.

In the distance, across the parking lot that led to the hospital, was a flash of color and movement. My eyes widened as I recognized what it was.

Nicole and McCray, racing from the hospital grounds toward us. And behind them . . . a mob of at least ten slobbering zombies.

CHAPTER 14

Money can't buy happiness, but killing shit helps.

Shit!" Dave said as he bolted to his feet. "Hand me the gun."

"I'm empty, remember?" I popped open the chamber so he could see.

"Fuck!" he muttered before he sprinted up the slanted roof and dove through the open window back into the house.

I stayed where I was. What? Someone had to be the lookout so we didn't lose them!

But being lookout really *sucked* because all I could do was watch in helpless horror as Nicole practically dragged McCray toward the potential safety of the houses. The zombies were on their tails, and their reaching dead fingers were pretty much ready to grab McCray's ragged leather jacket with every swipe. If he slowed down at all... if he missed a step (and since he was staggering, that was a pretty good bet)... he was toast and Nicole might go right down with him. The zombies would swarm and that would be it.

Though I guess, in retrospect, if Nicole got zombiefied, Dave and I wouldn't have a problem with her suspicious little mind anymore. But that wasn't how we rolled. I didn't want the girl dead. Or living dead.

"Hurry up!" I called into the house in the hopes Dave would hear me. "They're getting closer."

The sound of my voice must have carried across what was left of the hospital parking lot and the yard because Nicole jerked her gaze toward me. Her face softened with relief as she found me on the roof and sprinted harder in my direction.

I heard her voice, broken by the distance and the sound of zombie moans, but I'm pretty sure she was saying, "Come...hurry...*asshole*!"

"Hurry, hurry," I whispered, though I had no idea what exactly would happen if the two of them actually reached me. It wasn't like I had a ladder to get them up onto the roof and so far no weapons to...I don't know, save their asses from certain walking death.

So why didn't I yell for Nicole? Um, loud noises attract zombies (have you not been paying attention?) and I didn't want to bring any more of them scrambling toward our new friends and making this already wretched situation even more precarious.

"Sarah!"

I spun around and found Dave in the window. He was holding out a rifle for me in one hand and had another for himself. He also had a box of shells. Only half full, but still twenty or twenty-five shots was nothing to sneeze at.

At the sight of the guns, I almost sobbed with relief, but bit it back. We still had to, you know, save Nicole and

McCray before I could really relax and we could start congratulating ourselves.

I snatched the rifle from Dave's hand. It was the kind you'd hunt with, and I was going to do some goddamned hunting ASAP. Actually, at some point, I was willing to bet we'd start doing taxidermy on zombie heads and hanging them in the living room, but for now it wasn't the time to think about the specifics of post-apocalyptic décor.

I dropped on my ass onto the roof and used my knee as a way to settle my shaking hands before I took aim at the first zombie. He was right behind McCray and still dressed in what was left of doctor's scrubs. In fact, several of the chasing zombies were in some kind of medical-related rags. Apparently the hospital hadn't been all that empty after all.

I stared through the site. The first two zombies were actually side by side, so if I lined up my shot just right, I might be able to drop them both and save some ammo. Carefully I aimed, took a deep breath, and fired.

Bull's-eye!

As the bullet zinged through one skull and then the other, both zombies dropped like sandbags in a pile. Better yet, the two zombies behind them tripped over the fresh corpses and went sprawling head over feet in a humorous display of legs and arms, which slowed them down considerably.

Unfortunately, the other six in hot pursuit had enough time to react and went around the pile-up, groaning and grunting as they continued their jog for dinner. To make matters worse, the two zombies who had fallen over their dead dragged themselves up almost immediately and were soon back in the mob.

I do have to say that at least one of them had broken his arm in the fall. Even from this distance, I could see his elbow was now turned at a terrible, unnatural angle. But he didn't care. Zombies never care about little subjects like shattered bones. They're all about the big picture. And the big picture is always BRRRAAAAINS.

In some way, you have to admire their single-mindedness, I guess. In another way ... fuck, that's messed up. I mean, you should *care* if you break a bone. You should *care*!

"The sliding glass door is unlocked," Dave called down once Nicole and McCray had entered the edge of the yard where Dave and I had gone not an hour before.

Nicole didn't acknowledge what he said, but she bolted straight for the door. McCray still staggered behind her, but he was making good time, especially for someone who I suspected was totally high—and not on believing or a feeling or whatever that old song said. Though I had no idea what exactly he *could* be high on. It didn't seem like there were that many choices left in the wreck of a hospital.

I shook my head. This was not the time to go all day dreamy about a rocker's poison of choice. If we wanted the two of them to get into the house, we were going to have to kill some zombies.

Dave fired off his first shot as Nicole vaulted onto the cement pad at the back sliding door and yanked. They were underneath the roofline now, but I heard the door fling back on its track and then swing shut again. And yet I didn't hear it close.

"Mother fucker!" Nicole's voice came from below, slightly muffled but not enough to give me any illusion that she and McCray were safe.

"I'll keep sniping from up here," Dave said as he took another shot and dropped another zombie. "Go down there and help them if you can."

He didn't have to tell me twice. I fired off one last shot and didn't even wait to watch the zombie drop before I crawled up the roof and dove headfirst back inside.

I'll admit what I did next was kind of silly. I rolled. You know, that movie thing where the hero or heroine does a summersault dive into a room. That's the thing I did. It ended up with me on my ass with a rather painful thud. Reaching back, I rubbed my abused tailbone before I checked behind me to be sure Dave hadn't seen.

He was busy with other things. You know, zombies and all. Thank goodness. I hated to look stupid.

I scrambled to my feet and rushed out of the master bedroom and down the stairs. The sounds of grunts and fighting were getting louder with each step; by the time I jumped past the last three stairs to the landing, it was more than clear that the zombies were storming our little fortress.

I careened around the corner past the kitchen and into the living room area to find Nicole smashing a zombie in the head with a folding chair. Very WWE. Meanwhile, McCray was kicking at another one from a precarious perch on the back of the couch. Several more were wedged in the partly open door, too stupid to come in one at a time or . . . I don't know, *push the door open*.

Lucky for us.

I braced against the wall and fired off the rifle. The zombie attacking McCray's head exploded like a firework; McCray blinked over at me in confusion and foggy disbelief.

"Hello, love."

I shook my head as I popped another shell in the chamber. "Shut the door, McCray!"

He blinked again and this time shot his gaze over at the pile-up at the door.

"Oh, yeah," he said and then he strolled, I'm serious, he *strolled* over to the door, nonchalant as can be.

Once he was out of my line of site, I fired into the crowd of undead at the door. I hit more than one of the moaning beasts and a few collapsed on the others. McCray started kicking at the corpses, driving back the injured and pushing the dead clear until he finally managed to get the door shut.

"Lock it, asshole!" Nicole wailed as she swung the back of the folding chair (which was already coated in sludge and blood) against the temple of her attacking zombie.

His poor head was already half bashed in and this last blow dropped him out of my sight behind the couch. Nicole stomped downward—I assume on what was left of him—and then sighed in exasperation.

"Some help you are, dickhead!" she said as she came around the couch and smacked McCray across the arm. Hard.

"No need to resort to violence," he said as he backed away, rubbing his arm.

"But this is your fault. I said, don't go into the room with all the zombies, but did you listen? No! You had to go check for your stupid drugs!"

McCray shrugged. "Rather die happy than not!"

I ignored their childish pissing and moaning. I was too distracted by what was at the sliding glass door. The zombies we hadn't killed were still clawing at the glass, leaving it smudged with goo and mung and blood as their teeth and fingers scraped along the thin barrier between us.

Worse than that, there were more coming. Across the yard behind them. From the parking lot in the distance and the other yards. They had heard us shooting. They had heard the hungry moans.

And yet Nicole kept slapping at McCray and he kept whining about it like our lives weren't in pretty much mortal danger.

"Okay, I don't mean to be a stick-in-the-mud and interrupt your little issue," I snapped as I stepped between them like a referee. Or a babysitter. "But there are like ten zombies outside the door and I can already see more coming thanks to all the gunfire and other noise we're making. So for the love of everything holy, can we focus?"

I motioned wildly to the horrifying scene outside, and Nicole and McCray finally looked out the window. McCray bolted backward like he'd never seen a horde before and Nicole's face paled.

"Oh shit," she muttered, her hand lifting to her neck.

I thought I'd gotten through to them, really I did. But that moment faded as soon as Nicole smacked McCray again.

"See? All your fault!"

"It doesn't matter whose fault it is," I all but screamed, and the two of them straightened up like they were getting yelled at by their mom or something. "We have to go up, get David, and figure out how to get out of here! NOW!"

I guess my grown-up "teacher" voice must have worked because the two of them stopped smacking at each other and fussing and both of them nodded.

"Yeah, sorry," McCray muttered.

"Sorry," Nicole added, her cheeks coloring dark red, though I'm not sure if it was from continued anger at McCray or embarrassment at her childish behavior. I'm afraid it was probably the first, but I didn't have time to deal with it.

"Grab anything that can be used as a weapon, keep an eye out for more ammo, and let's go," I ground out through clenched teeth as I headed for the stairs.

"Right, just one minute," McCray said.

I turned and watched as he pulled the shade across the sliding glass door.

"How is that going to help?" Nicole asked blankly.

He shrugged. "At least we don't have to look at them. And maybe they'll forget we're in here if they can't see inside."

I stared. So McCray was obviously immature, infantile, and, judging by his ridiculously dilated pupils, high as a kite. But that wasn't actually the worst idea in the world. Zombies *did* sometimes forget about their prey if they were out of sight, out of mind. It wasn't like they had super-high-functioning brains or whatever.

"Um, great," I said as I turned for the stairs again.

We bounded up in double time and I turned for the master suite. Nicole motioned to the other bedrooms and I nodded. If she wanted to search for more weapons or ammo, she was my guest. I just hoped she'd find something Dave had overlooked in his hurry to grab a gun and save our new friends.

McCray followed me, of course, never one to take the initiative to...I don't know, save himself. From the master bedroom, I heard the occasional pop of gunfire, clear signs that Dave was still taking out a few zombies here and there while he waited to hear if our new friends had been saved from zombie death and dismemberment.

"Hey," I said as I popped my head out the open window. "We're okay."

Dave was perched up against one of the furnace vents that jutted out from the roof, using it as a brace so he could aim better. He fired his rifle again before he gave me a half-glance, but it was one of brief relief.

"Great," he said with a quick smile. Then he looked down at the gathering crowd below. "Unfortunately, more and more are coming. I think we put out the zombie dinner bell for the whole town. Maybe the whole county."

"Yeah, we noticed that," McCray said with a sarcastic sigh as he pushed past me to climb out onto the roof. As he approached the edge, he wobbled slightly and I tensed as Dave reached out an arm to steady him. "Whoa. Trippy."

"Yeah," Dave grunted, pure annoyance lacing his voice. If McCray wasn't careful, our entire group was going to hate him as much as Nicole seemed to already. "So I've been thinking about a way to get out of this."

"Please, I'd love to hear it because I'm having a hard time thinking of one besides 'hole up here and see if it works out better for us than the family who lived here before,'" I said as I stared down at the horde.

Even to a seasoned zombie hunter like me, it was a terrifying sight. There were probably fifty zombies down below and more straggling up from the parking lot and adjoining yards with every passing moment. Fifty zombies meeting maybe twelve shells left from two rifles equaled dead, and eventually walking dead, humans.

So seriously, if Dave had a plan, I was way more than willing to hear it at that moment.

"If I keep shooting, that's only going to bring the zombies to the back of the house," he explained, and as if he was punctuating that statement, he fired another shot and took out three zombies at once. Five more replaced them from the yard and proved his point exactly.

Despite that, I muttered, "Nice."

Hey, I was always appreciative of a good zombie kill. You can't lose sight of these small victories, even in the face of certain death.

"Thanks." Dave sent me a brief smile. "Anyway, I'll keep drawing them to the back by firing."

"How's that going to help us, mate?" McCray snapped, voicing the same question I had on the tip of my tongue (only he voiced it with a British accent, which is always better).

Dave glared at him. "Well, *that* will give *you* guys a chance to escape out the front."

I wrinkled my brow, but he kept talking.

"So you guys will go to a safer building, using quiet kills when needed and trying to attract as little attention as possible. Okay?"

I stared at him. "Um, no. Totally not okay."

"Why?" he asked.

I shook my head. "Why? You're really asking me why? Um, because that plan leaves us even further from our vehicle, which is back there by the hospital, in the same direction as the zombies you'll be gathering in the backyard. Not to mention the tiny little problem that it leaves *you* on the roof with a bunch of fucking zombies surrounding the house."

"Well, I've got a solution for both those problems," Dave said as he turned to face me head-on.

I blinked. I didn't like his look. Not at all. "What?"

He was silent, just staring at me, and I hated how calm his expression was, like he was surrendering to something, and I didn't want to lose him to it, whatever it was.

"What?" I repeated, this time louder. Loud enough that a few zombie heads swiveled toward me and their groans echoed from below.

"He's going to walk through them."

I spun around to find Nicole standing at the window. She had a new gun in her hand, a pistol, and another box of ammo for it, as well as a full box of shells for Dave's rifle. She was staring at my husband, but her expression wasn't one of smug certainty like I'd figured it would be.

It was respect. And not even grudging respect. Like full on respect-respect.

But she couldn't be right when she said what she said! This was just her fucked-up reporter mind trying to keep pushing at the story, make it more interesting. To try to prove David was... well, whatever she thought he was.

I spun away from her to look at him. He didn't look shocked by her suggestion. He didn't even look scared. He had that same calm, even look on his face that he had when I asked him to clarify his crazy-person plan.

Except it was pretty clear now that Nicole had just done that for him.

"No," I whispered. I could hardly breathe and had to work to drag in air before I continued, "No, David."

"Sarah," he whispered, still so very calm as he reached for my arm.

I yanked it away. "No! Tell me she's wrong. Tell me

that you don't actually intend to walk through the zombies."

He tilted his head and smiled at me gently. "I can tell you whatever you want to hear, babe, but it would be a lie. Because that's *exactly* what I intend to do."

CHAPTER 15

Who you are is not what you do.
Unless you eat brains.

Dave and I stared at each other. I couldn't even speak. I could hardly breathe, my mind was racing so fast with thoughts of David becoming a...what would you even call what he was describing? A zombie whisperer or something?

And I was also haunted by even more detailed thoughts of David being torn to shreds by the zombies outside because what had happened in the pool at the camp turned out to be nothing more than a fluke.

"How the fuck do you think you're going to survive that, mate?" McCray snorted, breaking the silence.

Nicole leaned back against the outside of the house and stared at us. "He did it before."

"What?" McCray asked.

He blinked and took a step away from us. One precariously close to the edge of the roof.

"Wait, are you guys just a dream? Am I awake? Is this a hallucination?" he asked in a terrified faux whisper.

I shut my eyes hard. I *wished,* and not for the first time since the outbreak, that this *was* a dream or a hallucination... maybe brought on by eating bad cheese. But it wasn't. This was real as real could get. You couldn't wake up or snap out of it, no matter how hard you tried.

"First, you're going to fall off the roof and I'm not coming after you and saving your ass again," Nicole snapped.

McCray took a look behind him and then scurried forward.

"*And* if you have to ask if the people you're hanging with are real, I *really* think you should try detox," Nicole continued with a shake of her head.

"Because reality is so fucking awesome, right?" McCray snapped and his voice was surprisingly lucid.

I expected them to start in on each other once again, but instead Nicole looked at him a long moment and then shrugged. "Well, you *do* have a point. Maybe start sharing whatever you're taking instead."

"Will you two just *shut up,*" I snapped.

Both of them looked at me and for once they had the same expression. Like they were annoyed at *me* for daring to interrupt their idiotfest!

I ignored the look and turned my attention back to David. I took in a couple of deep breaths. What I needed to be was the calm voice of reason here. Hysteria wasn't going to get my point across. Too bad that right now I just wanted to grab my husband and shake him and hold him back to prevent him from committing what amounted to suicide, but I could control that.

Mostly.

So instead I said, "You can't walk through the zombies, honey."

He smiled at me. "Like Nicole said, I did it before."

I shook my head. "And you have no clue if it will work again," I insisted as I grabbed for his hand. Like if I somehow touched him, it would snap him out of this craziness.

It didn't. Stupid, stubborn boy. Who I did *not* want to lose even if he was convinced he was the Zombie Jesus or some other nonsense.

"I think we both know it *probably* will work." He tilted his head. "As per our conversation before Nicole and McCray started across the parking lot like the Pied Pipers of Zombieville."

Nicole's eyes narrowed. "You know, I'm going to figure this all out. You two speaking in idiot code isn't going to stop me. I'm a reporter."

"Barely! I don't think stalkerazzi count," I snapped.

She glared daggers into me that could have killed even a zombie. Luckily I was a bit more resilient.

Dave glanced at me. "Look, if I'm going to do this walk-into-the-zombies thing, maybe we *should* just tell them the truth."

I raised my hands. "Whoa, whoa, whoa. First off, I still don't agree with the walk-into-the-zombies thing. And second, as per our conversation *before* the Pied Piper thing, I thought we weren't going to tell them anything!"

Nicole was snapping her gaze back and forth between us, her lids and brow getting lower with each look. Seriously, she wasn't even going to be able to see soon if she didn't knock it off.

"Guys—" she started.

Dave lifted his hand in the universal gesture of "Shut the hell up" but his gaze never left me. "Sarah, we need all the help we can get. And like Nicole said—" He looked at her briefly. "She's going to figure it out. Why not just skip all the sneaking around and lying and extra explaining we may have to do later?"

"Besides," Nicole said, folding her arms. "If you're going to trust me to watch your ass, I need to know the truth. In fact, I'm not leaving this damn roof until I hear it. So spill."

McCray leaned forward. He seemed completely freaking oblivious to everything around him. I swear, he was worse than a child with ADD.

"We are *really* high up, aren't we?" he muttered, I think more to himself than to us. "Like what, ten feet?"

I shut my eyes and counted to ten in my head, mostly so that I wouldn't end up pushing him down into the zombies just to get him to stop irritating me.

"Fine," I said through clenched teeth as I lifted my hands in surrender. "It's your ass, so it's your call."

Dave reached out and briefly touched my hand before he turned to face Nicole. He drew a deep breath and was about to speak when McCray looked at us.

"So do you two bang or what?" he slurred.

I shook my head. "Um, we're married."

He clucked his tongue. "So that's a no?"

Nicole spun on him. "Hey, McCray, how about we try the quiet game? I will find you some heroin if you just shut the fuck up for ten minutes and let David tell me his big secret. Deal?"

"Shit, Nicole, don't encourage him," I muttered as I watched McCray's eyes light up like someone had offered him Christmas candy or something.

"Do *you* want to babysit him, then, while the grown-ups talk?" Nicole asked, hands on her hips.

I glanced at our resident rocker. He looked so damn happy at the idea of more drugs to come and he *was* being very good now that the word *heroin* had come into play.

"Fine." I shrugged. "Nicole can find whatever she wants for you. You're an adult. Sort of."

"Great," Nicole sighed. "Now can we talk about David's big confession? Let's go, buddy. What's the deal?"

Dave sat down on the roof and stared out at the rolling sea of zombies that was now gathered under the house, looking up at us, brainlessly waiting to eat us. Then he looked at his scarred hand and slowly, quietly started to talk.

He told Nicole about our time in Phoenix and how we'd met Dr. Benson, a mad scientist if there ever was one, and started catching zombies for him. I was happy when he didn't add that I'd taken Benson's side over his and hadn't believed him when he warned me about the asshole.

And then he told her how he'd gotten bitten.

I turned my face away as he explained his feelings that day: His fear and despair as he waited for me to come back with what we hoped was a cure. His acceptance that it probably wouldn't work and that he'd be turned into a zombie and lose everything he cared about and hoped for.

In my head, I tried not to go back to that day, myself, but I couldn't help it. All I could think about was the memory of running through the corridors of Benson's underground bunker, praying I'd get back to David in time. Of nearly watching him turn into a monster I couldn't save.

Nicole blinked. Her eyes were wide and dilated and

she looked freaked the fuck out. She had been silent
through his story, but now she swallowed hard.

"So the cure worked," she whispered, voice cracking
as she stared at Dave like he'd sprouted a second head. Or
walked on water.

He was our own miracle, come to life. Maybe he *was*
Zombie Jesus, come to think of it.

"Yeah," he said. "Sarah saved me, though it was completely the last minute. I felt myself starting to change and
then...I was me again."

"Whoa," McCray muttered. To be honest, I hadn't even
thought he was paying attention, but now he stared at
Dave with a healthy dose of awe. "So is that where you
got that wicked cool scar?" He winked at me. "Chicks
love scars. And tattoos. And guitars."

"I could live without it," I whispered past a suddenly
very dry throat.

"But ever since then, things have been different," Dave
continued. "Slowly my body, my mind have changed."

Nicole backed up one big step and then lifted her gun
level with Dave's face. "What do you mean, *changed*?"

"Hey, oh!" McCray shouted as he unexpectedly staggered between them. "No need to get all pointy with Mr.
Pistol there, love."

Okay, so McCray was annoying as piss, but, shit, I
could have hugged him at that moment. I didn't, of course,
because he probably would have humped my leg and given
me God only knew what kind of communicable diseases,
but I could have. His distraction gave me enough time to
swing my own rifle into the ready and point it at Nicole.

"Shoot my husband and your brains won't be fit for the
zombies," I promised, low and serious.

Nicole's gaze slipped to me and I saw the fear behind even her hard eyes. The confusion. I could have felt sorry for her, were she not threatening, you know, the love of my life.

McCray started yelling some sort of incoherent Brit speak and then Nicole started shouting, too, I think half at him and half at me. That, of course, made *me* join in until we all sounded like a bunch of talking heads on one of those court shows that used to be on TV. You know, the ones hosted by that annoying, screeching blonde woman. Nancy-What's-Her-Face? I bet she made a really charming zombie.

But the cacophony of our yelling was disrupted when David pointed his rifle toward the sky and wasted a precious piece of ammo by discharging the weapon.

All three of us stopped talking and stared at him.

"We can scream and yell and eventually shoot each other, but then what's the point of everything we've been through?" Dave said, his voice quiet, especially in comparison to our ridiculousness up to this point. He looked at me and his pointed gaze made me blush even before he continued talking.

"Sarah, I appreciate you want to defend me, but I think Nicole would be stupid not to freak out a little when a person who admits he's been bitten by a zombie starts talking about changing."

I frowned, but shit, he was right. *Again*. It seems like that jerk is always right and he knows it, which makes it all the more irritating. But Dave had already turned his attention elsewhere.

"And Nicole, if you would just wait and *listen* to me before you threaten to shoot my face off for being a zombie, I'll tell you that I don't feel *zombie* different."

"What other kind of different is there?" she asked.

"Clearly the 'cure' mixed with the virus in my system and it did *something* to me. But the *something* doesn't include wanting to eat anyone's brains. And if it did, Sarah and I have already agreed that she'd shoot me." I couldn't help but wince, and he must have noticed it because he added, "And if she wouldn't, I have every confidence that *you* would."

Nicole bit her lip and then slowly lowered her pistol, so I did the same with my rifle.

"Sorry," she whispered after an awkward silence.

I wasn't sure if she was directing that to David or to me or both, but I nodded regardless. "I'm sorry, too."

"And McCray," Dave finished, turning on the rocker, who was weaving in front of Nicole, "seriously, dude, how did you survive this many months if you're *this* strung out?"

McCray stared at him and then he shook his head. "Months? I thought it had only been a few days…"

Dave covered his eyes with one hand. "Okay, well at least take a seat. You're going to fall off the roof and, like Nicole said, we aren't going after you if you do."

To my surprise, McCray did as Dave told him and sank down on his ass like he was a dog who'd been given an order by his beloved master. If his tail had wagged, it would have completed the picture.

Seriously, I was beginning to think this "Zombie Whisperer" thing had some merit. New Dave *definitely* had a way about him.

"Look, I'd love to talk about this even more with you, since I'm sure you have questions out the ass," Dave said, turning back to Nicole, "but right now we're on a roof, surrounded by zombies, and if we don't haul ass, we're going to be facing nightfall. I don't think we want to spend a night in this house."

"Especially since eventually those blokes will break the glass door," McCray muttered in one of his interesting moments of intelligence.

All three of us stared at him for a moment, and then Nicole shook her head like she was snapping herself out of a dream. "Okay, you're right. But just because I'm willing to table this 'Dave is partially a zombie' conversation—"

"He's not a zombie!" I interrupted as I clenched my rifle with both hands.

She shot me a glance, almost apologetic but not quite. "—well, this 'Dave is whatever Dave is' conversation then! But just because I'm willing to set it aside to get our asses out of this situation doesn't mean I'm forgetting it or that we're done talking about him getting bitten by zombies and you guys finding a cure."

Dave nodded. "Understood. Now why don't Sarah and I head over to the front side of the house and see if we can find a building that would make a good place for you guys to run to while I distract the zombies. Nicole, you stay here and fire at the zombies to keep them interested."

"Sounds good," I agreed with a sigh of relief.

Okay, crisis averted, at least for now and even though I didn't like the *Dave walks through zombies* thing, we could discuss it while—

Nicole shook her head. "No! No way!"

Dave shut his eyes and I could see from the throbbing vein in his neck that he was swiftly nearing the edge of his patience. Even Zombie Jesus had a limit, I guess.

"What now, Nicole," he ground through clenched teeth. "*What*?"

"There's no way I'm letting you and wifey just take off together after you admitted the zombie thing."

I rolled my eyes. "What do you think we're going to do, skip town?"

"Maybe," Nicole snapped.

"Okay, then come with us," Dave sighed.

"And leave doofus alone?" Nicole laughed. "It's not like *he's* going to be able to keep the zombies' attention. Unless he falls into the mosh pit they've got going on down there."

"Mosh pit?" McCray asked, looking up.

I shut my eyes. She was right. And from the way Dave pursed his lips, he knew it, too.

"Okay," he said, dragging out the word as he thought of some kind of solution. "I would say you and Sarah go, but then I won't know which building to drive the truck to."

I rubbed my eyes. "You and Nicole go," I said, though I didn't like the idea of Dave being alone with Miss Itchy Trigger Finger. "And I'll stay here and babysit McCray and shoot the zombies the best I can. Is *that* agreeable, Nicole?"

She thought about it for a minute and I could see she was actually looking for a reason to be contrary, but finally she bobbed out a nod. "Yeah, okay."

"Thanks, your highness," I muttered as I put myself in position and started firing at the zombies below. I dropped a handful with the shot, but there seemed to be always be more around to fill the hole.

Dave leaned forward and pressed a quick kiss to my cheek. "Thanks," he whispered.

I lowered my gun and turned into his arms. As I hugged him, I murmured, "Be careful of Nicole. She still might shoot you."

"Naw," he said with a smile as he turned to follow her into the house. "She knows if she did that, you'd blow her into tiny pieces."

I glowered as I refocused on the zombies below. Damn straight I'd blow her to pieces if she hurt my Dave. And then I'd feed said pieces to the zombies just for good measure.

Huh, a bit bloodthirsty, I know. But you have to admit, the bitch had it coming if she screwed with my husband. There are lines, even in a zombie apocalypse, people. And Nicole was treading dangerously close to mine.

"So your brother," McCray said, and his voice dragged me from my murderous thoughts.

"Who?" I asked as I stared at him.

"The guy, the zombie guy," McCray said as he motioned toward where Dave and Nicole had gone.

"We're *married*," I clarified without much patience.

Now McCray looked up at me with a twisted face of horror. "You're married to your brother? I don't care if there are zombies, that's just wrong."

I resisted the urge to swing my rifle on McCray and put him out of his misery, and instead said, "No. I mean, David isn't my brother. He's my husband. And he's not a zombie."

"He got bitten by a zombie and everyone bitten by a zombie gets turned into a zombie. So he's a zombie," McCray said with a dismissive wave of his multiringed hand.

I took a deep breath and fought to find a new subject

since this one was becoming progressively more dangerous for everyone in our group.

"So what's your deal?" I asked as I fired into the crowd
again. "Why didn't you just make a run for it after the
outbreak? Why did you stay here? I'd think you'd want to
get as far away as you could from the place where you got
imprisoned in rehab."

McCray stared out over the zombie sea below. "Yeah,
well, it was actually my idea to come here and get sober."

I blinked. "No fucking way."

He glanced up. "Yeah. We fired our manager last year,
my best friend from school, because he was so doped up
he couldn't do his job. He died a few months later from an
overdose and I told the mates it was time for us to clean
up. So we came here. And then they all died."

I stared at him. There wasn't any slurring to his voice
now. There wasn't any teasing. "Do you think that's your
fault?"

He glanced at me and then shrugged. "Dunno. But if
they didn't get to leave, why should I?"

I fired another time and then glanced at him. "Because
you survived, McCray. So you owe it to them to get your
act together and *live*. You're coming with us when we go."

He shook his head. "Where do you think you're going,
anyway? You and reporter bitch and zombie boy."

I shrugged. "Midwest Wall."

He blinked. "You believe in that rot?"

"I don't know," I admitted. "But I'd rather believe in
the rot than not believe in anything. So we're going. And
you're coming with us."

"No—" he started.

"Hey," I interrupted. "I'm not asking."

He looked over at me and for a long moment we held gazes. He looked like he wanted to answer; hell, he actually looked grateful on some fucked-up level. But before he could do anything, Dave and Nicole popped back through the window.

"We've got a place picked out," Nicole said as she pulled her gun from her waistband. "But it may not stay safe for long. So let's get a move on."

She turned to Dave, who had moved to stand next to me. Then, to my absolute surprise, she handed over the pistol to him and all the slugs from her pockets.

"Here. You need the guns to keep their attention," she said softly. "We'll go the shovel/machete/baseball-bat route. It's quieter anyway."

Dave blinked and then took her gun. "Thanks," he said softly.

She backed away and worked on dragging poor McCray up from his seated position. Which left me and Dave to face each other.

"I don't want you to do this," I whispered.

He nodded. "I know. But it's the only way off this roof."

I sighed. I knew that look in his eyes. The look that said he couldn't be swayed. The one that said he was going to do what he was going to do and that was it. And we could argue about it and get all bitter before we split up for the first time in...weeks, or I could just give him my gun and a kiss and hope my fears were unfounded.

I decided to go with the second one.

CHAPTER 16

Banish the doubt. You can *totally*
walk through the zombies without dying!

Nicole and I crouched on either side of the front door
with McCray leaning against the wall behind her, checking his nails. The people who lived here had also barri-
caded this area, but we managed to yank the useless
boards free in about five seconds and now we were ready
to go out and face the world.

Or something.

Our eyes met across the foyer and we both lifted the
weapons we'd found around the house.

I'd gone with Dave's abandoned shovel, partly for sen-
timental reasons, partly because shovels are good for so
many kinds of zombie kills and even burying the bodies if
you have the time (which you never do). Nicole had a
rolling pin and also a butcher knife she had slung through
a belt loop.

Even McCray had gotten in on the action. He'd found a
baseball bat (though the Brit insisted on calling it a cricket
mallet for some reason), which he held in one fist even as

he looked totally distracted from matters at hand. Seriously, he had the attention span of a gnat. I don't think either Nicole or I had any illusion that we could depend on him if and when the going got zombie tough.

"One," Nicole said as she reached for the doorknob. "Two."

My heart started throbbing and I could hardly breathe. It was weird. I was accustomed to the zombies by now. I guess the thing I *wasn't* used to was leaving Dave behind. The one time I'd done that before had not ended well.

But there was no choice this time. Not if we wanted to survive.

"Three," we said together, then she opened the door.

After all the build-up, the end result was pretty anticlimactic. The sunny fall day was pretty quiet, aside from the moans of the zombies we could hear echoing from the backyard and the occasional gunshot as Dave fired to take them down and draw them in. But in the front yard you might not have even known there was an outbreak. Well, except for the overgrown grass, sludgy sidewalk, and wrecked cars scattered up and down the street. And the bodies, of course. Headless dead who had apparently gone zombie and been slaughtered by the survivors and ones who had been so torn up in the attacks that they hadn't reanimated at all.

Nicole and I were equally jaded, though, so as we started out of the house, we just stepped over the detached arm still gripping a machete on the ground. I guess that hadn't worked out for him. Or her. Too hard to tell when it was just a rotting arm.

"Okay," Nicole whispered. "There's a church about five blocks up. It has a low roof we can wait on for Dave with the truck. We might even be able to see him when he makes a run for the hospital."

I nodded, even though I felt a little queasy when Nicole said "church." We'd had some bad experiences with churches and zombies in the past. But that was where Dave was going to meet us and since we couldn't exactly call him on a cell phone and change the location to some-place that *didn't* make me break out in hives, it was too late to argue the point now.

"Okay," I simply agreed. "And Dave said he'd give us twenty minutes to get over there before he starts his, er, zombie walk."

Zombie walks. Those things had *rocked* before the apocalypse. Seattle had even broken a record for one, though I hadn't been able to go since I had to work at my shitty job. Dave had stopped by, of course, and said it was flipping awesome. I had been so jealous at the time.

And yet... here we were. The real thing was far less cool.

"Hey," Nicole said as we stepped out onto the side-walk. She looked at me sideways. "He's going to be okay, you know."

I stared at her. "Um, is this you trying to be all support-ive and counseling and shit?"

She shrugged. "I guess. You just looked worried."

I smiled slightly. This girl was going to make me like her despite myself. "Well, I appreciate the gesture, but I don't think I'm going to be *not* worried until Dave pulls up with the truck and no zombie wounds."

"Um, speaking of zombie wounds," McCray said, motioning with his baseball bat toward the corner of the street.

A zombie stood next to a bus stop. The sign had been bent over in half, probably after being hit by a car months ago. It was rusted out, but you could still see the cheerful bus logo under the dried sludge and rust.

The zombie was a man dressed in what seemed to be remnants of one of those "Mr. Clucker" fast-food chicken costumes. People used to wear them and stand out by the side of the road with the chicken head all smiling and stupid. It was supposed to make me want to eat chicken, I guess, but it always just made me want to smack whoever came up with the idea.

There wasn't a lot left of the costume after all these months. Most of the feathers had worn away, but the red, rubber cockscomb flopped sadly around his rotting, gray head.

"Man, if it wasn't bad enough that the poor sap had to wear that thing in life, he died in it, too," I muttered.

McCray stared, probably wondering if he was having another hallucination. "Damn, look at his chicken feet."

We all did. Part of the costume were a pair of ridiculous, clown-big, red chicken feet. Since they were made of rubber, they'd survived better than the rest of the get-up.

"Yeah, that must have slowed him down," Nicole sighed.

I nodded slowly. "Poor guy. Never had a chance."

There was a moment of respectful silence. Okay, more like a second, and then Nicole said, "Okay, let's kill the fucker, guys."

I nodded as I lifted up my shovel into death-grip mode. "Yeah, but quietly, please. Quietly, or else all of Dave's distracting will be for nothing!"

We tiptoed forward and then Nicole dropped down behind a big hedge that hadn't been trimmed since hell came to town a few months before. I crouched beside her and we peeked around the bush.

"Okay, we can wait him out," I whispered. "See if he goes running next time Dave fires his gun."

She nodded. "Yeah, or we could—"

She didn't finish. She didn't have a chance. Instead of waiting, McCray stepped out from behind the bushes and did a flat-footed, almost zombie-esque stride toward the corpse on the corner. The thing noticed him when he was about five feet away and spun around. He had a broken arm that dangled at its side and occasionally a dirty feather would lightly drop from it and meander its way to the sidewalk like it was from the movie *American Beauty* or something.

The zombie hissed a sound of hunger and some kind of blood lust.

McCray didn't even flinch. He swung his bat as the zombie launched toward him and the thing dropped on the sidewalk where our coked-up rock'n'roller, the guy who was impressed by heights and had never quite figured out what Dave and I were to each other, proceeded to pummel its head into oblivion. His shots were massive and precise and pretty soon there was another headless corpse with a bloodstain at its neck on the sidewalk.

Nicole and I stared at McCray, then exchanged a quick glance. She looked as freaked out and impressed as I felt. Slowly, we got up and joined McCray where he waited for us at the corner. I stared, waiting for him to say something about his little "kill" moment. But he didn't even seem to remember it.

"This way, right?" he asked, motioning with his blood-stained bat toward the church in the distance.

Nicole nodded wordlessly and we watched as he took off down the street, flicking shit off the end of his weapon and whistling one of his own number one tunes from the early nineties.

"Um, I guess *that's* how he survived this long," I whispered. I was sort of afraid to say anything too loud.

I mean, the guy had just beaten one corpse into submission without even batting an eye. I wouldn't want to piss him off or anything.

"Yeah, I guess we'll have to tell Dave since he asked earlier," Nicole whispered back.

I rolled my eyes. "I'll add it to the list of shit to talk to him about. If he makes it."

Nicole sent me a side-glance as we began walking again. "He'll make it, Sarah."

I didn't answer; it was too hard to say anything when it came to the subject of Dave's survival. Instead I focused on what *we* had to do. That's all I could do.

McCray continued up the street and I could see that despite his occasional swaying step, he was actually paying attention to what was going on around him. Somewhere in that drug-addled brain, it turned out that our friend had a survival instinct and a killing frenzy.

Both of which: very useful in a zombie outbreak.

Behind us, we still heard Dave shooting and I breathed a sigh of relief every time I heard the crack of the rifle echo in the air. If he was still firing, that meant he hadn't started his walkabout yet. The moment the shooting stopped, *then* I'd have to worry. And I would. Oh, I would.

With most of the zombies distracted, it took us about

ten minutes to creep our way to the church. It was an old Methodist establishment with a steeple but a new addition with a flat roof had been attached in the last few years.

"How are we getting up there?" McCray asked as we stared at the husk of a building.

The fire from the main area of the town hadn't been the only one. This neighborhood had burned at some point, too, and the building looked pretty well gutted.

I looked around. Since I hadn't had a chance to look at the place when Nicole and Dave picked it, I had no idea. But Nicole didn't seem worried. She pointed across the way.

"See that rusted-out ambulance that's right underneath the awning?"

I looked. "The one on its side?"

She nodded. "That's the one. If we climb up there, we should be able to drag ass up on top of the roof. And we might even be able to see Dave run his way across the hospital parking lot."

I froze at the idea. Did I really want to *see* my husband make a mad dash through a hundred moaning zombies? Um, yeah. I totally did.

"Let's get to it, then," I said as I hurried toward the ambulance. I climbed up and made a jump for the edge of the roof. McCray was right behind me and he gave me a shove that helped vault me up onto the flat surface. I popped up and offered a hand to Nicole. With McCray's help, she soon joined me and somehow we managed to haul him up, too.

I stared out toward the house we'd left behind. Nicole was right, I could see it through the trees. I couldn't see the back roof where Dave was, but I *could* see part of the parking lot of the hospital beyond the neighborhood.

"Shit, I wish I had a rifle scope," I muttered as I squinted like somehow that would give me supersight or something.

"Here," Nicole said, and suddenly a pair of cheap binoculars were shoved under my nose.

I stared at her as I took them. "Where the hell—?"

She smiled. "I found them in the house and I figured we might need them for just this very thing."

Yeah, I was going to end up liking this girl despite myself.

I lifted the binoculars and scanned the hospital lot. There was a tree in the way, but I had a partial view of the truck we'd driven in with, still sitting by the emergency room door less than a mile away.

It might as well have been a hundred miles, though, since Dave had to walk through the zombies to get there.

"Hey, I haven't heard any rifle fire for a bit now," McCray said.

I froze as the image in my viewfinder began to shake. He was right. Dave hadn't fired a shot for well over a minute. Which meant he was probably on his way down to see his zombie friends.

"Fuck, there he is!" McCray said.

I spun to look at him. He was standing on the edge of the roof pointing toward the hospital, but when I looked through the binoculars, I couldn't see anything. I rushed to McCray's side of the roof.

"Where?"

"There," Nicole said as she lifted her damn camera to point it in the same direction McCray was facing.

I might have taken the time to argue with her about filming, but since I still couldn't see Dave, I didn't.

"Where?" I repeated and I couldn't keep the desperation from my voice.

McCray stepped back and then positioned me where he had been standing. He pointed again and there, even without the help of the binoculars, I could see Dave's small figure in the distance, just leaving the yard and starting across the parking lot.

And he was surrounded by zombies. I couldn't hear them from so far away, of course, but I could certainly see the way they looked at Dave with that weird cocked head. I held my breath, ready for any one of them to suddenly pounce and rip my husband to shreds before he could even react.

But like the zombies in the pool had the previous day, they just...ignored him. They looked, they smelled, and then they went back to milling aimlessly. Some even shambled after him, slower than him so that they formed a weird conga line in his wake. A conga line of death. Cha. Cha. Cha.

"Shit, he's really doing it," Nicole whispered from behind me, though I didn't think she was talking to me.

What we were seeing was nothing short of a miracle. Even McCray was silent as we stared at Dave, leading his group of zombies, making his way in slow and steady fashion across the parking lot to the safety of the truck.

"You weren't kidding about a cure," Nicole said, and this time she glanced at me.

I lifted my hand without even thinking and covered the vial under my T-shirt to make sure it was still there. Inside was the thing that had done this to David. The thing that had saved his ass and was currently saving the rest of ours.

Well, it would save our asses *if* he could get to the truck and *if* he could get the truck back to us without bringing the zombies to us and trapping us on a new roof.

"Why did you touch your neck?" Nicole asked.

I ignored her question even though my throat closed. I always touched the vial when I thought about the cure. It was like a Pavlov's dogs kind of response now. Cure = check to see if still have cure.

"No reason," I lied.

"You have something under your shirt," Nicole pressed, tilting her head.

I ignored her, still focusing on David. He was almost to the truck now and the zombies still followed him or shambled like a herd of cows in the parking lot.

"Seriously, I thought it was a necklace, but you don't seem like the jewelry type of girl," Nicole said. "So what are you wearing?"

"Yeah, lift up your shirt!" McCray encouraged.

"Wait," I whispered, watching as Dave opened the truck door. One of the zombies leaned in after him and my heart just about stopped.

But he wasn't trying to eat Dave, and when Dave pushed him, he staggered back and then turned to wander off and join the rest of the group. The truck rocked slightly as my husband started the engine. I breathed a big sigh of relief when he rolled through the parking lot and started to head in our direction. Relief that faded when Nicole snatched the binoculars away from me and stared at me evenly.

"Seriously, Sarah. *What* are you wearing around your neck?" she snapped.

Now I could have probably smacked her with the

shovel. The problem was that I wasn't sure she wouldn't get in a couple of whacks with her rolling pin before I incapacitated her, and there was no telling what McCray would do if I started playing Whack-A-Bitch with Nicole's head.

Plus, I was totally willing to beat the shit out of a zombie or a cult leader; . . . anyone threatening me or Dave physically was fair game.

But Nicole wasn't really doing that. At least, not yet. And I was still sort of stuck on "Thou Shalt Not Kill" when it came to humans who had saved my ass and weren't currently trying to eat it.

"It's the cure," I whispered. "We managed to get a sample of it out of the lab down in Arizona. *That's* why we're trying to get to the Midwest Wall. What we did for Dave, we might be able to do for anyone bitten from now on. If we could get this thing into the right hands, it might even be a way to wipe out the zombies who are roaming around currently."

Nicole backed away from me, staring at me in total disbelief. I could hardly blame her. I mean, I was holding the future of the world on a chain around my neck. That was a pretty big deal.

She swallowed and it looked like she was going to say something. But before she could, Dave slid up underneath the awning in the truck, rolled down his window, and said, "Well, what are you waiting for? Get the fuck in!"

CHAPTER 17

Be prepared for all contingencies.
Especially zombies, liars, and highway traffic.

As we pulled away from the town and back onto the highway east, the truck was filled with uncomfortable silence. I sat in the front next to Dave, but I could feel Nicole staring daggers into my back. Even McCray shifted around, staring out the window between quick glances at me, then Dave, then me again.

"Seriously, no one has *anything* to say about what I just did?" Dave finally asked as he glanced in the rearview mirror at our new friends. "I mean, I just about walked on zombie water, people."

No one said a word, but he didn't seem to care. He slammed his palms on the steering wheel with a hoot of pride and amazement.

"I got to a truck through at least a hundred, maybe a hundred and fifty of them without getting eaten alive. Surely *someone* wants to pat me on the back."

He was greeted with more silence, this time silence he seemed to notice, and he frowned.

"Um, thanks Dave!" he said, making his voice high pitched the way he did when he was teasing me. "You were awesome Dave." Now he switched to a British accent and dropped his voice lower like he was pretending to be McCray. "Good show, mate. Thanks for saving our asses."

"Great job, babe," I managed to croak out since that seemed to be what he wanted. I just had my mind on other things at the moment.

He looked at me very briefly (we were on the highway, remember, so you kind of had to go with brief to avoid wrecks and zombies).

"Okay, what the hell is going on?" he snapped. "You three are acting bizarre. You've hardly talked since you all jumped into the truck and that was like fifteen, twenty minutes ago. Did something happen while you were getting from the house to the church?"

More silence. I *really* didn't want to tell him that I'd spilled my guts about our cure. I wasn't sure how he'd take it. I mean, these were decisions we were supposed to discuss together, I was always saying that, reminding him (sometimes none-too-gently) about that. And yet I was the one who had broken that trust. Big time.

Suddenly, Dave hit the brakes and the truck squealed to a stop in the middle of the road. He threw it in Park and then half-turned so he could see all of us.

"Was someone bitten?" he asked quietly.

I blinked. Shit, of course that's what he would assume when we were all being weird.

"No," I whispered.

"Sarah—" he said, his voice drawn into a warning.

"I promise, no one was bitten."

"Though if they were, it sounds like it wouldn't be a

big fucking deal," Nicole said. She leaned back in her seat and folded her arms. "Being that you have a supercure or whatever on you."

Dave's eyes went wide and he slowly looked at me. "They know?"

I nodded once and then looked away. "Sorry," I whispered. "I didn't mean for it to come out."

"I should have known," Nicole muttered. "You two are like goddamn folk heroes—"

"Wait," Dave said and he faced her more squarely. "Folk heroes? I thought you didn't know who we were when we found you."

Now it was Nicole's face that went pale and she looked at me with guilt in her gaze. "Um, yeah. About that…"

I sat up straighter, my own feelings of being an asshole fading in the face of her apparent lies. "Shit, you knew who we were?"

After a hesitation, she nodded. "Yeah."

"What?" Dave said in blank disbelief.

Nicole shifted. "Well, I mean I'd heard about you and the extermination business you had in Phoenix. It was the talk in camps all over the Southwest, so pretty much the second I popped up over the border back into the U.S., I couldn't ignore it. It was a *huge* story in the making."

"So you came looking for us?" I asked as I shook my head in disbelief.

She nodded. "I kind of had to. People were saying you'd just packed up one day and disappeared without any explanation, but that it was like you had something to do. At that point, I *knew* there was a story there so, yeah. I-I set up meeting you, hoping you would take me along with you and I could figure out what it was."

I stared at her. "But when we met you, you were getting chased by zombies. You'd had a motorcycle wreck, you had road rash... all that shit..."

She shrugged. "Yeah. All a set-up. Except for the road rash. I didn't mean to get hurt quite that badly."

"You little con artist," McCray said with a wide grin on his face like this made her more interesting to him rather than more repugnant. "I *knew* I liked you even if you were a reporter strumpet."

She glared at him, apparently unimpressed by his "compliment."

"Well, now you know what you tricked us into finding," I said with a shake of my head. "You got your story, Nicole. Dave is sort of... zombie benefits without zombie disadvantages and we have a sample of the cure that made him that way. *Bravo,* I'm sure a Pulitzer isn't far behind. Oh wait, do they still give those out since the fucking world pretty much blew up?"

She flinched and at least she had the decency to look embarrassed. "Yeah, I probably should have told you I knew who you were, but I didn't think you'd let me come with you if I did."

Dave shrugged as he sent me a side-glance. "Well, that may be true."

"No," I protested. "No, no, no. There's no way I'm going to be made to feel like Nicole's lies are my fault somehow. We wouldn't have just left her there by the side of the road even if she said straight out what her motives were. We're not that awful." I glared at her. "Though I'm starting to think we *should* be."

"Oh, like you two don't have secrets out the ass!" Nicole said with a huff of breath. "David gotten bitten by a zombie and is all superpowers now, but you let me ride around with you for days before you brought that up. What if he'd flipped and gone all zombie on me?"

"Come on, that's not going to happen!" I snapped.

She shook her head. "You don't know that. Plus you have a cure around your neck that you never mentioned even after you knew me pretty well."

"It's my cure, why should I tell you?"

She folded her arms. "What if something had happened to you on the way to the church and we *needed* that cure? I wouldn't have known and neither would McCray. So somebody could have died or gone zombie and we could have stopped it except we didn't know."

I blinked. I guess I had no answer for that. Even if I wanted to pretend she didn't, she had a point. It wasn't like we'd told anyone about the cure since we had it, but Nicole wasn't exactly just anyone. We'd never ridden with anyone else we'd come in contact with over the past month, or been in a position to help if they needed it. I could see how she might be irritated by that and that we hadn't mentioned the "Dave bitten by a zombie" thing since that could have resulted in her eminent death and dismemberment.

Dave sighed. "Clearly, we all have our issues. But I think we should find a way to forgive each other, being that it's the apocalypse and all. If there's a time to go a little nutbar, this is it."

I looked at him from the corner of my eye. He was going to be the bigger man, the grown-up. It was time to follow that lead. "Are all the secrets out on the table at this point?" I asked. "Just so we can all be honest from this point forward."

There was a brief moment of silence and then McCray slowly raised his hand like we were in elementary school. Dave shook his head.

"You don't have to wait for permission, just tell us what we need to know."

"I accidentally banged my cousin after a show in Liverpool eight years ago," McCray piped up. All of us looked at him and he shrugged. "I was pretty drunk at the time. Didn't know she was related until the next morning."

Dave opened and shut his mouth a few times, almost like he didn't really know how to respond to that interesting admission (and who could blame him) but then he nodded. "Great. Glad you felt comfortable enough to finally share that, McCray. I'm sure that knowledge will come in handy in the future. So are all the secrets out on the table *now*?"

I nodded. McCray gave a sigh filled with relief and shrugged. Only Nicole sat stoic.

"What?" I asked, feeling a strong urge to toss her out on the side of the road like I'd claimed we wouldn't have done before.

"I want to see it," she said softly.

"What?" I asked. "McCray's cousin?"

She narrowed her eyes. "No. The cure. I want to see the cure."

Dave and I exchanged a quick glance. I hadn't let anyone see or touch the vial besides him from the moment we obtained it back in the lab. My throat constricted just at the thought. But he nodded slowly. I glanced at Nicole. She didn't look like she was going to back down from this request.

And maybe she shouldn't. I wouldn't have.

I reached under the neckline of my T-shirt and gently tugged the vial over it. Against the shirt's black background, iridescent purple sparkled in the fading afternoon sunlight that filtered through the truck window behind me.

"Wow, that's it?" Nicole whispered. Both she and McCray leaned forward to look at it. She even picked up the vial and rolled it between her fingers.

I fought the urge to snap it away from her, but nodded.

"Yes," I whispered. "I injected David with the same stuff after he was bitten. It's the cure."

"My third album cover was the same color," McCray mused before he lost interest and flopped back against the seat.

Nicole let go of the vial with a semi-contented sigh. "To think, all that power in one tiny container."

I nodded. "So are we good? Did you get a good enough look?"

Nicole nodded and I flopped the vial back under my shirt. Funny, the fabric really provided *no* security, but I still breathed easier when it wasn't out for the world to see.

"Great, so that's all settled." Dave glanced at me. "There's just one more thing for us to discuss."

"You two are really the president and first lady of the United States," McCray offered.

"No." Dave shook his head. "Sarah and I are still going to the Midwest Wall. It's our best possible chance to getting this cure to people who might be able to use it to help the survivors in the Badlands."

Nicole nodded. "Yeah, I figured as much."

McCray just stared out the window. I looked at the two

of them and when I cast David a side-glance, I could tell we were thinking the same thing.

"Look, now that all the cards are on the table and you know what we're doing and why...if you want to come, you're welcome to tag along," I said. I couldn't believe the words were coming from my mouth, but there they were. "Or we can find you another vehicle and you're welcome to go your own way. We'd understand either decision, you just need to tell us."

There was a long silence and then McCray shrugged. "Yeah, I'll go with you. Why not? I've always sold well in Chicago-land."

I smiled despite myself. Even if he was a major irritant, I was happy to know McCray wouldn't be killing himself in Oklahoma any time soon.

Nicole nodded, too. "Yeah, I'm in. This is the story of the century, I can't bail now."

Relief worked its way through me. I might not have warm fuzzies about either of these two morons, but the more, the merrier at this point. There was safety in having extra hands to fire extra guns.

"*But*," Nicole added and my heart sank again. "If you really have the cure, I don't think we can meander our way to the Wall like we're on a school field trip."

"Hey, I wouldn't call it meandering," Dave said with a frown.

Nicole shook her head. "It took you a month to get to the point where you found me. Long enough for me to suspect you two had an angle, formulate a plan, and ambush you with my damsel-in-distress routine. That's meandering."

Dave pursed his lips, but didn't argue with her again.

"So maybe we meandered a *little*," I admitted. "What do you want to do about it?"

"I think we have to get there and get there *now*, before something happens to the cure and we lose any chance of getting it into the right hands." She shook her head. "That means no more thirty-miles-a-day driving and shit."

"And how do you propose we do more than that?" I asked. "We're not exactly in optimal driving conditions."

Dave stared at the deserted road. "We'd have to stay on the highway," he mused.

I shook my head as I thought of all the trouble we'd found on the highway. "No, no—"

"I know you don't like that," he said as he grabbed my hand. "But it *is* the fastest and most direct route. Half of our slowdowns have been because of the roads we've been traveling since we started east."

"And there are four of us," Nicole added. "Which means lots of people to clear wrecks or butcher zombies if we need to do that. And we should also drive in shifts."

"You mean drive at night?" I burst out. Yup, my chest was closing. No air. Death immediate.

"Yes," Nicole said with a short, military-like nod. "We'll have to be slow and careful when it's dark, of course. Two people awake. One driver, one lookout."

"Oh yeah, that will make it better," I wheezed as I fought for breath.

"I think the past few days have proved that stopping to camp every day is just as dangerous," Dave said, his tone gentle like he knew I needed more reassurance than even he could give. "Every time we stop, we have to clear places, find food, deal with hostile survivors."

"But it's over six hundred fifty miles to Normal right

now," I insisted, even though I could see I was about to be outvoted. But I'd never been one to give up without a fight, hence why I was still alive.

"*So?* That's like ten hours of driving!" Nicole said.

"*If* we could average above sixty and never stop for gas or to pee," I snorted. "You think that's going to happen on Interstate Zombie? *Really*?"

Dave sighed. "Okay, you're right. But we could probably average thirty even with stops and unforeseen circumstances. That would be..."

We all hesitated, doing math in our heads.

"Less than twenty-four hours," McCray piped up from the back.

All of us stared and he shifted with a bit of discomfort.

"*What?* I went to school, too, you know," he muttered.

"It's like he's Rainman," Nicole muttered. "But he is right. So what do you think?"

I stared at her. The girl already looked like she'd won, which was superannoying. McCray wasn't really paying attention. Finally, I looked at Dave. He was waiting for me. But I think we all knew what I'd have to say. They hadn't really given me much choice, being all reasonable and everything.

"Fine," I said as I rubbed my eyes.

Nicole let out a whoop and grabbed for the atlas that was on the console between Dave and me. "I'll start charting the best course and our switch and gas points."

I turned around in my seat as Dave put the truck in gear and we started rolling again.

"Hey," he said quietly. "You ready for this?"

I laughed, though at the moment I was feeling more nervous than amused. "Well, ready or not, here we come."

CHAPTER 18

Pay attention to nonverbal communication.
People almost always signal in some
way before they try to kill you.

Getting to the outskirts of Normal, Illinois, took a little *longer* than twenty-four hours. McCray refused to sleep (or maybe he *couldn't*), so that left three drivers to trade shifts rather than four, which meant a bit more switching and figuring out rest schedules. But about thirty hours and three zombie fights later, we did roll up a low hill on Interstate 55 and came to a slow stop right before the Main Street Exit.

Main Street, Normal, Illinois.

Could you get any more Norman Rockwellian? All we needed was a kid to come by tossing a ball to his dog and we'd be set. Of course at this point, the kid would be a zombie and he'd be tossing a human hand to a demon mutt or something.

"Well, here we are," Dave whispered, even though we were in the car with our windows rolled up. But there *was* something about this situation that screamed *reverence.* After all, we were about to finally find out if the rumors of the Midwest Wall were true.

And if they weren't, I had no clue what we'd do. Keep heading east, I guess, until we ran out of real estate and hit the Atlantic Ocean.

But I wasn't looking forward to that, partly because it would be a long, grueling trip. If McCray and Nicole came along, I'd have to spend some portion of it listening to them fight in the backseat and resisting the urge to tell them, "If you don't stop that, I'll turn this car around."

I'd totally turn into my mother before a week was up.

But more importantly, I *needed* there to be a Midwest Wall. If there wasn't, it would pretty much guarantee that my entire family was dead. My dad had been heading this way last I heard from him (which was, admittedly, about five seconds after the attack) and my mom had lived in Normal for the last five years. I didn't see her as the running-for-cover type. Even if the zombies came to her door. In fact, she might make them coffee just because she was so polite.

Yeah, I know, I hadn't exactly inherited that trait. We all have our failings.

In the backseat, Nicole was loading shells into a shotgun we'd found at a gas station along the route. McCray was next to her, sharpening the blade of a machete with enough careful precision that I figured he'd done it before. Sometimes I wondered how much of his "drunken rock star" thing was an act and how much was real. At this point, I didn't have the answer.

"Now I heard the Wall should be right over the bluff of the freeway," Dave said while he pocketed shells and checked his own weapon. "So we'll need to take a peek over the overpass and just get our bearings."

"Yeah," I whispered as I opened my door. "We'd hate to lose those."

"A bearing is a terrible thing to waste," he quipped, but he followed me, as did the others.

We crept up to the metal barrier that had once kept cars from plummeting onto the street below (though considering there was a smoke-streaked hole in it now, I'm guessing that had stopped working months ago) and peeked over.

And there it was.

I don't know what I'd pictured when I thought about a Midwest Wall. Maybe some kind of fortress like you see in China, I guess, built of steel or rock or brick . . . or heck, all three for good measure. But now that I saw it, I realized those kinds of reinforcements would take decades to build, not months under the worst kind of circumstances.

Instead, this "wall" was more like a fence. In fact, it *was* a fence made of chain link with reinforced towers at specific intervals as far as the eye could see. Along the top ran sharp razor wire coiled in unavoidable loops so no one could climb over. All that made the other side look more like a prison than a safe haven.

Or maybe *we* were on the prison side. It sort of felt like that because there didn't seem to be any way to escape and get to the safe side. Not only was the fence marked with big CAUTION: ELECTRIC signs, but there were other barriers that would keep us right where we were.

Namely zombies.

Lots and lots and lots of zombies. A shitload of zombies was probably the most accurate measurement.

Like back at the house near the hospital the previous day, these zombies could obviously smell the survivors on the other side of that fence. The idea of getting to those survivors called to them, an undeniable siren song that had them bouncing up against the electrified fence.

"Whoa!" McCray breathed as yet another one shambled forward, arms flailing like a fish out of water, and did just that.

The fence was definitely really electrified because the moment the rotting body hit it, there was a huge spark and the power threw him backward at least ten feet.

For a moment the creature lay still and I straightened up. Was this a new killing method? Because if electricity would do it, I was pretty sure there were ways to rig huge arcs that could wipe out dozens of zombies at a time.

But no, after a few seconds the pathetic creature popped back up to his feet and lumbered back toward the fence. Only this time his hair smoked gently, sending wispy puffs off in the fall breeze. If he did that enough times, he was going to catch fire.

Now you might think a fire zombie would be great. Or that it would kill them. Not so much. Unless the flames burned hot enough to destroy their brain, which normally took a *long* time, fire didn't do shit. All you ended up with was a flaming corpse running around roasting everyone in sight like a campfire marshmallow before he ate them. Not good.

"Look at them all," I said as I stared down at the zombie mob. "There's no way we can get by."

"Yeah, I'm not sure even *I* would risk it," Dave agreed. "Especially since even if I walked through them and made it to the Wall, I'm guessing those guards would just shoot me thinking I was one of them."

"What guards?" Nicole asked. She crouched down next to us and craned her neck.

Dave pointed and both of us followed his direction. Shit, how had I missed that? Behind the first line of barbed wire and chain link was a second, elevated platform made of much sturdier steel and wood. And standing on it were at least thirty soldiers, in formation, guns raised and ready to fire if a zombie dared to even put their pinky through the fence.

"They don't look like they're fucking around," McCray whispered.

"I'm guessing these guys are of the 'shoot first, ask questions later' vein when it comes to the zombies." Dave shook his head.

"But you're not a zombie," I whispered. "*We're* not zombies. If we could get their attention, maybe they'd send a helicopter for us or a rescue unit."

I gazed around, but I didn't see any helicopters in the sky, circling around to assist potential survivors. But then again, it *had* been months. Probably the survivor faction had thinned considerably during that time. Maybe they only sent out troops to assist when they knew for sure survivors were there.

"Yeah, maybe," Nicole muttered, but she didn't sound so certain.

I rolled over to look at her. Her eyes were narrowed and worried. I was going to ask her why, but before I could, I saw a truck coming from the distance on the other side of the road that went under the freeway overpass. It was booking, too, heading straight for the zombies and the gate.

"Hey, we're about to find out how they let people in," I said as I flopped back on my stomach and peeked through my rifle site. "There's a truck coming and it's driving too steadily to be someone infected."

The other three looked back and then we all leaned forward as the truck barreled under the overpass and
squealed to a stop in front of the gate.

Now that it was closer, we could actually see it. It was
an older model, big truck with some kind of camper shell
attached to its bed. The whole thing had been heavily
armored, sort of like you always see in the best zombie
movies.

Clearly someone was a smart person and handy with a
welding torch, because when the zombies starting bang-
ing on the vehicle, it didn't even rock. They clawed at it,
trying to find purchase to climb up, but there wasn't any
chance of that, either. They merely slid down because
there were no handholds or footholds to be found.

I wanted one. You know me and new toys.

After a couple of seconds, a hatch at the top of the
truck slowly opened and a man's head popped out. We
were probably a hundred yards away but the breeze blew
toward us, so I could actually hear him when he bellowed,
"You can't lock the uninfected out!"

I blinked. Maybe I *couldn't* hear him so well after all.

"Did he say they're locking the uninfected out?" I
hissed beneath my breath.

Nicole's face had paled considerably and she took a
moment before she swallowed and said, "That's what I
heard."

"Shhh," Dave barked. "We have to listen."

We all shut up. The man on the truck spoke again. "I
know you have ways of testing us, of proving we're not
infected, but still you refuse to let us in."

Nothing but silence from the soldiers greeted the man's
stunning accusations.

He continued, "You can't hide what happened from the survivors on the other side of your wall. You can't keep up the lie that we all died. Even if you blow up all the radios, even if you cut off the cell phone service from this side, even if you bomb the cities. The truth is going to come out eventually."

Even McCray, lost in his own universe at least 80 percent of the time, understood what this new guy below us was saying.

What it meant was that the government was actively working to keep out the survivors.

"My wife is on the other side," the man pleaded. "And I'm coming in."

Finally one soldier stepped out from formation and drew a bullhorn up from somewhere within the crowd of soldiers behind him.

"Sir, you are in a red zone. You are ordered to back away from the fence or you *will* be fired upon."

"I'm not backing away!" the man on the outside with us insisted at a near-scream. "You have to let me in!"

"You have five seconds to comply," the soldier's voice came again over the bullhorn. "Five."

"Please, let me in!"

"Four."

"You can't do this to an American citizen!" the man screamed.

"Three, . . . two," the guard continued, apparently unmoved by the pleas.

"Get back in the truck," I whispered, praying he would somehow listen. "Please!"

But he didn't.

"One."

The guns went off all at once in a haze of smoke and flame and bullets that ricocheted off the armored truck and struck zombies all around.

But what they mostly found was their mark. The man on the truck slumped forward and blood began to trickle from the porthole he had opened and down the sides of the truck. The zombies raced to the vehicle, licking the blood like it was fudge on a sundae.

"No!" Dave gasped.

I turned away from the scene and lay on the dirt at the side of the highway for a long time before I was able to speak again.

"H-He wasn't doing anything," I stammered, as much to myself as to anyone else. "Just trying to get inside. He wasn't infected. Why didn't they help him?"

Nicole pushed away and crawled back to our truck on the overpass. She sat with her back against the wheel and stared at us. I'd never seen her look so pale. So worn. All her reporter bravado was gone, replaced by jaded, heart-broken certainty. She already had a theory. And she was ready to tell us.

"In all these months, the only time I saw any military presence was when they were firebombing the cities," she said softly.

I bit my lip as I tried to think back. She was right. From pretty much the moment the outbreak started, all air traf-fic ceased. I'd certainly never seen the National Guard or the Army or anything.

"There's only one reason they wouldn't come out to help us in all this time." Nicole shook her head. "It's a cover-up."

"No," I whispered. "No, that can't be right."

Nicole shook her head. "You heard that guy in the truck as well as I did, Sarah. He said they weren't letting survivors in off the Badlands."

"In fact, he said they were telling everyone on the other side that we're all dead," Dave said in a hollow, empty voice.

She nodded. "If that's not a cover-up, then tell me what it is?"

"Your friend is right," came an unfamiliar voice from beside the truck.

All of us swiveled, weaponry at the ready, toward the voice. A woman stood at the tailgate of our truck. She was totally Resident Eviled out, too. Loose-fitting pants, tight black tank top, military-style jacket, thick blonde hair tied back in a braid. I would guess she was around forty, though she was one of those people who had genetics on their side when it came to the way they aged.

Oh, and she was pointing a missile launcher at us like we were in a Halo game or something. Suddenly our little rifles and shotguns seemed way less scary. Especially since about ten other people came strolling up behind her with a variety of weapons that even the military jerks down below would have coveted . . . if they hadn't, you know, shot us all first.

"As you can see, you're outnumbered here, so it would be a good idea if you lower your weapons and come with us," the Missile Launcher Woman said.

Dave shook his head. "No, we've played this game two times before. We don't go with cults. Stranger Danger and all."

The woman laughed. "We're not a cult, my dear. And the reason I ask you to come with me is because in about ten minutes those military forces down there will send a rocket up here and blow you all to smithereens. Come with us and you'll live."

She shrugged as she lowered her weapon. "Or stay and die. It's really your choice."

I glanced at Dave and he looked pissed because there was no way to prove what she said was wrong. And if the military was really trying to keep all of us out, she was probably right. They most likely already knew our position and were scrambling...um...bogies (sorry, most of my military lingo comes from *Top Gun*) to wipe us out.

"Well, when you put it that way," I muttered. "How can we refuse your invitation?"

We all got to our feet and in a flurry of activity we were walked down the highway away from the Wall and the military. At the bottom of the hill where we'd just come from was another one of the armored trucks just like the one the military had blown up down at the Wall.

"After you," the woman with the missile launcher said as she motioned to a wide open door on the dark back of the vehicle.

Leading into the truck was a ramp that we marched up like the best little minions being led to certain death. But as the door swung shut and left us in cool darkness, I had to shake my head.

"We do have the best luck in finding the crazies, don't we?" I sighed as I rested my chin on Dave's shoulder.

His laugh was drowned out by the voice of the woman who had spoken to us earlier. "Like I said, we're not crazy."

The big vehicle started up and a dim, blue light snapped to life in the cargo area we sat in. I blinked as I looked at

our...captor? Except we weren't tied up; she hadn't confiscated our guns and ammo...hell, she wasn't even holding a weapon on us anymore. So she wasn't like anyone
else who'd ever taken us hostage before.

"So what's your deal, lady?" Dave asked, his voice
tired like he was so over this. And who could blame him?

"My name is Kathleen Domingo," she said and she
reached out her hand to shake his.

He did it, but he never smiled. "So what's your deal,
Kathleen?" he repeated in the very same tone. "Do you
need virgins for a sacrifice or just bodies to feed to your
pet zombies or what?"

The woman chuckled again. "If we were looking for
virgins, I doubt any of *you* would qualify."

The four of us looked at each other and then shrugged
in turn. She had us there.

"As for our 'deal,' we're just survivors like you. And
we're trying to find a way to communicate with those over
the Wall, just like I think you'd like to do." Her smile fell
and a hardness entered her eyes. "Just like Isaac tried to
do earlier."

"Is that the guy with the truck like this one?" Nicole
asked. "The one who got—"

The woman nodded. "Yes."

I looked at her. Her eyes were so sad, so hollow.

"He was your friend," I whispered. "Sorry."

"It's not your fault." Kathleen shook her head sadly.
There was a moment's hesitation, but then she continued,
"Isaac was married, but he and his wife were separated
after the attack. He worked outside the perimeter they
ultimately set up and lived within. When they shut the
'border,' he was trapped out here."

I shut my eyes. Dave and I had fought to stay together. I couldn't imagine being separated and not knowing what had happened to the other. It was so...Berlin Wall–Cold War.

Kathleen stared off at nothing. "She was pregnant at the time of the attack. His baby was due today. He's been desperate to get to his family, tried everything. I think something snapped in him this morning. When we realized he'd taken a vehicle and headed for the Wall, we followed him. But it was too late."

Her gaze dropped down and her face looked long and tired for a moment. Then she shook her head.

"But we found you even if we couldn't save him. At least we could stop you from trying something equally foolhardy to get inside."

The truck bumped and lumbered before it came to a stop. The doors to the holding area opened, but the outside was dark. We all hesitated.

"I promise you," the woman said as she got up and walked out into the ominous dark. "We're not going to harm you. And if you don't decide to stay with us, we'll load you up on supplies and send you on your way."

I arched a brow of disbelief. Was this woman kidding? Or had we actually found some kind of savior?

She motioned around her. "But come with me, hear me out, share whatever news you have, before you make any decisions."

Dave looked at me for a moment and then he nodded. "Okay. But just so you know, we've killed better cult leaders than you."

She laughed again and it was a pleasant sound. "That's duly noted."

We got up and followed her. The moment we stepped off the truck, I realized why it was so dark. We were underground. I smelled earth and green, and there was a pleasant damp coolness to the air. Very different from the rotting death that permeated the air above us.

"What is this place?" I asked.

A few lanterns strung up along the ceiling lit the room...or whatever we were in...which became clearer. Though hardly. The lamps weren't very strong and they cast everything around us in a sort of scary shadow and light.

"It *was* a storage area for crops at one time, a long time ago before refrigeration became standard," the woman explained. "And then it was upgraded by the farmer who lived here as a nuclear bomb shelter in the fifties. Luckily he decided to keep it up as a tornado shelter once the Red Menace was gone."

"Yeah, who knew we'd all have to worry about the Gray Menace eventually," McCray muttered, inspiring another brief grin of appreciation from Kathleen.

"He might not have anticipated the, er, Gray Menace, but that didn't mean he wasn't prepared. When the zombies attacked and the government started to work on the border, he guessed where it was all going to lead. And he was nice enough to let us all come down here to hide."

One of the others in the room smiled, but it was sad. "Good old Jacob."

"The zombies got him?" McCray asked. Always tactful, that one.

"No, just old age, about a month ago," Kathleen reassured us. "But sit."

She motioned to a worn-out table that had been set up

in the middle of the big, empty room. There was food there. Real food! Piles of apples and pears, as well as some dried meat and fish that made my mouth water.

It also pretty much erased all our remaining misgivings. We might be wary by nature by now, but we weren't going to turn down a real meal.

There was a flurry as all of us flung ourselves into the chairs. McCray grabbed for the closest thing to him, a pear that looked like it was perfectly ripe, but the rest of us waited. Stupid leftover manners.

Kathleen smiled. "Go ahead and join Mr. McCray. You must be hungry."

"How do you know his name?" Dave asked, his hand hesitating above an apple as he glared at Kathleen with renewed suspicion.

"Um, I own all his CDs?" Kathleen laughed.

"Thanks, love!" McCray said, his mouth full of pear juice, which sprayed all over the table. Lovely.

"Maybe I could even get an autograph later." Kathleen blushed.

"Oh God, don't encourage him, he's useless already!" Nicole groaned.

Kathleen's cheeks darkened with girlish embarrassment even further. "Anyway, I can answer any of your questions while you eat."

I bit into an apple and barely contained my moan of pleasure. Oh fresh fruit, how I'd missed you and your awesome vitamins and minerals and sweetness and...oh, sorry.

"I have a question, but it's not going to be quick," Dave said.

She nodded. "Go ahead."

"What the fuck happened here?"

Kathleen's smile fell. "Same thing that happened everywhere, I guess. When the outbreak started in Seattle, the news was everywhere and as it spread, it was the usual 'Zombie Watch 2010' on all the stations. But then...the news stopped. They kept saying 'technical difficulties' and had those 'Please Stand By' things on all the stations. Within a couple of days, we noticed the Wall going up."

I swallowed my bite of fruit, which was now hard and flavorless as sand. "A couple of days?"

She nodded. "Apparently the government knew almost immediately that the West would be a loss. I'm guessing there was some serious loss-versus-cost analyses during those days. Whatever happened, they decided to draw a line right on the edge of Normal and keep the virus from coming any farther than here. Except they weren't about to let a flood of refugees from outside come in and maybe bring the infection. That's when they started 'clearing out' the towns within fifteen miles of the Wall."

"Clearing out?" Dave said. "What does that mean?"

Kathleen arched a brow as she stared at us evenly and let her words sink in. They seemed to hit McCray, of all people, first.

"Wait, you mean they...they *killed* people?" McCray choked.

One of the others in the group who was standing back around the wall of the underground compound nodded. "If we hadn't had Jacob's help and the help of other farmers with underground bunkers, we'd all be dead."

I shook my head. "And here I thought *we* had it bad, running from the zombies. No one official was shooting at us. Trying to eat our brains, sure. Occasionally trying to convert us to their religion or take us as sacrifices, why not? But officially kill us, never."

Kathleen's eyes went wide. "Sounds like you've had your own interesting time, but yes. It was a shock when it first happened. We got over it, though. There wasn't a lot of choice in the matter. For the past few months we've been building a bigger and bigger circle of survivors as a kind of resistance movement."

"Resist what? The zombies or the government?" Nicole asked.

She hadn't touched any of the food, but just leaned back in one of the chairs, watching all of us carefully. She looked very reporter-y at present. And not trashy celebrity reporter, either. This was Nicole, Future CNN goddess, multiple Pulitzer prize winner at work.

"Both, I guess," Kathleen said with a wry smile. "The zombies have to be dealt with, of course. They're a constant threat and their forces never seem to get smaller. Plus, they don't surrender like a human force would if you wiped out half of them. They just... keep... coming."

We were all silent for a moment, pondering that horrible truth that had been our world for so many months.

"Okay, so you all kill the zombies, but what do you do about the soldiers?" Dave asked. "I mean, I'm guessing the group we saw down below the overpass isn't the only platoon or whatever guarding the Wall. So even with that cool missile launcher you have and all these people, you're a *little* outnumbered."

Kathleen nodded. "You're right about that. Plus, we don't want to kill the soldiers if we can avoid it. They're following orders from people much higher up and I know for a fact that when they don't, they're set out for the zombies without any protection."

"Sounds familiar," I muttered as I thought of all our experiences over the past few months.

Dave nodded. "Sounds like the government has gone a little crazy culty, themselves."

Kathleen pursed her lips. "We've rescued several of those poor men after they were put out. The only good thing about the expulsion is that their expertise does come in handy for our movement."

"So how do you resist if you don't shoot the soldiers?" Nicole pressed.

"By trying to get the word out to the people on the other side of the Wall," Kathleen explained. "Most of them don't have any idea we're still alive out here. When the television eventually came back on their side, their 'news' had changed. A lot of the anchors and reporters had been replaced by government scabs who were willing to repeat the party line for cash and protection."

Nicole flinched and I couldn't help but join her. So much for First Amendment rights.

"All they've been showing on television or online are all kinds of pictures of the burned-out cities and the zombies, but they never show the living. They never talk about the camps or the people fighting to survive. So the majority of those inside the Wall think that everything and everyone in the West is dead and that the whole area has to be quarantined until the government can destroy all the zombies."

Nicole shut her eyes. "And if they see it on TV ..."

Kathleen nodded. "Then it must be true. Unfortunately, that's the way it is."

"Which is why they can't let us get in," I moaned. "If we did, we'd ruin their story. People would start asking a hell of a lot of questions."

"And they wouldn't want that," one of Kathleen's minions grunted in anger.

She sighed. "*But* there are several groups on the other side who *are* fighting to get the truth out. An underground network of reporters, regular people and scientists who are working on proving the virus was created by the government and that thousands of people survived."

"Did you say reporters?" Nicole asked and I could practically see her ears perking up at the thought of her brethren working to save the world.

"Forget the reporters. Did you say scientists?" Dave asked and he cast a quick glance at me. Well, my chest, but not for the nookie. I could see he was looking where the vial of our cure hung.

Sounded like exactly the kind of people we'd need to reach to make sure that precious vial ended up in the right hands.

"But how does this resistance movement work?" Nicole asked. "I mean, before the soldiers shot him, your friend was shouting about cell phone service being cut off out here and radios being destroyed."

"And they have control of the Internet," one of Kathleen's people added helpfully.

"How does that work?" David said with a blink.

"Ever heard of China?" McCray laughed. "They were doing it for years. I would guess our government might be even better."

Kathleen nodded. "Exactly. They monitor everything online, they edit everything, they block everything. When something does manage to get out, it's debunked as insanity and the source is... *taken care of.* It's a full-on crackdown."

Nicole shut her eyes briefly. When she opened them again, they were hard and angry. "If there's no communication, how can you *resist* anything by spreading the truth?"

"The government *did* confiscate and destroy most shortwave radios, but...". Kathleen smiled. "They didn't get all of them. There's a woman in Normal with one and she and her husband help us disseminate all our information to the other resistance members all over the East. By radio, by hand-printed newsletter, by information tree. It's old fashioned, but it's been working so far."

"So who are these people?" Nicole asked. "Were they military or something beforehand?"

"Nope, just ordinary folks just like us." Kathleen gave an affectionate smile. "Her name is Molly Lexington."

I blinked and Dave turned on me with a look of shock I hadn't seen since we came into our marriage counselor's office and found her going all Zombie Bitch on the couple who were her clients before us.

"Did... did you say Molly Lexington?" I whispered and my voice cracked. Honestly, I was surprised I had a voice at all.

Kathleen nodded slowly and her brow wrinkled as she looked at me. "Yeah, why?"

I didn't answer but grabbed for Dave's hand. I could actually feel the blood draining from my face and I suddenly felt super lightheaded.

"What?" Nicole asked as she glanced at us. "What is *that* look for?"

I guess maybe I should have hidden my thoughts, since we didn't really know these people all that well. I guess I should have kept what I was about to say to myself. But I couldn't. I was too freaked the fuck out to try, say, *discretion* at this moment.

My voice shook. "Um, Lexington was my maiden name; my mom's name is Molly *and* she lives in Normal." I shot Dave a quick look. "But she and my dad have been divorced for years and she went back to her own maiden name. So it can't be her. It can't be her."

Kathleen stared at me. "Well, her husband's name is John, if that helps."

If I hadn't been sitting down, I would have fallen over. As it was, I gripped the table edge to keep from tumbling from the chair. "T-That's my dad's name."

Kathleen stepped closer. Her hands were shaking as hard as mine were. "Their daughter and son-in-law were from Seattle. Part of the reason they help us is in the hope that the two of them are among the survivors. You wouldn't happen to be from Seattle, would you?"

I couldn't move, so David was the one who jerked out a short nod.

Now Kathleen had as freaked out an expression as I could feel I did. "Sarah was her name. And David?"

I swallowed. Twice. Hard. And then I croaked out, "Get me to your radio. I want to talk to my mommy."

CHAPTER 19

Know yourself. Also know your friends.
Sometimes both will amaze you.

The first fifteen minutes I talked to my mom was pretty much an incoherent mass of blubbering. I won't go into all the messy, snotty details, partly because it would bore you and partly because I think I've established myself here as a pretty tough broad. I wouldn't want to tell you how I cried until I blocked a sinus the moment I heard my mom's voice.

"Where's Dad, over?" I finally said when I could do more than hiccup incoherent sounds.

"He's at the store, but he'll be back in a few minutes, over," she answered.

I shook my head. The last time my parents had been together, my mom had thrown dishes at my dad's head. I couldn't exactly picture them in the same house without imagining bloodshed that had nothing to do with zombies.

"So are you two back together or something?"

There was a hesitation since I hadn't said "over." Or

maybe because she didn't want to say it out loud after all the custody fighting and putting me in the middle over the years. But then her voice crackled over the radio.

"Um, yes. He showed up here about a week after the outbreak."

"How the fuck did he get over—"

"What?"

I shook my head. "I wasn't finished."

"Oh, sorry. You said over. Over."

I rolled my eyes. Apparently I had entered a twilight zone. An Abbot and Costello, "Who's on first?" twilight zone.

"I was asking, how did he get across the Wall? They were killing people by a week in, weren't they?"

I could hear the smile in her voice when she replied. "Well, you know your father. He's resourceful. He was the last one to smuggle in before the government got its act together."

"And so you two ended up back together," I said, giving Dave a blank stare. He shrugged. He'd seen the two of them trying to be civil in a room together and failing (at our engagement party, our wedding, one time when Dave broke his arm and they both showed up at the hospital . . . I could go on). It was as much a mystery to him as it was to me.

"Yes. These kinds of situations will do that." She hesitated. "How are you and David? Did the counseling work, over?"

I looked at Dave and he shook his head with a grin even though my mom was sort of publicly airing our issues to the group of resistance fighters who were now all staring at us with speculation.

"Um, well, like you said, zombie apocalypses will bring you closer together," I answered. "He's right here."

There was an audible sigh of relief on the other end of the radio. "Oh good. I really thought the two of you would break up and—"

"Um, Mom!" I burst out as I looked at the others in pure embarrassment. Seriously, this was as bad as her commenting on my status updates on Facebook. "Other people present."

"Sorry," she said. "But you're okay? No one was bitten?"

I glanced at David. He was rubbing his scar on his hand and McCray and Nicole were both watching him do it. And now we were in a quandary. Apparently my mother was the Ma Barker of the Zombie Underground. If that was true, she needed to know about the cure and the superzombie thing so that we could somehow get what we had across to the scientists she knew and trusted.

But that meant spilling our secret in front of all these "rebels." And I wasn't sure how they would take it.

Dave stepped forward and gently took the radio receiver from my hand. "Hi Molly," he said.

"David! How are you, honey?"

The relief in her voice was palpable, almost like she hadn't fully trusted that I was telling the truth about his whereabouts. Thanks, Mom.

"Molly, I need you to listen, okay?" he said as he shot me a look. "I was...I *was* bitten."

Suddenly the feeling in the room around us shifted. Guns cocked and lifted, pointing at my husband.

"Wait, please!" I begged, standing between them, though I was pretty sure these people wouldn't hesitate to shoot right through me to kill a zombie in their safe haven. "Let him explain."

My mom's voice was strained. "Oh, honey. When?"

He looked at the group before he lifted the radio receiver and said. "Almost a month ago, Molly."

Around the room were looks of confusion, and the same was definitely reflected in my mom's tone when she responded. "Then how are you still...talking?"

"We have a cure," he explained.

Half the guns dropped immediately and all the eyes in the room widened at once.

Kathleen blinked. "Shit, change channels," she burst out.

Dave lowered the receiver. "What?"

"Tell them you're changing channels, they'll know which one to switch to," Kathleen snapped.

He did as she told him and my mom didn't seem fazed.

"What the hell?" he asked as he turned the knob to the channel Kathleen told him to move to.

She shook her head. "In case they're trying to monitor us. The radio system works well, but there's no security. And we *don't* want them hearing this."

I stared. Apparently we'd gotten dropped into the real-life version of Big Brother. Only there wasn't any half-a-million-dollar prize at the end. Not that money had any value out here besides as a fire starter.

My mom's voice crackled on the other side of the radio. "David?"

He raised the radio to his lips again. "Hey, Molly."

"Tell us everything," she said with a shaky tone. "Fast before we have to change channels again."

"This cure, it stopped me from changing." He shrugged. "Pretty much. I don't kill others. I don't want to."

"A-a cure?" my mom whispered.

"Truly?" Kathleen said as she took a step toward us. She was pale as paper and her mouth was tense.

I started to nod, but before I could say anything, Nicole interrupted.

"I've seen it," she explained. "And Dave isn't lying. I've been with these two for days and I've seen his...powers. But I've never felt threatened. What about you, McCray?"

The rocker jolted at the sound of his name and he glanced at Nicole blankly. "Huh?" She elbowed him... hard, and he grunted with pain. "Fuck, I agree with whatever she's talking about!"

"David?" my mom's voice crackled over the radio.

Dave gave a smile to Nicole and McCray before he lifted the receiver back to his mouth. "Sorry, Molly. Yes, you heard me right. A cure. We have a sample, but there's nothing we can do with it out here with no electricity. Is it true there are scientists in your Underground? People who might be able to do something with this if we could get it to you?"

"Oh my God," my Mom said.

"Mom?" I leaned closer and said into the radio. "Please tell me we didn't carry this here for nothing."

"No!" she burst out. "We can definitely do something with it. Hang on, your father just came in."

Oh, dear old Mom. She might have been a leader of the Zombie Underground, but she still was no good at technology. Instead of turning the mic off, she left it open, so we all got to hear her muffled explanation of our survival, my dad's whoops of joy, and then the story of Dave being bitten and our potential cure.

My dad was the next to get on the line. "Sarah?"

He sounded like he was crying and that got me started. I took the receiver from David. "Daddy?"

"Oh, thank God, it's you. Change channels, baby."

I pursed my lips. Damn, this security thing was a buzz kill. I turned the knob to the next number Kathleen said and soon enough my dad was back on the line.

"Chickadee," he said, using a childhood nickname I'd always hated, but now loved. "Mom tells me you have a cure?"

I nodded and then realized he couldn't see me. Duh.

"Yes. But how can we get it to you? Those soldiers at the gate on this side have pretty much proven they're not going to just let us waltz in."

There was a moment of hesitation, then my dad again, strong and sure of himself, as always: "I know some people. We'll get you and that cure through at any cost. I'll need some time to get it set up, though. Can you wait a few more hours?"

I almost laughed. Almost. For months Dave and I had been fighting our way through zombie hell, and my dad wanted to know if we could sit in a safe bunker for what amounted to the blink of an eye.

"Yeah, I think we can manage that," I chuckled. "Contact us when you have more information on where we should go."

"Yeah, are you in Kathleen's camp? Outside the northeast platform?"

Now Kathleen stepped up and quickly gave my dad some coordinates, I'm guessing to the camp we were at.

"Great. We'll see you soon, Chickadee."

Kathleen laughed as she handed the receiver back over to me. "I think he's talking to you."

I nodded as I took it back. "Thanks, Dad. I'll wait for your call with the details. Can't wait to be home!"

My dad signed off and I set the receiver back on the machine and snapped it off as I stared at David.

"We did it," I whispered.

He shook his head. "We can say that *after* we get across the Wall and into the regular world."

Kathleen nodded. "Yeah, he's right. It's going to be hard. Your dad didn't say it, but we haven't been able to get anyone across in over a month and a half. The security is brutal."

"So we might not be able to get in?" I repeated.

Dave shook his head and the scary thing was, he actually looked defeated. We'd spent so much time debating this place, thinking about it, now that we were here, it wasn't exactly what we'd planned.

"Come on, you two!" McCray snapped.

Everyone turned to look at him. He pushed back from the table and leaned over it like a weird general about to lead his troops into battle.

"Did the Americans give up when they took over Vietnam?" he asked.

I wrinkled my brow. "Um—"

"And when Lead Tongue got lost on the way to Rockfest '99, did *we* give up?"

Dave blinked. "I have no idea. Um…no?"

"No. We drove around until we found some groupies who told us the way. Also gave us wicked good hand jobs. So you can't give up now!" McCray said, wrapping his knuckles on the table with force. "We've got to find a way to get this cure past the Wall. Who's with me?"

He didn't wait for an answer; he just turned and ran

from the main room of the bunker and out of our sight. We all watched him go.

"Um, what's down that hall?" Dave finally asked.

Kathleen was shaking her head. "Just barracks."

"Good," Nicole sighed. "He'll probably forget what he was doing when he gets in there and take a nap. But his point is a good one. We can't give up. What you guys have is just too important."

Kathleen sat down in the place McCray had vacated. "So is it *really* a cure?"

I nodded. "It stopped David from turning into a zombie. And the man who made it…"

I trailed off as I thought of the madman who had all but convinced me to take his side against Dave's.

"Well, he was pretty strenuous that he'd used it on other zombies with similar results."

Kathleen rubbed her eyes. "Then we have to get you and it across the border as soon as possible. You three stay here, eat as much as you'd like, and take a nap in our barracks if you can. You're going to need the rest. I'll work on the specifics from our side of the Wall."

I stared at her as she got up and motioned her people to move out with her. Apparently she hadn't been lying. We weren't prisoners here.

"Hey, why are you doing this?" I asked as she reached the exit. "I mean, you don't know us. We could be totally full of shit."

Kathleen turned toward us and shrugged. "I'd rather help you and find out you were full of shit later than not do it and lose a chance to end this madness." She smiled. "Plus, I don't think you're full of shit. McCray may be, but you aren't. See you later."

Then they all left and the three of us were alone.

"So what do we do?" I asked.

Nicole shrugged. "Well, you two can nap if you want, but I'm going to take a look around." She dug into the bag she'd carried in and grabbed her camera. "And get some shots. If we do get smuggled across the border, the video I've taken will be worth millions."

She smiled and then went in the direction that Kathleen and her people had gone. Which left me and Dave.

"Come on," he said, grabbing my hand and practically dragging me toward the barracks. "You haven't slept for twenty-four hours. And it sounds like we're going to need the rest in the next twenty-four."

I followed him. In the barracks, it turned out Nicole was right. McCray was already completely passed out, sprawled across a cot in the corner. I took another. Dave picked the one beside mine and lay so that he faced me.

"How did you know I didn't sleep?" I asked as exhaustion overtook me.

He laughed. "I guess I'm just that good. Sleep well."

And I did. Until all hell broke loose.

CHAPTER 20

Remember to care for yourself while
you're caring for others. Otherwise,
you might get shot or something.

When the shouting started, I was dead asleep. Not *undead* asleep; just put the guns down and breathe, okay?

The yelling echoing from the not-so-distant distance roused me and .the smell of cordite from guns firing filled my nostrils with acrid warning. I was fully awake in less than a second.

Old habits. If you don't wake on a hair trigger in the apocalypse, you pretty much go zombie the first or second night because you didn't hear your front door being broken down by a shambling mob of the living dead. Oops, should have invested in that alarm system, I guess.

I sat up but found myself in complete darkness. And not "someone took pity on me and turned off the lights so I could sleep better" darkness; I mean total pitch blackness that could only mean every light in the bunker was out. And *that* meant that at some point something or someone had taken out the generators that supplied the dim, bluish light in the compound. This was one of the disadvantages to being underground.

That and the worms. Gross.

"Dave?" I whispered into the darkness, but there was no response. "David?" I repeated.

Still nothing and now my heart started to pound. Dave had an even sharper "wakey-wakey" response than I did. And it had only been made more intense by his zombie-cure experience. Seriously, the sound of the breeze against a solitary leaf would sometimes wake him up. So the fact that he hadn't said *my* name and tried to bring *me* around was a little bit freaky.

I found the edge of the cot and slid my feet to the floor. I was still wearing my boots (in a zombie apocalypse, sleep with your boots on...just another handy-dandy hint). I felt around on the ground with my feet, but he wasn't down there, crouched and at the ready or even incapacitated in some unknown way.

I *did* manage to find the foot of his cot and reached out to it. I felt rumpled blankets, a really flat pillow, but otherwise...

Empty.

"David?" I asked again, this time louder.

Shit, where was he? And why did I feel so foggy and have such a screwed-up taste in my mouth? Like Rainbow Brite barfed in there, a combination of sweet and dead cat.

I wanted to run from the room to find my husband, but I knew better. That would only lead to falling down, open wounds, broken bones, infection (regular or zombie) and possible death. So I had to calm down, think rationally, and just stay cool.

I got up and felt around with my hands and feet as I

inched my way toward the hallway. I went toward the sounds of activity—and there were plenty. And the closer I got, the more intense and desperate they sounded.

Shit was clearly going down.

"Get a light, get a light," I heard someone yelling. It was a familiar voice, too. "He's been shot."

I froze and then all thoughts of calm fled my mind. It was Nicole's voice talking. And she sounded panicked, like it was someone she knew who was hurt.

David. *David!*

I stopped worrying about stubbing my toe or breaking my arm and bolted through the dirt hallway. About half-way down someone managed to get a light into the bunker and I could finally follow that back into the main room where we'd eaten just a few hours before.

A crowd stood around the table, jostling one another as they tried to help or even just see what was happening.

"Give me something to clean this wound!" another voice barked out. It was Kathleen.

"How badly is he hurt?" I burst out as I elbowed my way through the group.

I expected to see my husband laid out on the table, fighting for his life. But it wasn't David.

It was McCray. His leather jacket had been torn off and his black button-down shirt, stripped open so that it gaped and revealed a skinny white chest. And a hole the size of a quarter right in the gut.

"Sarah," Nicole breathed and yanked me into an expected hug. "Thank God you're awake. That stuff wore off."

"Stuff?" I repeated as I pulled from her arms and watched as a few of the rebels worked on McCray. He moaned painfully and a couple of others moved to hold him down. "What are you talking about? What happened?"

Kathleen glanced up at me and then went back to her work.

"We were ambushed by troops." She shook her head as she put pressure on the wound to try to stop the bleeding. "I *knew* they were trying to tap into our signals. I told Carter that a dozen times. They must have heard the coordinates I gave your father. They slipped in and gassed the compound."

I staggered back. "Gassed?"

"I'm sorry I have to concentrate," Kathleen snapped. "He's losing a lot of blood."

I stared. McCray was pale and he looked at me with wide, glassy eyes.

"Oh shit," I whispered.

"Yeah," Nicole said as she dragged me away from table so that the others could do their work.

"Where's David?" I asked her.

She turned her face away and every fiber and nerve in my body went totally numb. I grabbed for her arms out of pure instinct and shook her hard.

"Where is David?" I repeated, louder.

Kathleen was the one who answered. "They took him."

Her tone was clipped and no nonsense; she never even looked up from McCray.

Nicole caught me as my knees buckled and I nearly went down on the floor in a heap.

"Breathe," she ordered me in a no-nonsense tone. "We think that's why they didn't just kill everyone. If they did overhear our coordinates, they probably also overheard

everything you told your parents about Dave and your cure
and all that. We think they stormed the camp and knocked
everyone out so that they could find you and Dave. Then
they probably intended to kill everyone else, only..."

She trailed off and tears filled her eyes.

"What?" I almost screamed.

"Turns out one side effect of being a total junkie is that
McCray isn't all that affected by knock-out gas. Shit, it's
like smelling flowers to him. So he didn't go down and
he..." She blinked a few times and her eyes cleared.
"Apparently he fought back to keep them from taking you
guys. They shot him in the fight before they just bolted
out of here with David."

I staggered from her supporting arms and spun back
toward McCray, laying on that table. He looked at me.

"Sorry...it...didn't work out...so well," he croaked.
His accent was even heavier when he was, you know,
totally dying.

I moved to his side and grabbed for his hand. "You
tried to save us," I whispered. "Shit man, that's way more
than most people try to do in zombie hell. Thank you."

Kathleen sighed and backed away. "That's the best I
can do with what we have. The bleeding is stopped but..."

I grabbed her arm and pulled her away from the rocker.
"But?"

"I can't get the bullet out. He needs a real doctor with
real equipment." Kathleen shook her head. "We've got to
get him over the Wall."

I rubbed my eyes. I had to shake off my fears and my
freak-outs and pull it together. I had to get a plan.

"Okay. Have we heard from my dad yet?" I asked as I
cleared my head the best I could.

Kathleen nodded. "Right after we all woke up and realized what had happened, he called through. We switched to a different frequency since our security had obviously been compromised, but I wouldn't be surprised if that didn't work this time any better than it did last time."

"So he knows our situation?" I asked. She nodded. "And how much is he freaking out?"

"Your dad? Well, he's not much of a freaking-out kind of guy," Kathleen said with a shadow of a smile. "But he's not happy that we were ambushed or that David's been taken. Relieved that you're okay."

I shook my head. Okay was relative. Without David, I wasn't sure it was possible anymore.

"So in the midst of all this, did he tell you if he worked out a way to get us across the Wall?" I asked.

Again Kathleen nodded. "Yeah, they have a plan to get you guys through to the other side with your cure. He didn't want to give me too many details since we had no idea anymore who was listening, even with the new frequency. We're supposed to meet them at a rendezvous spot in two hours. A place along the Wall that has the fewest guards."

I glanced at McCray. "Can he make it that long?"

Kathleen shrugged and cast a furtive glance at the rocker. "I-I think so, but who knows." Her gaze slipped downward. "I'm not a doctor."

I tilted my head. "What are you?"

"Huh?"

"What *were* you?" I corrected myself.

She smiled. It was a nice smile. "I *was* a high school math teacher."

"Well, you did a fucking amazing job, math teacher," I said.

She smiled, but I saw the strain that being the leader of a rebel faction put on her. Fortunately, chaos tends to bring out the best in some people. I hoped it would in me. David needed my best.

I turned away and looked around the room. A couple of Kathleen's people were monitoring McCray, but the rest stood in small groups. There were fewer than twenty of them in total and that included the addition of our little band of misfits. Not exactly a big force to fight the freakin' army. I was going to have to use mind power, not brute force on this one.

"So what do we know about the operation that took David?"

One of the men in the group stared at me. "What do you mean, what do we know?"

I shrugged. "You guys have been battling it out with these people in some kind of cold war for months, right?"

Kathleen nodded. "Sometimes hot, but mostly cold since they stopped coming out and shooting at us on a regular basis, yes."

I shrugged. "Then I *know* you have information about them and the way they operate."

"Some," one of the men admitted slowly.

I breathed a sigh of relief. "Some" was better than nothing. "I need to find out where they could possibly be going with David. Across the Wall right away, or do they have some kind of holding area on this side?"

Kathleen·stared at me. "W-Well, there's a barracks they keep here in the red zone. It's the only military compound outside the Wall. I would guess they'll take him there for interrogation, maybe even decontamination and then decide if they're going to take him inside."

I nodded, though my mind was racing with thoughts of what "decontamination" might entail. Especially for a person who had been bitten and cured.

"Okay. Any educated guesses about how long he'll be held at this facility?" I was met with a small sea of blank expressions and I clenched my fists at my sides in utter frustration. "Come on, people. This isn't that hard. You must know these things. What kind of rebel alliance are you? This is your Death Star! Help me blow it the hell up!"

The same guy who had answered me first shook his head. "I've seen them hold people there as little as three hours and as long as twenty-four."

"And how long has it been since he was taken?"

The same guy shrugged. "Almost an hour."

"Great, thanks, er . . . ," I said with a nod toward him.

"Rick," he supplied, though his tone was more question than answer.

"Rick. Thanks." Now I turned toward Nicole. "I need you to do something for me."

She tilted her head. "What?"

Carefully I slipped my hand under my T-shirt and found the vial of cure I had been carrying for over a month now. For the first time, I slipped it from around my neck and held it out to the very same reporter I had not trusted less than twenty-four hours before. But things were different now.

Everything was different.

"What the fuck are you doing?" she asked, backing away like she feared the stuff would burn her face off or something.

I shut my eyes and tried to keep my voice calm.

"This *has* to get across the border. And so does McCray or he'll die. So I need for you to take them both there and meet my dad."

"What are you talking about?" Kathleen interrupted as she stepped up next to Nicole and both of them stared at me like I was a crazy lady just released from Asylum Island (it's like Candyland, only prettier).

"Yeah," Nicole said. "*You* are going to the rendezvous point with me, so you can hold on to that freaky purple shit yourself!"

"No," I said softly and grabbed her hand to shove the liquid into her palm. She closed her fingers around it with a bit of urging from me. Okay, so I squashed her fingers until she had no choice. "I'm not."

"You have lost your fucking mind," Kathleen said with a roll of her eyes. "Of course you're going."

"I'm not."

I looked at McCray from the corner of my eye. He had listed into unconsciousness and that was probably for the best considering how painful that gut shot had to be. Even our coked-up rocker had limits, it seemed.

I shut my eyes and tried not to think of my husband's limits and if they were being pushed further than McCray's.

"*I'm* going after David."

CHAPTER 21

See the beauty all around you. Like in
night-vision goggles, a fully loaded AK-47,
and a souped-up SUV.

The others stared at me—and I swear the silence seemed
to stretch out forever.

"Honey, I think that gas gave you a little aneurism,
because you cannot be serious," Nicole finally said as she
reached out and patted my hand half-heartedly.

Kathleen nodded. "Nicole is right, Sarah. You're talking about a military establishment here. With trained soldiers who think that killing you is a way to further their
goals. You can't just waltz in there and steal David away
from them."

"Really?" I laughed, but there was really nothing funny
about the situation. "Since August, I've fought zombie
therapists, killed my own sister-in-law, matched wits with
both a mad scientist *and* his annoying child, and trekked
across the zombie wasteland that is the South and Midwest. And I've done all this to keep my marriage together.
So if you think I'm going to let some soldier boys who
want to play Test The Freakazoid with my husband

destroy that . . . you are dead wrong. They're *not* making my David into a pincushion to see if his zombie super-powers are transferable. I'm going after him."

Nicole stared at me. "Let me just save us all some time. Is this up for debate?"

I shook my head. "Nope."

She turned to Kathleen with a heavy sigh. "She's not going to change her mind." Kathleen opened her mouth to speak, but Nicole waved her off. "Seriously, you can save your breath. I've never met anyone as stubborn as this girl. Totally pig-headed."

"Um, thank you, still standing in the room," I said as I stared at Nicole.

She shrugged. "Sorry."

But she totally wasn't. And yet, I kind of loved her for it in that moment.

Kathleen shook her head in utter disbelief. "But-but we have a plan to get you across the border."

I nodded. "And I'm not interfering with that plan. We've got about two hours and I have every intention of getting David back and meeting you at the rendezvous point before our window of opportunity closes. But I don't want to risk McCray's surprisingly brave ass or Nicole's chance to take credit for bringing the cure across. She has a Pulitzer to win after all."

"And an Emmy," Nicole interrupted. "And doesn't Edward R. Murrow have an award, too? I'd like one of those, as well."

I ignored her. "So they'll go, and Dave and I will meet you there afterward. All I need from you guys are some weapons, the directions to the barracks where they might have David, and the coordinates for the rendezvous."

Kathleen stared at me for a long, charged moment. Then she sighed. "I can do the weapons, no problem. But the rest is going to take too long to explain. So I'll just come with you."

Rick, the one who had been telling me about the barracks, jumped forward. "What the fuck, Katy! You can't be serious."

She looked at him with a shrug. "And yet, somehow I am. Rick, you get those two to the rendezvous and for God's sake, protect them both. That cure has to get across to John and Molly."

"Does that mean using full force against the military?" Rick asked.

Kathleen hesitated for a moment and then she nodded once. "Yeah. Use full force if you have to." She looked at me evenly. "Dave and Sarah and I will meet you there."

"But don't wait for us if we don't," I hastened to add. I looked at Nicole. "Promise me that you'll make my dad leave us behind if we're late. I don't want to risk your lives or his or the chance of getting the cure into the right hands."

Nicole hesitated a moment and then sighed. "You are going to owe me *so* fucking big time by the time this is done."

I laughed. "Pulitzer, remember? We'll call it even."

Nicole stepped forward and then I was enveloped in a hard hug that I'd never seen coming. I hugged her back, at first out of reflex, but then out of relief and gratitude. She might be a pain-in-the-ass stalkerazzi, but she was *our* pain-in-the-ass stalkerazzi.

"Thanks," I whispered.

She nodded against my shoulder. "Get Dave back. And I'll see you in a couple hours."

She pulled away and moved toward McCray. Without looking at me, she barked. "Now get going. You don't have a lot of time and I won't wait for your bitch ass if you're not there in time."

"Gotcha!" I said. Then Kathleen and I walked out of the bunker and into the dusk of early evening.

I was pleased I didn't cry as we walked away. Especially since I was pretty certain I'd never see that girl again.

Kathleen led me to another bunker about a quarter of a mile away. We didn't speak as we went because, well, what was there to say? This was a suicide mission, or it very well could be. I knew why I was doing it.

But why she was participating was beyond me.

She opened the doors and flicked a lantern that was hanging near the entryway. It sputtered and I stepped back in shock.

"Shit, you weren't kidding about the weapons," I breathed.

You know that scene in *The Matrix* when Neo has all the weapons go flying up next to him. This was kind of like that, only we weren't dressed as well and there was more mud.

Their collection was amazing. All kinds of guns, cannons, even hand grenades lined the walls, organized by type and size. Without hesitating, Kathleen marched into the bunker, grabbed a rusty grocery cart parked by the door, and started yanking weapons off the wall.

"Flash grenades," she muttered to herself as she placed

each item on the cart in succession. "Tear gas canisters. Rubber bullets."

I shook my head. "Okay, I get that these guys are just following orders, but what's with all the nonlethal weapons?"

Kathleen turned to me. "Oh, these are just so we can get to David. Once we have him, then we won't worry so much about who we hit and we'll switch to..."

She trailed off and grabbed for a selection of carbine machine guns. "The real shit."

I grinned and grabbed my own selection, including a twin of the missile launcher she'd been carrying earlier that I'd so coveted.

"Oh, and grab a couple of shotguns," she suggested as she turned the heavy cart toward the bunker door, "There will be zombies, too, all the way up to the perimeter of the barracks."

"Oh, I could never forget the zombies," I said as I grabbed what she'd requested and followed her up an incline out into the night air again.

The sun was almost fully set as we loaded up a vehicle. This time it wasn't one of those souped-up ones with the body armor but something less conspicuous: an SUV, though it did have leather seats. The back ones were covered in dried blood, but still. Nice.

Kathleen said a few words to her people. They had gathered out beside the car and were standing around looking worried. I sat with the windows rolled up and watched her try to comfort them. It didn't seem to work very well. But it didn't stop her as she got into the car and we rolled off into the night.

"Hey, can you open the glove compartment and grab

those night-vision goggles?" she asked after we'd rolled along in semisilence for about ten miles. And not on the road, either. Kathleen just took a straight route through dead fields and dirt yards.

What? The zombie highway system is way different. No tolls (which made the I-Pass attached to the SUV window pretty useless)!

My eyes went wide as I popped the glove compartment, then I held out one of the three pair of the precious glasses before I slipped on my own.

"Just flip the switch on the side," she directed as she did the same and then cut her headlights.

There was a moment of total darkness (without city lights, dark is pretty damn dark) and then the world flashed into Paris-Hilton-Does-a-Porno green.

"Sweet," I breathed while I looked around.

When you got past the weird color, these things really were a game changer. I could see everything clear as day, from the underbrush to the animals to the zombies who milled around in the distance, checking out the fields for hiding survivors.

"Dave and I have been looking for a pair of these for months," I said as I pressed my face to the glass like a kid at a store's Christmas window. "They were always cleaned out. Stupid shortages to create a false demand. It's like this apocalypse was being run by Apple or something."

"Except my iPad is a coaster now." Kathleen smiled. "And if we manage to get you two back across the border, you won't need night vision anymore. The other side still has electricity, running water, television, even Facebook, though everything that is posted has a massive lag time so that the government can censor it."

I shook my head in disbelief. After so many months of living in the way-back world, I wasn't sure I was ready to dive back into technology heaven.

"So people just went back to their normal lives?" I asked.

Shit, even if they thought we were all dead, didn't we deserve some kind of freaking mourning period before everyone logged back on to Twitter?

Kathleen nodded. "But it's not really that abnormal. Think of how it was after September 11. Everyone freaked out and watched nothing but news for a few weeks, but then we went back to reality TV and petty movie-star scandals. It's pretty much the same with this, only with way more restrictions. But most people don't have any clue what's going on even just a few miles away on the other side of the Wall."

"We're going to change that," I promised, more to myself than to her.

Kathleen shook her head. "I sure hope so. If people start seeing the truth, maybe they'll wake the hell up and start dealing with the outbreak in more ways than watching the zombie cams the government provides online."

"Ew," I said as I gave her a look. "They really watch zombie cams?"

She nodded. "Apparently they're some of the highest rated shows on TV. Right behind football and ahead of *The Bachelor.*"

"Shit, we don't even outrank *The Bachelor*?" I huffed. "Jesus, that sucks! None of those people even stay together. We've got zombies! Death! Dismemberment."

Kathleen laughed. "You have to remember, Sarah,

these people have no idea that they're being so tightly controlled."

"What do you mean?"

She shrugged. "They think the cams are live. They never see any survivors on screen. To them, they're seeing an unfiltered view of what's going on in the West, including heroic firefights where the soldiers clear out zombies and bravely hope to find people still alive and hiding out. But it's all a bunch of bullshit. Produced in Indianapolis, the L.A. of the new United States. All the stars who survived moved there."

"Eh, depressing," I groaned. "I love Indy, but really? The place where they run the 500 is now the heart of television and movies?"

She nodded and we were quiet for a minute.

"So, I get why you want to help us get over the Wall since we have the cure and Nicole's video footage is uncensored and might help start your revolution and all. But why help me go after David?"

Kathleen glanced at me briefly. "I was married before this all went down, too. With two kids. A dog. We were the perfect family. A teacher and an insurance agent living the dream in a cozy town just outside the city limits."

"Did the zombies end it all?" I asked softly. That was a story I'd heard a hundred times, and I didn't really need to make this poor woman go into it again.

"Well, sort of," she said after a painful pause. "At first we battled. But then...they got our older son."

"I'm sorry," I whispered.

"Me too," she responded, just as quietly. Then she continued, "After that, my husband didn't want to fight anymore. We argued about it endlessly. I was already starting to see the writing on the wall and had hooked up with people who were fighting the zombies and watching the government start its sweeps and firebombings."

"What happened?" I asked.

She hesitated for a long moment. "Greg told me I was obsessed and an unfit parent and he ran with our younger daughter. I have no idea where they are now. I hope maybe over the Wall since he was a resourceful guy with some connections. But the zombie apocalypse *didn't* save my marriage, though it seems like it did wonders for yours. So why not try to help you salvage your family since I can't find my own?"

I stared at her. She was so stoic as she looked straight ahead at the path before her. She didn't reveal her feelings, even with a twitch of her mouth. And yet I felt her pain.

"Well, thanks," I said softly.

She shrugged, but then she slowed the car and cut the engine. "The barracks are just over the crest and across a stream. We'll have to walk from here."

We got out of the SUV and loaded up. As I struggled with the weight of all my weapons, I grunted. "This is going to be a lot easier when we have Dave and his zombie-strength thing to help."

She smiled at me, but there was hesitation on her face, even in the green glow of the night-vision goggles. "Do you ever worry he'll go full zombie?"

I didn't stop loading, even though my hands faltered for a second. "Yes, of course. But no, too. I mean, to me, he's just my Dave. Only like, Super Dave. And I can freak myself out about my future or I can just live every moment in the present. I think that's what I learned in the zombie apocalypse." I cocked my gun. "Live in the now."

She motioned me across a few more feet of field and then we were standing on the top of a slightly elevated area that looked down over a small building. Well, a shack was more like it. The roof was missing some shingles and one of the windows had been boarded up. The whole thing couldn't be more than five or six hundred square feet. Not exactly the barracks I'd been picturing out of a dozen different military movies.

But the fact that there were like thirty soldiers present, patrolling the perimeter, told me it wasn't your ordinary Unibomber-esque hovel.

Kathleen flattened down almost on her belly and then we started a quick crawl across the rest of the distance. Let me tell you, no one on TV or in movies ever lets on a truth about a belly crawl. It hurts!

Sticks and twigs kept poking me through my T-shirt and some kind of prickle plant itched like a son of a bitch. Oh, and dirt kept dragging into the top of my boot until I could feel it shifting around in my sock.

Basically, it's annoying and dirty and superslow. But after about five horrible minutes, we managed to cross the last couple of hundred yards and lay together within fifty feet of the circling soldiers.

Kathleen looked at me and in the green glow of the goggles she indicated a few brief actions with a few hand motions. I hoped to God I was reading them right and nodded.

Everything that happened next was a blur. Kathleen threw a flash bomb. I closed my eyes as it popped off; the explosion of sound made my ears ring. When I opened my eyes, the soldiers were staggering around from the blinding combination of light and sound and fury.

I burst forward, praying no one was going to be aware enough to shoot me. I shoved past the blinking guards, some of whom seem to recognize I was there. A few grabbed for their guns, but none of them was okay enough to actually aim or fire at me, and I wasn't about to stick around long enough to let them get over the flash. I skidded to a stop and kicked in the door to the shack with my steel-toed boot.

In these situations, you really only have a second to take in everything. Luckily, I'd had plenty of practice, though always with mindless zombies, not thinking humans. But still, all those zombie battles were a pretty fertile practice ground for now.

Time seemed to slow as the door popped open and I flew inside. A quick scan of the room showed Dave tied to a chair straight across from me. A man in an officer's uniform was positioned in front of him, half-turned in his chair to face the door and all the sound and chaos outside.

I drew my pistol and fired, hitting him between the eyes. There were two more guards, each at the door. I kicked one, sending him flying backward while I punched the other.

Kung fu movie awesome, right?

But kicking and punching don't really hold people off like they do in those movies and these weren't super-soft-skull zombies, so they came back pretty quickly and pretty pissed and also armed with submachine guns.

Luckily, I also had guns. My pistol took out the first, but before I could swing on the second, he grabbed my arm and flipped me around so that I was on my back, staring up at the business end of a machine gun.

"Hold still," the soldier said with a scowl. "Or I'll plaster your brains all over the floor, orders or not."

I stared up at him. Well, this hadn't gone well. And now all that running and hiding and hoping and battling had turned out to be for nothing. I hadn't saved Dave, and I had probably just killed poor Kathleen if she hadn't figured out my plan had gone to shit and booked it back to her people (and somehow she didn't seem like the "abandon ship" kind of friend).

Basically, it was a clusterfuck. But before I could manage a good, solid cry before I was taken into custody and probably turned into a pincushion for the government, there was a quite zombie-like roar from across the room.

Both the guard and I turned our gazes toward David just in time to see him go all "Hulk Smash" on the ropes that were looped around him, tying him to the chair. He tore through them like they were nothing, and the soldier paled as he swung his weapon toward Dave instead of me.

I didn't really think; I just reacted. One swift upkick and I sent the machine gun flying just as the soldier started firing. Bullets scattered up into the ceiling as the gun went spiraling away and hit the ground too far away to be of any use to him.

He stared at me, then at Dave, and then backed up toward the door. "I don't want any trouble," he said, his voice cracking.

Dave took a long step toward him. "Then you better run. RUN!"

The man dove out the broken-up door and into the night, past his comrades who were all starting to come out of their flash bomb fog (uh-oh) and into the dark. I was guessing he wouldn't be back.

I turned toward Dave as I got to my feet. He was grinning at me.

"Hey," I said as I hurried to his side and enveloped him in a hug. When I pulled away, he was still looking at me with that goofy expression. "What's that look for?"

"You are just freaking awesome, that's all," he said before he swept up our friend's abandoned machine gun. "And nice goggles, are those night vision?"

"I know and yes, night vision. AWESOME!" I said as I motioned to the glasses with my own grin.

"Where did you get—?" he started.

I waved my hand. "I promise I'll tell you all about it later, but right now there are a shitload of other guys outside and they want to sort of kill us dead. Well, *me* dead anyway since they want you for science or something. So let's boogie, huh?"

He didn't have to be asked twice. The busted door was not going to be the way to go, though. Outside Kathleen was firing off her machine gun at the soldiers and they were starting to be aware enough now to fire back.

Dave motioned to a side window and I nodded. "Kick it, Zombie Boy."

He laughed as he did just that. "See, there are advantages to being part zombie."

"Yeah, that rope thing was awesome," I admitted as we dove through the hole he'd created in the window.

Unfortunately, there were two guards just outside and both of them raised weapons as we rolled clear of the building.

But Dave hadn't been playing video games for years without learning *something* for the effort. He swept his legs toward one guard and tripped him up as he fired off his first shot.

Now Dave will forever tell me that he did this on purpose, but I contend it was all just luck. You see, as guard number one staggered, his shots went wild and *he* actually shot his own buddy. Between the eyes, no less.

Dave blinked, but he didn't savor his luck for too long. He couldn't. Instead, he threw himself on the soldier who he'd tripped and slammed a hard, heavy shot right to his temple, knocking him unconscious with one blow.

"Nice," I admitted before I motioned him behind me and crouched low as I stared into the night. "Stay behind me," I whispered. "I can see in the dark."

He grabbed the back of my shirt and did as I asked, staying right on my ass (though he did snatch a pistol from my belt before he did it... almost like he thought I might not finish up this "save the day" superhero shit! The nerve). We crept away from the house, inch by inch.

Only of course it wasn't going to be so easy.

We were almost to the base of the hill where we could climb up and I could "distract" the guards by using a missile launcher on the shack when I stopped.

We weren't alone. At the top of the hill were figures moving in the dark. They weren't soldiers. They weren't rebels.

They were zombies.

CHAPTER 22

Let go. It won't be as bad as you think. Maybe.

Oh, fuck an elf," I muttered as I stared at the milling zombie horde.

Darkness doesn't really bother zombies; they don't have such great eyesight anyway (rotting eyeballs and all). But they can still smell meat and brains. And hear firing guns.

"What?" Dave whispered.

"Sound brought zombies," I answered. "Of course."

"Fuck an elf," he agreed softly.

"Okay," I said as I stepped to the side and pulled him forward. "Aim your gun this way...."

I maneuvered him so that he was pointing uphill in the general direction of the zombies. "And fire."

"Oh yeah," he said as he pulled the trigger. "Like Halo when one of us used to use the sniper rifle scope with night vision while the other one fired."

"Sure," I sighed. "Just like that, dear."

If video-game references helped him do this, I wasn't

going to argue. I pulled my carbine and started firing. The zombies lurched between the combined accuracy of our bullets (though Dave did go wild more often than not, I have to point out) and they fell in big rows. Some of them even tumbled down the hill and landed pretty much at our feet.

I glanced over my shoulder.

"Oh crap," I muttered as I grabbed for Dave and started hauling him up the hill.

"What?" he asked, tripping over zombies and swinging his arms wildly as he tried to get some purchase over what he couldn't see.

"The soldiers heard us killing the zombies."

"And the zombies hear us killing the soldiers. Damn, it's like a catch-22."

"I'd *kill* for a .22," I muttered as we reached the top of the hill.

Through the darkness I saw more groups of zombies staggering toward us. They were pretty far off, though. I dove flat on my stomach and yanked Dave next to me. Once again, I pointed his gun at an angle.

"Trigger," I said as I struggled to get the big missile launcher I'd been carrying into position. I looked down at it. There were actually a lot of pulleys and levers on this thing. Huh.

"What are you doing?" Dave whispered. He was hitting soldiers, but not with too many kill shots. Lots of knee hits, though. Ouch!

"Trying to figure out how to shoot a missile launcher."

What? I'd never fired one before.

"Give it to me!" Dave snapped. He reached out and started slapping at me, grabbing at my face (and catching me a few times in the process); he got my goggles and pulled them off.

"Ouch, Grabby McGee! You could ask me to do that myself, you know," I muttered, though I surrendered the missile launcher and went back to the carbine. I fired into the dark toward where I'd last seen the soldiers coming. "Big jerk."

"*You're* the one who rescued me," he pointed out and then there was a huge crash and the shack exploded, filling the area with fire and light.

"Bull's-eye!" I cried before I used the new light to fire off a couple more precise shots at Dave's former captors.

He yanked the night-vision goggles down around his neck since the light was too bright for them now and smiled. "Thanks!"

"Wow, how'd you know how to do that?" I asked as we scrambled to our feet and started running back toward the vehicle that was outlined by the fire of the shack. I just prayed to God Kathleen had made a beeline for it, too.

He shrugged. "Halo, right?"

"Ah, of course," I laughed.

We reached the SUV, but it was empty and I stared toward the hilltop with worry. I couldn't see the shack from this angle, but the glow from its fire was more than visible. People were yelling down below and pretty soon they'd start coming up the hill toward us.

"What are we waiting for?" Dave asked as he got into the passenger side.

"Kath—" I started and at that moment she came half-running, half-limping up the hill toward us. "—leen!" I finished.

"Get in the vehicle!" She screamed. "Get in the fucking truck and start it!"

I didn't wait for more instruction. I dove into the driver's seat, turned the key, and gunned the engine hard enough that the smell of gas filled the air. Kathleen wrenched the back door open, dove in, and tossed a grenade over her shoulder, all while screeching, "Drive, drive, drive!"

I peeled away and the only thing that kept smoke from billowing from my tires was the fact that we were on dirt. But dust did flow behind us, though not enough to block out the huge explosion that rocked from Kathleen's grenade. And this one wasn't of a flash persuasion. It was the real deal.

I floored the truck as we barreled across the field.

"Um, goggles, please!" I shouted as we bumped and battered against the doors. "Can't see in the dark!"

"Fuck," Dave hollered and dragged them over his head and across mine. They were cockeyed when I finally was able to see, and there, in front of me, was a tree. A *big* fucking tree, rising up in the not-so-distant distance before me.

"Hold on!" I screamed as I turned the wheel.

The SUV had pretty good handling (came with the leather seats, I guess) and we stayed upright as we swerved around the tree. Unfortunately, more zombies were right behind it in a shambling mob. I barreled through the line of them without even slowing down. Rotting flesh hit my windshield, cracking the glass as arms and legs bounced off the doors and roof of the car.

"Where do I go?" I asked as we passed through that gauntlet. There was blood and goo on my windshield and the wipers were not helping at all.

"Hang on, I have to remember how to breathe," Kathleen panted from the back. "Just go straight for a while."

Dave looked back at her. "How badly you hurt?"

She shook her head. "Not bad. Got shot in the thigh and it stings, but I'll be okay."

"Thanks for coming for me," Dave said as he reached back to squeeze her hand.

She nodded. "Of course, but thank your wife. She's the one who put this party together even though she *could* have just gone to her daddy at the Wall and gotten free."

Dave spun on me. "What? You mean, you could have gotten out with the cure?"

"Relax," I said as I got us back on something resembling a road and clicked out headlights back on now that I felt like we were far enough from the chaos. "I sent the cure with Nicole and McCray."

He stared at me. "What the fuck? You handed over the cure to that drug addict?"

"Well, first that drug addict took a bullet to the gut trying to save you when those people knocked you out," I said, watching Dave's face pale in the dim light. "And secondly, I gave the cure to *Nicole.* I'm not so stupid as to give it to McCray, who'd probably take it just because he liked the color."

"I hate to interrupt this little spat, but turn left," Kathleen said from the back.

I did as she asked while Dave laughed. "You think this is a spat? You should have seen us before the apocalypse."

I grinned at him, but then looked at Kathleen. "How long to get to the rendezvous?"

She shrugged. "Depends. Maybe twenty minutes."

I glanced at the clock on the dash. "And that's just about as much time as we have left before we're supposed to be there. It's going to be tight."

"What happens if we don't make it on time?" Dave asked.

I tilted my head. "Actually, I'm not so clear on that, myself. Kathleen?"

"Well, you know all the soldiers guarding the place where we just got Dave?"

"Yeah?" he said.

"Well, multiply that by one to two hundred and add a thousand zombies. Your dad is good and if they have a solid plan, they can probably cut a hole in the wire and keep it clear for around three to five minutes."

"And then?"

"Then all hell breaks loose and they're going to have to run. The military closes that bitch up and that's it. It's going to be double protection for at least three months."

I blinked. Shit. This really was a make-or-break kind of deal. So I put my pedal to the metal and drove faster into the dark.

Twenty minutes can feel like an eternity. But after a bunch more turns and a couple passes of "dodge that zombie pod" in the middle of the road (they are worse than cows, I swear to God), we managed to reach...something.

"Stop here," Kathleen said. "And cut your lights."

I did as she asked and then clicked the night-vision goggles back on. In the hazy green I saw the high fence of the Wall in the distance. There were people standing around it.

"There," Kathleen said. "Dave, there's another set of

goggles in the glove compartment. Put them on and let's haul."

"Can't we drive closer?" Dave asked as he slung the third pair of goggles on. "It's like three hundred yards or more."

She shrugged. "Too much noise, too many vehicles, and it's only going to draw attention that much faster."

We got out of the car and started running across the field. We were about halfway there when I could finally see the people at the fence more clearly. McCray was being helped through a cut in the wire by Nicole. My dad was on the other side, pulling them through and hustling them both toward a vehicle parked close by.

He turned and searched through the darkness with a rifle scope that I prayed had night vision. Apparently, my prayer was answered because he raised an arm and waved toward us.

Relief washed over me. We were here. And in a few minutes we'd be through. Yeah, we'd still be running, but we'd be on the other side, away from the zombies and able to work on getting the word out about the truth of the outbreak. That was something.

We were a hundred yards away now, seventy-five.

That's when the three military Humvees tore up from behind. Doors slammed, orders were shouted, and suddenly a hail of bullets starting falling around us like rain.

Kathleen dove down on her stomach and Dave and I did the same. It was pretty barren and there was no protection out in the field. It was only going to be a matter of moments before the bullet shower started hitting and we ended up dead.

I lifted my head. I really hoped my dad wasn't going to

see this. But in the distance, people started to pour out of the vehicle where McCray and Nicole had gone. They had weapons, ones just as impressive as the military, and suddenly the soldiers who had come for us had to turn their attention on the firefight instead of shoot at us.

"Crawl for the SUV," Kathleen said, her voice laced with pain from the shot she'd already taken to the leg.

I sent one final glance toward the fence. If we crawled for the vehicle, we would be going in the wrong direction.

We wouldn't make it through the fence. There was no way with all the soldiers firing and more lights coming toward us from the distance with even more military types in them, no doubt.

"Go! Dad, just go!" I screamed out into the night as we started to hurry toward our abandoned car. "Run!"

My dad hesitated, sending me one final, furtive look before he did as I said and ran. Before he even had the door shut, the car took off and disappeared around a bend, with a couple of military jeeps tearing after it. But the car was superfast (I think it might have had a turbo engine) and I doubted they'd be caught.

Us on the other hand...

Kathleen tossed her last grenade toward the fence and we all started running back toward the SUV. I heard it explode and then a voice crying out, "Wall breach, wall breach! Focus on shoring up the Wall before the zombies come."

And that's how we got away. The zombies, or the threat of zombies, saved us.

And you know what, after all the time we'd spent running from those fuckers, they owed us one escape.

CHAPTER 23

Make the decision to be free. Whenever you can.

We couldn't go back to the bunker. It had been compromised since the military knew about it, and before the night was out, Kathleen's crew had relocated. It took us over an hour to get to the new camp and by the time we unloaded and fixed up Kathleen's leg, dawn had lit up the sky to the east.

Dave and I sat outside on the dead grass, blanket wrapped around us to ward off the winter morning chill, watching pinks and purples light the sky.

Still on the outside of the Wall.

"Think McCray and Nicole made it?" Dave asked.

"That's what I came out here to tell you," Kathleen said.

We turned and she hobbled up behind us. Her jeans were torn and her leg was bandaged. She leaned on an ornately carved cane, but she didn't appear much the worse for the wear.

"You have news?" I asked, as we both jolted to our feet and took a few steps toward her.

She nodded. "Come on."

We followed her to another underground tornado shelter. It wasn't as nicely fixed up as the other, but the radio equipment had already been set up, along with some heaters and some temporary lights. Within a few days, it would be a cozy little home again.

A guy sat at a small table, listening through headphones, but when we came in, he flipped a switch and the sound filled the room.

"This is J.L. on a repeating signal. This is not live. We are safe," my dad's voice crackled across the waves. "This is J.L. on a repeating signal. This is not live. We are safe."

I shut my eyes. "When did it start?"

"About five minutes ago," Kathleen said. We think he set it up on an open channel along their escape route. The government will shut it down within five or ten minutes, but it gets across the message. They made it."

As relief and regret both washed over me, I didn't say anything else, just turned and went back outside. I wanted the sunshine for a minute. Even if it seemed like we were going to spend the rest of our lives hiding underground and planning sneak attacks on military outposts and zombie pods.

Dave followed and put his arm around me without saying a word. I leaned into him as we watched the sunrise again.

Kathleen hobbled next to us. "So where will you go?"

I stared at her. "Go? Um, here. You guys need us, don't you?"

She shook her head. "Sarah, I won't lie. We would love to have you two here to help us. The more, the merrier and you would definitely be assets with all your skills and...

er . . . *attributes*." She hesitated. "But that just isn't going to work."

"Why?" I asked.

Dave looked down at me. "C'mon Sarah, you know why. The military *knows* I have this zombie thing. Even if they weren't sure before, they took my blood and stuff as soon as they captured me. I'm sure they're running tests on it right now. They'd love to run some more."

Kathleen nodded. "They won't stop looking for him. And that means they'll come for us over and over again. But if you leave . . ."

I stared at the horizon. Yeah, I got it.

"If we leave, they'll know that, too."

Kathleen smiled. "We'll make sure they do."

I nodded. "And they won't come for you because they'll figure the zombies will get you eventually. Everything will go back to . . . normal."

She nodded. "Something like that." We were all quiet for a minute and then she added, "But we have something for you. Come with me."

I looked at Dave and he shrugged so we followed her around to a big deserted barn on the property. The house had been destroyed but this structure remained standing, one fading beacon of what had been before zombies.

She opened up the doors and inside was a vehicle. One of those souped-up armored trucks that kept the zombies off.

"This is for you two," she explained with a wave of her hand.

"What?" Dave asked as he moved toward it. "No way!"

She smiled. "Yeah. We can convert the truck you came in within a week, so we won't lose much time with an extra vehicle. And you guys will need this wherever you go next. It's zombie proof, repels most ammo, and it has a converted engine so you get almost fifty a gallon."

"Whoa," I muttered as I reached up and let my fingers glide across the smooth surface of the vehicle.

"It's also full of supplies and weapons. Basically, it's a zombie killing machine." Kathleen smiled.

"Well, I've always wanted a zombie killing machine," I sighed. Then I turned to Kathleen for a brief hug. "Thanks."

"Thank you," she answered as we parted. "And I'll see you again."

"After the revolution, right?" I laughed as I got in the car.

"It's already begun," she said.

Dave waved and got into the driver's side. We started the engine and smiled at each other. Quiet and efficient. Awesome.

He pulled out of the barn. Everyone in Kathleen's group lined our way, waving to us, even saluting us. It was enough to bring a tear to a girl's eye.

But pretty soon we left it all behind and pulled up to the highway again.

"So," Dave said as he stopped in the middle of the road and threw it in Park. "Where do you want to go today, my dear?"

"Well," I said, "I've always wanted to see Montana. Plus it's the least populated state per square mile in this here union. Fewer zombies. Pretty mountains. Yellowstone park."

"All true," he mused. "But it's also *cold* this time of year."

I shrugged. "Well, there's got to be a mall near Des Moines. I hear everyplace is having a good sale on outerwear these days."

"Okay," Dave said as he pulled onto the highway. "To the mall it is."

extras

orbit

meet the author

A Facebook application once told **Jesse Petersen** that she'd only survive a day in a zombie outbreak, but she doesn't believe that. For one, she's a good shot, and two, she has an aversion to bodily fluids, so she'd never go digging around in zombie goo. Until the zombie apocalypse, she lives in the Midwest with her husband and two cats.

Find out more about the author at
www.jessepetersen.net.

introducing

If you enjoyed EAT SLAY LOVE,

look out for

SOULLESS

The Parasol Protectorate: Book the First

by Gail Carriger

Alexia Tarabotti is laboring under a great many social tribulations. First, she has no soul. Second, she's a spinster whose father is both Italian and dead. Third, she was rudely attacked by a vampire, breaking all standards of social etiquette.

Where to go from there? From bad to worse apparently, for Alexia accidentally kills the vampire—and then the appalling Lord Maccon (loud, messy, gorgeous, and werewolf) is sent by Queen Victoria to investigate.

With unexpected vampires appearing and expected vampires disappearing, everyone seems to believe Alexia is responsible. Can she figure out what is actually happening to London's high society? Will her soulless ability to negate supernatural powers prove useful or just plain embarrassing? Finally, who is the real enemy, and do they have treacle tart?

CHAPTER ONE

In Which Parasols Prove Useful

Miss Alexia Tarabotti was not enjoying her evening. Private balls were never more than middling amusements for spinsters, and Miss Tarabotti was not the kind of spinster who could garner even that much pleasure from the event. To put the pudding in the puff: she had retreated to the library, her favorite sanctuary in any house, only to happen upon an unexpected vampire.

She glared at the vampire.

For his part, the vampire seemed to feel that their encounter had improved his ball experience immeasurably. For there she sat, without escort, in a low-necked ball gown.

In this particular case, what he did not know *could* hurt him. For Miss Alexia had been born without a soul, which, as any decent vampire of good blooding knew, made her a lady to avoid most assiduously.

Yet he moved toward her, darkly shimmering out of the library shadows with feeding fangs ready. However, the moment he touched Miss Tarabotti, he was suddenly no longer darkly doing anything at all. He was simply standing there, the faint sounds of a string quartet in the background as he foolishly fished about with his tongue for fangs unaccountably mislaid.

Miss Tarabotti was not in the least surprised; soullessness always neutralized supernatural abilities. She issued the vampire a very dour look. Certainly, most daylight folk wouldn't peg her as anything less than a standard English prig, but had this man not even bothered to *read* the vampire's official abnormality roster for London and its greater environs?

The vampire recovered his equanimity quickly enough. He reared away from Alexia, knocking over a nearby tea trolley. Physical contact broken, his fangs reappeared. Clearly not the sharpest of prongs, he then darted forward from the neck like a serpent, diving in for another chomp.

"I say!" said Alexia to the vampire. "We have not even been introduced!"

Miss Tarabotti had never actually had a vampire try to bite her. She knew one or two by reputation, of course, and was friendly with Lord Akeldama. *Who was* not *friendly with Lord Akeldama?* But no vampire had ever actually attempted to *feed* on her before!

So Alexia, who abhorred violence, was forced to grab the miscreant by his nostrils, a delicate and therefore painful area, and shove him away. He stumbled over the fallen tea trolley, lost his balance in a manner astonishingly graceless for a vampire, and fell to the floor. He landed right on top of a plate of treacle tart.

Miss Tarabotti was most distressed by this. She was particularly fond of treacle tart and had been looking forward to consuming that precise plateful. She picked up her parasol. It was terribly tasteless for her to be carrying a parasol at an evening ball, but Miss Tarabotti rarely went anywhere without it. It was of a style entirely of her own devising: a black frilly confection with purple satin pansies sewn about, brass hardware, and buckshot in its silver tip.

She whacked the vampire right on top of the head with it as he tried to extract himself from his newly intimate relations with the tea trolley. The buckshot gave the brass parasol just enough heft to make a deliciously satisfying *thunk*.

"Manners!" instructed Miss Tarabotti.

The vampire howled in pain and sat back down on the treacle tart.

Alexia followed up her advantage with a vicious prod between the vampire's legs. His howl went quite a bit higher in pitch, and he crumpled into a fetal position. While Miss Tarabotti was a proper English young lady, aside from not having a soul and being half Italian, she did spend quite a bit more time than most other young ladies riding and walking and was therefore unexpectedly strong.

Miss Tarabotti leaped forward—as much as one could leap in full triple-layered underskirts, draped bustle, and ruffled taffeta top-skirt—and bent over the vampire. He was clutching at his indelicate bits and writhing about. The pain would not last long given his supernatural healing ability, but it hurt most decidedly in the interim.

Alexia pulled a long wooden hair stick out of her elaborate coiffure. Blushing at her own temerity, she ripped open his shirtfront, which was cheap and overly starched, and poked at his chest, right over the heart. Miss Tarabotti sported a particularly large and sharp hair stick. With her free hand, she made certain to touch his chest, as only physical contact would nullify his supernatural abilities.

"Desist that horrible noise immediately," she instructed the creature.

The vampire quit his squealing and lay perfectly still. His beautiful blue eyes watered slightly as he stared fixedly at the wooden hair stick. Or, as Alexia liked to call it, hair *stake*.

"Explain yourself!" Miss Tarabotti demanded, increasing the pressure.

"A thousand apologies." The vampire looked confused. "Who are you?" Tentatively he reached for his fangs. Gone.

To make her position perfectly clear, Alexia stopped touching him (though she kept her sharp hair stick in place). His fangs grew back.

He gasped in amazement. "*What* are you? I thought you were a lady, alone. It would be my right to feed, if you were left this carelethly unattended. Pleathe, I did not mean to prethume," he lisped around his fangs, real panic in his eyes.

Alexia, finding it hard not to laugh at the lisp, said, "There is no cause for you to be so overly dramatic. Your hive queen will have told you of my kind." She returned her hand to his chest once more. The vampire's fangs retracted.

He looked at her as though she had suddenly sprouted whiskers and hissed at him.

Miss Tarabotti was surprised. Supernatural creatures, be they vampires, werewolves, or ghosts, owed their exis-

tence to an overabundance of soul, an excess that refused
to die. Most knew that others like Miss Tarabotti existed,
born without any soul at all. The estimable Bureau of
Unnatural Registry (BUR), a division of Her Majesty's
Civil Service, called her ilk *preternatural.* Alexia thought
the term nicely dignified. What vampires called her was
far less complimentary. After all, preternaturals had once
hunted *them,* and vampires had long memories. Natural,
daylight persons were kept in the dark, so to speak,
but any vampire worth his blood should know a preternatural's touch. This one's ignorance was untenable.
Alexia said, as though to a very small child, "I am a
preternatural."

The vampire looked embarrassed. "Of course you are,"
he agreed, obviously still not quite comprehending.
"Again, my apologies, lovely one. I am overwhelmed to
meet you. You are my first"—he stumbled over the
word—"preternatural." He frowned. "Not supernatural,
not natural, of course! How foolish of me not to see the
dichotomy." His eyes narrowed into craftiness. He was
now studiously ignoring the hair stick and looking ten-
derly up into Alexia's face.

Miss Tarabotti knew full well her own feminine appeal.
The kindest compliment her face could ever hope to garner was "exotic," never "lovely." Not that it had ever
received either. Alexia figured that vampires, like all pred-
ators, were at their most charming when cornered.

The vampire's hands shot forward, going for her neck.
Apparently, he had decided if he could not suck her blood,
strangulation was an acceptable alternative. Alexia jerked
back, at the same time pressing her hair stick into the
creature's white flesh. It slid in about half an inch. The

vampire reacted with a desperate wriggle that, even without superhuman strength, unbalanced Alexia in her heeled velvet dancing shoes. She fell back. He stood, roaring in pain, with her hair stick half in and half out of his chest.

Miss Tarabotti scrabbled for her parasol, rolling about inelegantly among the tea things, hoping her new dress would miss the fallen foodstuffs. She found the parasol and came upright, swinging it in a wide arc. Purely by chance, the heavy tip struck the end of her wooden hair stick, driving it straight into the vampire's heart.

The creature stood stock-still, a look of intense surprise on his handsome face. Then he fell backward onto the much-abused plate of treacle tart, flopping in a limp-overcooked-asparagus kind of way. His alabaster face turned a yellowish gray, as though he were afflicted with the jaundice, and he went still. Alexia's books called this end of the vampire life cycle *dissanimation*. Alexia, who thought the action astoundingly similar to a soufflé going flat, decided at that moment to call it the Grand Collapse.

She intended to waltz directly out of the library without anyone the wiser to her presence there. This would have resulted in the loss of her best hair stick and her well-deserved tea, as well as a good deal of drama. Unfortunately, a small group of young dandies came traipsing in at that precise moment. What young men of such dress were doing in a *library* was anyone's guess. Alexia felt the most likely explanation was that they had become lost while looking for the card room. Regardless, their presence forced her to pretend that she, too, had just discovered the dead vampire. With a resigned shrug, she screamed and collapsed into a faint.

She stayed resolutely fainted, despite the liberal application of smelling salts, which made her eyes water most tremendously, a cramp in the back of one knee, and the fact that her new ball gown was getting most awfully wrinkled. All its many layers of green trim, picked to the height of fashion in lightening shades to complement the cuirasse bodice, were being crushed into oblivion under her weight. The expected noises ensued: a good deal of yelling, much bustling about, and several loud clatters as one of the housemaids cleared away the fallen tea.

Then came the sound she had half anticipated, half dreaded. An authoritative voice cleared the library of both young dandies and all other interested parties who had flowed into the room upon discovery of the tableau. The voice instructed everyone to "get out!" while he "gained the particulars from the young lady" in tones that brooked no refusal.

Silence descended.

"Mark my words, I will use something much, much stronger than smelling salts," came a growl in Miss Tarabotti's left ear. The voice was low and tinged with a hint of Scotland. It would have caused Alexia to shiver and think primal monkey thoughts about moons and running far and fast, if she'd had a soul. Instead it caused her to sigh in exasperation and sit up.

"And a good evening to you, too, Lord Maccon. Lovely weather we are having for this time of year, is it not?" She patted at her hair, which was threatening to fall down without the hair stick in its proper place. Surreptitiously, she looked about for Lord Conall Maccon's second in command, Professor Lyall. Lord Maccon tended to maintain a much calmer temper when his Beta was present. But, then, as Alexia had come to comprehend, that appeared to be the main role of a Beta—especially one attached to Lord Maccon.

"Ah, Professor Lyall, how nice to see you again." She smiled in relief.

Professor Lyall, the Beta in question, was a slight, sandy-haired gentleman of indeterminate age and pleasant disposition, as agreeable, in fact, as his Alpha was sour. He grinned at her and doffed his hat, which was of first-class design and sensible material. His cravat was similarly subtle, for, while it was tied expertly, the knot was a humble one.

"Miss Tarabotti, how delicious to find ourselves in your company once more." His voice was soft and mild-mannered.

"Stop humoring her, Randolph," barked Lord Maccon. The fourth Earl of Woolsey was much larger than Professor Lyall and in possession of a near-permanent frown. Or at least he always seemed to be frowning when he was in the presence of Miss Alexia Tarabotti, ever since the hedgehog incident (which really, honestly, had not been her fault). He also had unreasonably pretty tawny eyes, mahogany-colored hair, and a particularly nice nose. The eyes were currently glaring at Alexia from a shockingly intimate distance.

"Why is it, Miss Tarabotti, every time I have to clean up a mess in a library, you just happen to be in the middle of it?" the earl demanded of her.

Alexia gave him a withering look and brushed down the front of her green taffeta gown, checking for bloodstains.

Lord Maccon appreciatively watched her do it. Miss Tarabotti might examine her face in the mirror each morning with a large degree of censure, but there was nothing at all wrong with her figure. He would have to have had far less soul and a good fewer urges not to notice that appetizing fact. Of course, she always went and spoiled the appeal by opening her mouth. In his humble experience, the world had yet to produce a more vexingly verbose female.

"Lovely but unnecessary," he said, indicating her efforts to brush away nonexistent blood drops.

Alexia reminded herself that Lord Maccon and his kind were only *just* civilized. One simply could not expect too much from them, especially under delicate circumstances such as these. Of course, that failed to explain Professor Lyall, who was always utterly urbane. She glanced with appreciation in the professor's direction.

Lord Maccon's frown intensified.

Miss Tarabotti considered that the lack of civilized behavior might be the sole provenance of Lord Maccon. Rumor had it, he had only lived in London a comparatively short while—and he had relocated from Scotland of all barbaric places.

The professor coughed delicately to get his Alpha's attention. The earl's yellow gaze focused on him with such intensity it should have actually burned. "Aye?"

Professor Lyall was crouched over the vampire, examining the hair stick with interest. He was poking about the wound, a spotless white lawn handkerchief wrapped around his hand.

"Very little mess, actually. Almost complete lack of blood spatter." He leaned forward and sniffed. "Definitely Westminster," he stated.

The Earl of Woolsey seemed to understand. He turned

his piercing gaze onto the dead vampire. "He must have been very hungry."

Professor Lyall turned the body over. "What happened here?" He took out a small set of wooden tweezers from the pocket of his waistcoat and picked at the back of the vampire's trousers. He paused, rummaged about in his coat pockets, and produced a diminutive leather case. He clicked it open and removed a most bizarre pair of gog-glelike things. They were gold in color with multiple lenses on one side, between which there appeared to be some kind of liquid. The contraption was also riddled with small knobs and dials. Professor Lyall propped the ridiculous things onto his nose and bent back over the vampire, twiddling at the dials expertly.

"Goodness gracious me," exclaimed Alexia, "what *are* you wearing? It looks like the unfortunate progeny of an illicit union between a pair of binoculars and some opera glasses. What on earth are they called, binocticals, spectoculars?"

The earl snorted his amusement and then tried to pretend he hadn't. "How about glassicals?" he suggested, apparently unable to resist a contribution. There was a twinkle in his eye as he said it that Alexia found rather unsettling.

Professor Lyall looked up from his examination and glared at the both of them. His right eye was hideously magnified. It was quite gruesome and made Alexia start involuntarily.

"These are my monocular cross-magnification lenses with spectra-modifier attachment, and they are invaluable. I will thank you not to mock them so openly." He turned once more to the task at hand.

"Oh." Miss Tarabotti was suitably impressed. "How do they work?" she inquired.

Professor Lyall looked back up at her, suddenly animated. "Well, you see, it is really quite interesting. By turning this little knob here, you can change the distance between the two panes of glass here, allowing the liquid to—"

The earl's groan interrupted him. "Don't get him started, Miss Tarabotti, or we will be here all night."

Looking slightly crestfallen, Professor Lyall turned back to the dead vampire. "Now, what *is* this substance all over his clothing?"

His boss, preferring the direct approach, resumed his frown and looked accusingly at Alexia. "What on God's green earth is that muck?"

Miss Tarabotti said, "Ah. Sadly, treacle tart. A tragic loss, I daresay."